DREAM WEAVER

DREAM MATES
BOOK ONE

M. FRANCIS HASTINGS

CONTENTS

1. RenFest — 1
2. Amber Eyes — 5
3. Believer — 9
4. Cry Wolf — 15
5. Dinner and Dessert — 19
6. Take Me Home — 25
7. All in the Family — 31
8. Disapproval — 39
9. Shot in the Dark — 45
10. Two and a Half Hours — 49
11. Cold Reception — 55
12. Monsters and Men — 61
13. Sucker Punch — 65
14. Home Sweet Home — 69
15. Just a Kiss — 75
16. Bad Call — 81
17. Beta — 87
18. Succession — 93
19. Making Up — 97
20. Love Woes — 103
21. The Bite — 109
22. Seeing Doc Again — 115
23. Earth Shattering — 121
24. Breakfast Time — 129
25. Mated — 135
26. Stupid Is — 139
27. Misadventure — 145
28. Home in the Rearview — 149
29. What's Coming to Them — 153
30. Fooled or Foolish? — 159
31. The Call — 165
32. Loggerheads — 171
33. Melee — 177
34. Breaking In, Breaking Out — 181
35. Werewolf Down — 185

36. Death Defying 189
37. Deal Making 193
38. Deal Breaking 197
39. Done 203
40. Guilt 209
41. Back Home 213
42. Life and Death 217
43. A Man Walked into a Bar 223
44. Melting Moments 229
45. Getting Ready 233
46. She Said Yes 237
47. Kiss Kiss Kiss! 241
48. What If? 245
49. Up to Fate 251
50. Knowing 255
51. The Gift 261

Also by M. Francis Hastings 265

1

RENFEST

Carly

It was hot.

That was what most people didn't get, and what surprised traveling vendors at the Minnesota Renaissance Festival. In summer, Minnesota was HOT. Not an "it's fifty degrees in Florida and now I need a coat" type of thing, but an "it's 95 degrees and you could swim in the humidity" hot. Minnesota, land of 10,000 lakes, actually had more than 13,000 of them, and all of them were quite happy to add to the heavy moisture in the air.

Carolyn "Carly" Waite of "Dream Weaver" was fanning herself with a hand wool carder, sweating in the shade of the booth she shared with her friend Dawn Price. Dawn was a weaver and was working at a large loom in the shade of the shop. Carly was leaning over the rustic counter, trying to attract customers to their stall. Carly spun and dyed yarn, but right now, the skeins were in the kettle soaking. She'd run out of fiber to spin, and carding at high noon on this particular day was heatstroke waiting to happen.

It didn't help that they were in their garb—peasant-type clothes, complete with fitted bodices. Carly's breasts were nearly spilling out of the top, covered loosely by a white peasant blouse. Her long black hair was plaited into a braid down her back, and a crown of dried baby's breath completed the ensemble.

Sweat beaded on her skin ran between her overflowing cleavage and also and down her back and legs. If the costumes weren't so thick, she'd look like a wet mop.

At least she wasn't one of the characters who needed to be meandering out in the sun among the press of the first-day crowd. Then, the heavy costume might just have killed her.

"How's it going, sis?" a teasing voice asked before her younger brother, Matthew, came into view down the dusty path. He leaned on the counter, giving Carly a wink and Dawn a taste of his come-on-and-date-me smile.

"Same old, same old," Carly said, suppressing a smile as Dawn ignored her brother, per usual. "Another year, another heatwave. Global warming is real."

"True," Matthew said. "But hey, when the icebergs melt, we'll finally have beachfront property."

"Ha-ha," Carly replied. "So, what brings you in… shorts and a t-shirt… to our humble booth?"

Matthew made a face. "You're never gonna get me in tights, sorry, sis." He slung a backpack off his shoulder. "Mom wanted me to give you this." He plunked a cooler down on the counter. "Ham sandwiches and Jell-O salad, just enough for two." He made big puppy eyes at her.

"Oh, go get a turkey leg, you," Carly said. "You know Mom made them for Dawn and me."

"Bring some salted nut rolls back while you're at it," Dawn chimed in from her loom.

"You got it," Matthew said, perking up a bit now that Dawn had actually spoken to him.

Both women watched Matthew disappear into the crowd, Carly envying his cool outfit, Dawn checking out other assets.

Dawn gave a loud sigh. "Damn your brother is fine."

"Then why won't you go out with him?" Carly asked.

"It's the principle of the thing. If I wanted to be another notch on a bedpost, I'd still be with Eric," Dawn sniffed.

Ah yes. The cheating ex-husband. Just seeing Dawn's harrowing experience with that asshole was enough to make Carly swear off love for the rest of her life. That and the stiff relationship her parents had with each other had turned Carly off the idea of happily ever after. She'd much rather sit at home and spin than deal with all the headache—and heartache—of a relationship.

"Men take too much care and feeding," Carly agreed with a sigh.

"That's right," Dawn said. "If I need something that needs cleaning up after and its ego stroked, I'll get a cat."

Carly burst out laughing at that, "you have a cat."

"I could always get another six before going head first stupid into another—" Dawn trailed off, something catching her eye.

Carly turned around and found herself face-to-face with the most beautiful pair of amber eyes she had ever seen.

"Oh," she said once she found her words again. "Hello. Can I help you?"

"Yes," his deep voice rumbled, almost setting the counter to vibrating as he leaned across it. He sniffed the air and inclined his head, "I think you can."

———

Kiernan

Mate.

That had been the drumbeat of Kiernan Peters' whole morning.

Mate.

Mate.

MATE.

Usually, Kiernan would be at the Wisconsin Renaissance Festival this time of year, but circumstances had conspired against him being ready for it, so he'd opted for the later-opening Minnesota equivalent.

He had his tent. He had his woodworking wares. He had a vending spot. He had everything planned and prepared for the new venue, except for one major, unforeseen problem. Somehow, someway, this black-haired, green-eyed, porcelain-skinned beauty had activated his inner wolf with the oldest genetically ingrained imperative his people had.

Mate!

"Are you looking for yarn? Maybe a rug or a blanket? We've also got some nice table runners and..."

Kiernan didn't catch the rest, basking in the sound of her voice rather than the words. When she paused, it took him a moment to realize she was asking a question. Her soft words made his wolf rollover with a sigh and beg to be petted. If it hadn't been for the morning's influx of customers, Kiernan would have been glued to this booth the moment he'd first scented her.

As it was, the scent had gotten stronger and stronger until finally, at noon, Kiernan couldn't take it anymore. Though it was probably one of the peak times for customers to meander over to his tent, his wolf's mating call had gotten so overpowering that Kiernan felt lucky he hadn't shifted. Now, he saw why. She was sweating, pretty little rolling drops he longed to catch on his tongue.

"Sir?" his mate asked.

"Yes," Kiernan said, pulling his eyes from her cleavage back up to her face.

His porcelain beauty was blushing. "Um... yarn?" she asked again.

"Right," Kiernan said. She was normal, he could smell it, not a were-shifter of any kind. She also gave off a tang that made him frown. It brought back memories, bad ones. But he couldn't in his right mind believe that Fate would have given him a mate who was also a Hunter.

2

AMBER EYES

CARLY

Carly was fairly certain he'd just checked out her assets and not the ones in her stall. She didn't know whether to be pleased or offended. The sandy-haired hulk of a man was also staring at her expectantly, as though he'd asked for something. But he hadn't. At least, not that Carly could recall.

He smelled like cedar and cinnamon and was practically molded into his black pants, wearing a loose-fitting black shirt that was open at the collar and high boots. He looked something like the Dread Pirate Roberts from "The Princess Bride." She'd always liked Wesley. The only difference was the eyes.

"So... what kind of yarn were you looking for?" Carly asked. She figured if he could ogle, so could she.

The stranger smiled slowly. "What kind do you make?" he asked in his oh-so-sexy deep voice.

"Um... I use a variety of fibers, actually. Most people are looking for wool or cotton yarn... do you have a preference of color or combination of colors?" Carly asked. He wasn't sweating, and she had no idea how that was possible. Not a drop hindered her view of the delicious deep V in his shirt.

"I like wool," the stranger said. He tipped Carly's chin up so she was looking him in the eye again. "Reminds me of sheep."

"Well, that's where it comes from," Carly said lamely.

Dawn snorted in the background. "She's also got some nice alpaca back here."

The stranger flicked his gaze briefly to the auburn-haired, blue-eyed, curvy Dawn. Carly thought for a moment she was in the clear and could tamp down on the heart-pounding sensation in her chest. But his eyes came back to hers almost immediately. He might as well have put a NOT INTERESTED sign over Dawn's head. This was an incredibly unusual occurrence. Men tended to favor Dawn, as a rule.

"I'm Kiernan," the stranger said, extending his hand.

Carly self-consciously wiped her hand on her skirt and shook Kiernan's hand. The touch was so electric she wondered if there'd been a static shock between them.

"Carly," she said after staring at their hands a moment, belatedly pulling away. "So... wool yarn? Any particular color?"

"What's your favorite?" Kiernan asked.

This was by far the weirdest conversation Carly'd had with a customer. "I... er... scarlet?"

"Nice," Kiernan said. "It would go well with your skin tone."

"Uh... thanks?" Kiernan's slow smile made Carly's mouth go dry. "Do you mean you'd like a commission?"

"What do you make?" Kiernan asked.

To distract herself from the tantalizing V in his shirt, Carly began ticking items off on her fingers. "I make all kinds of things. Sweaters. Dolls. I crochet and knit."

"How about a scarlet sweater," Kiernan said. "My size."

"Oh, right, great," Carly said. "If you could just come back here and I can take your measurements..." She swallowed again, realizing she was going to get to touch him.

Carly felt Kiernan's rumbling laugh all the way down to her core. "I think I'd like that," Kiernan said with a wink.

"So much for getting a cat," Dawn chuckled behind her.

Kiernan

Kiernan knew he was missing some kind of inside joke, but wasn't that bothered by it, especially when the redhead stood up and said she was taking her lunch. He could have hugged the woman for her perfect timing. Now, he'd get to go into the booth with his mate alone. Well, not exactly alone—he doubted the red-haired friend would have allowed that. There were people bustling outside the stall, and the open counter left them in full view of the public.

"No funny business, then," Kiernan lamented aloud, his eyes twinkling at Carly.

"Uh..." Carly said.

"Relax," Kiernan said, holding up his hands. "I'm just kidding." For now.

"Right," Carly said, and she blushed again.

Everything in Kiernan wanted to see her flushed with pleasure while she lay underneath him, screaming his name while he marked her as his. It made his wolf howl inside, and Kiernan had to remind himself Carly wasn't a wolf. She was Normal. There was nothing inside her telling her anything right now except perhaps that he was a stalker. The idea made Kiernan laugh.

"What?" Carly asked, opening the booth's swinging counter door for him.

"Nothing." Kiernan stepped inside. This close, he couldn't help but notice how he dwarfed her small frame.

Apparently, she couldn't either, because Carly's eyes had gone wide as saucers.

Kiernan decided to have mercy on her and took a respectful step back. "I'm not going to eat you," he said.

"Right, no, of course not," Carly said with a nervous laugh. She stepped to the middle of the stall and got out a tape measure. "Um... would you mind removing your shirt?"

"With pleasure," Kiernan said, whipping the black pirate-esque shirt over his head. The way she stared at his body made his wolf give a self-satisfied growl.

"Yeah..." Carly said, shaking her head. "Right, measurements." Then she began pressing the tape measure across his shoulders, waist, and arms.

Kiernan wished she wouldn't be so professional about it. He wouldn't have minded one bit if that flicker of desire in her eyes had caused her to linger over her measurements. But, he also had to respect his mate for her businesslike demeanor. He certainly wasn't holding a whole lot back.

"I'm a woodworker," Kiernan said, breathing in her scent as she worked around him. There was that subtle, strange tang again that worried him, but her overreaching scent of citrus, sage, and something smoky and nice drowned it out. "You should come visit my tent sometime."

"Oh, I love woodwork! I thought you smelled like cedar," Carly said, then clamped a hand over her mouth.

So, his mate had scented him. Kiernan's wolf purred. "I'll bet I do. I work with a lot of cedar."

"That would make sense, yeah," Carly said. She finished notating down his measurements and put the tape measure away, much to Kiernan's disappointment.

"I'm just down the road there," Kiernan said, pointing. "I've got some comfortable chairs. We could sit and chat awhile." He pulled his shirt back on.

"Uh... sure," Carly said, her blush returning.

Kiernan beamed. "It's a date."

3

BELIEVER

Before Carly could respond to that final revelation, Kiernan was gone, whistling to himself as he wandered back down the path.

Dawn materialized out of nowhere, making Carly jump. "So," Dawn said. "How was your time with Mr. Tight Pants?"

"Kiernan," Carly said, still blinking in bewilderment. "I... I think he may have asked me out."

"Well, duh, yeah, I figured that much," Dawn said eagerly. "Details, woman! Is he as hot as I think he is under that shirt?"

"It's not like it left a lot to the imagination," Carly said with a blush. "You didn't miss much."

"Bullshit," Dawn said. "I may be divorced and jaded, but that was one YUMMY specimen of a man."

"No argument here," Carly said. "But he's a bit out of my league, don't you think?"

Dawn took Carly by the shoulders. "Listen you. You're always putting yourself down. You're a gorgeous, smart, talented woman and he'd be a fool not to want to date you."

"Date me? As in more than one date?" Carly squeaked. "Oh God, and here I thought I'd just go sit in an Adirondack chair for a minute and shoot the breeze with him."

"I think you should go sit on his lap and..." Dawn said.

Matthew arrived then with salted nut rolls. He frowned at Dawn. "Who's sitting on whose lap?"

"Carly's got a da-ate," Dawn grinned, snatching her salted nut roll from him and sitting down to munch. "Cashews! You remembered!"

"How could I forget?" Matthew said. He turned to Carly. "Don't go sitting in the guy's lap right away. Make him work for it," he teased.

"You two really are made for each other," Carly grumbled, going to check on the yarn she was kettle dyeing.

"Could you tell Dawn that? 'Cuz I don't think she's gotten on the Matt train," Matthew said.

"Oh, so it's a train and not a wagon?" Dawn sniffed.

Matthew grinned. "You'd better believe it, babe."

"Gross," Carly said. She reached in the cooler and handed Dawn her sandwich and Jell-O salad. "How's about we eat lunch."

"Sounds great. I'll eat here. You go see Mr. Tight Pants at his tent. I scoped it out already. He has some nice stuff," Dawn said, taking a big bite of sandwich.

"He's a vendor? Awesome, I'll come with you. I've gotta approve him before he gets all handsy on you," Matthew said, sticking Carly's salted nut roll in the cooler and waving her out from behind the counter.

"Matt, I'm going alone," Carly said.

"Aww, come on. What's a brother for if not to completely embarrass you and harass potential boyfriends?" Matthew asked.

"If you stay here, I'll let you eat lunch with me," Dawn said.

THANK YOU, Carly mouthed as Matthew slid into the booth and pulled up a stool.

YOU OWE ME, Dawn mouthed back.

"Whatever. Do everything I would do," Matthew said. "Just don't tell Dad."

Carly cringed at the very thought of her stern father finding out she'd even THOUGHT of having sex with Kiernan, much less acted on the impulse. Wait, when had this turned to sex? Stupid Matt. Still, if it got that far, Carly was sure her father would already have some sort of dossier on him. Even at twenty-three, her father still guarded her like she was Fort Knox. She wished she had more of Matthew's freedom. "You better not tell dad," she said.

"Would I do that to you?" Matthew asked innocently.

"Yes. You did it once in high school and then again in college," Carly reminded him. "I swear, if you do it again, I'm going to push you off Schaar's Bluff."

"Mendota Falls would be much more dramatic," Matthew called as Carly started on her way.

"Less chance of getting caught at the bluffs," Carly called back, and her brother's laughter followed her down the path.

It wasn't difficult to find Kiernan's setup, despite the crowd of costumed RenFest goers, characters, and people milling around in normal clothes. A thick, tan tent was staked down at the end of a row of vendors. Furniture of all shapes and sizes spilled out of it, as well as stained sculptures and children's toys. Kiernan was busy showing a small, mirrored cabinet to an elderly couple when his eyes met Carly's. The smile he gave her made Carly think she was going to melt, and it had nothing to do with the heat.

"Take a seat," Kiernan said, gesturing to, yes, Adirondack chairs. "I'll be with you in just a second." He turned back to the couple, describing the wood, process, and stains he'd used to create the cute little cabinet, complete with a rose relief at the top of the inset mirror.

Carly sat down in one of the chairs he'd indicated and just watched, smiling at the elderly couple as they held hands. Kiernan's eyes flicked up to hers occasionally, and Carly blushed.

The woman chatted a mile a minute, the husband hardly able to get a word in, but he didn't seem to mind. He just watched his wife fondly, then paid for the cabinet once she'd decided she wanted it.

"Do you need me to drop it off at your house?" Kiernan asked kindly, making Carly feel warm inside. A lot of vendors would have said, even to an elderly couple, that they needed to figure out a way to haul their purchases themselves.

"Oh aren't you a dear," the elderly woman said, pinching Kiernan's cheek. "No, my grandsons are coming tomorrow. They can pick it up then."

"Sounds good," Kiernan said. "You both take care now. Enjoy the rest of the fair."

The elderly couple smiled at him and tottered off, hand-in-hand.

"I want that someday," Kiernan said, sliding into the Adirondack chair next to Carly's.

"A cabinet with a rose on top?" Carly said with a grin.

"Cute," Kiernan chuckled. "No, I mean I want to be in a relationship like that. I want to be a hundred years old and still feel like the luckiest sonofabitch who ever lived."

Carly shrugged. "I guess. If you believe in that stuff."

Kiernan

Kiernan's attention snapped to Carly. "You don't?"

"I believe love like that is the exception that proves the rule," Carly said. "No offense."

"Some taken," Kiernan said, wondering what else he could possibly say to that. Not only was she still giving off that slight warning scent of Hunter, she also didn't believe in happily ever after. If only she knew she was his mate—that he would love and adore her forever. Not that the love bit had happened yet. Mostly it was just the biology at this point. But Kiernan found unhappy mates in his pack to be few and far between.

"Sorry," Carly said, blushing. "Probably not the most hopeful beginning to a first date conversation."

"At least you agree it's a date," Kiernan said, a bit of his smile coming back. If he could turn hickory into a desk, he could get past her barriers.

Color rose in Carly's cheeks, and Kiernan's inner wolf licked his lips. Down boy. "Well, you did SAY 'it's a date,' so I'm taking you at your word," Carly said.

"You set the bar pretty low for me. I appreciate that," Kiernan said, realizing he'd been grinning like an idiot since she first arrived. "How about, after we talk for a bit, we go out to dinner. My treat."

"I'm afraid you won't like me very much," Carly said. She was fidgeting her hands in her lap.

Kiernan couldn't help himself. He took one of her hands and kissed the back, then held her hand between them, resting on the arms of the Adirondack chairs. "I think you're wrong," he said.

4

CRY WOLF

Carly's heart thumped loudly as they held hands, having fluttered like butterfly wings when he kissed the back of her hand. She was drawn to him, no question, and she wanted to believe him. But she'd seen it all go wrong a time or seven too many. Perhaps she was even more jaded than Dawn.

"We'll see," she replied, and left it at that.

Kiernan smiled at her. "Ah, a glimmer of hope. I'll take it."

Carly couldn't help but laugh at his easy confidence. "Okay, okay. You've known me for all of thirty minutes, but let's leave it there for now. On to less serious topics?"

"Sure. What's your ring size?" Kiernan said.

"What?!" Carly said, her heart suddenly thundering for some reason.

"Kidding, kidding," Kiernan said, his grin completely unrepentant. "So, it's Saturday. What do you usually do on a Saturday night? Aside from having dinner with me."

"Oh, it gets pretty wild," Carly said. "I might go back to my parents' farm and knit some slippers. Maybe do a little spinning. Sometimes, I even read a book. Crazy stuff."

"What do you read?" Kiernan asked.

Carly was getting accustomed to the way her hand fit in his, and her heart started slowing down a bit. That was until he squeezed her hand, ramping things right back up. "Um..." Carly said, feeling herself blush. "I read... fantasy."

"Really? Me, too," Kiernan said. "Among other things. Who's your favorite author?"

"Terry Pratchett. I like how he's funny, while at the same time tackling serious topics," Carly said.

"He's great, isn't he," Kiernan said. "Though I'm not sure about his depiction of werewolves."

"Werewolves?" Carly said, confused. "That's random. What don't you like about it?"

Kiernan's eyes twinkled. "I don't like how they get stupid if they shift into wolf form too much."

Carly blinked at him. "You're weird, Kiernan. Next you're going to tell me you don't like his depiction of vampires."

"Well, now that you mention it..." Kiernan said.

It was too ridiculous. Carly began laughing. "Of all the things you could say, werewolves is really your sticking point."

"Let's say it's a topic near and dear to my heart," Kiernan said.

"Nutball," Carly giggled. She actually giggled. Like a schoolgirl with a crush.

Kiernan's wide smile made her heart pound. "Nutball? Is that some new insult I'm not familiar with?"

"Sorry. It's my word," Carly said. "And I really didn't mean to insult you-"

Kiernan squeezed her hand again, and Carly thought she might actually have a heart attack. "You're fun to tease," he said. "I don't feel insulted, don't worry so much." He broke their hand-holding, and Carly felt the loss keenly, until Kiernan stroked a finger down her cheek. "I like it when you blush. It's cute."

"Er... okay," Carly said, and wanted to kick herself for stuttering. She was twenty-three after all, not thirteen.

Still, when Kiernan's hand drifted back down to hers, Carly felt an inexplicable sense of coming home. Oh boy, was she in trouble.

***

Kiernan

He knew he was being a bastard, but every time he made her heart pound, like just now when he'd touched her cheek, it gave him a deep sense of satisfaction. Kiernan also enjoyed hearing her speak. His mate was intelligent, well-read, wanted to travel but had never actually gotten further than Iowa. As she spoke, he just basked in the light of her smile and the passionate way she waved her free hand in the air to illustrate her points.

Carly's hand was warm and delicate in his. He imagined her deft little fingers spinning yarn, feeding the fiber through her fingertips. Of course, he imagined her delicate hands doing other things, but that was for later. Right now, he was happy with their easy conversation, and his wolf seemed satisfied just to be with their mate. It would do no good to push her, that much he knew, and his wolf, mercifully, agreed. They wanted Carly for life, and if that required taking it slow and pushing past all the barriers she'd put up around her heart, well, Kiernan was ready to do that.

She was open now, however, animated and happy.

"What about you?" Carly finally said, drawing Kiernan out of his reverie. "You didn't say what you do on a wild Saturday night. Actually, aside from Pratchett, I think I've done all the talking." She was blushing again, looking just like a porcelain doll.

"Me?" Kiernan said. "Oh, I get pretty wild. I might take a lathe to a dresser. You'd better watch out." He was pleased she was a bit of a homebody, like him.

"Wow. I'll be sure to watch out for my virtue," Carly laughed.

You'd better believe it, Kiernan thought to himself. He didn't care either way, but her comment had his mind wandering elsewhere.

"... hobbies?" Kiernan caught the end of her question.

"Hmm?" he said, bringing his mind up out of the gutter. With effort.

"Do you have any other hobbies? Besides reading. I know woodworking isn't a hobby," Carly said.

He liked how she respected his profession. Kiernan was sure that, like him, she got a lot of comments about how her chosen profession was more of a "hobby."

"I hunt," Kiernan said. "Fish. Hike. I like the outdoors."

"Me, too," Carly said. "I mean, I don't hunt, but as for the rest, I'm game. I used to fish with my grandfather. I kind of miss it."

"Then I'll have to take you fishing," Kiernan said.

"I'd like that," Carly said.

Kiernan's mind filled with a long, sunny afternoon spent in a boat, just the two of them. "So that's two dates we've got set up now. See? Throw in a library date and that's three."

"You really are determined, aren't you," Carly said, shaking her head.

"You have no idea," Kiernan replied.

5

DINNER AND DESSERT

CARLY

"You can't wear that," Dawn said, frowning at Carly's current outfit. "You're having dinner with a handsome guy, not churning milk."

Carly looked at her rose-patterned dress in the mirror. "What's wrong with it?"

"You look like a couch," Dawn said. "God, if I'd known your wardrobe was this bad, I would have brought you something of mine."

"Oh right. Like it'd fit," Carly said.

Dawn shrugged. "You've got enough boobs to carry off one of my dresses."

"Ahuh. You keep telling yourself that," Carly said. She stripped off the dress and went to her closet to hunt down another.

"You really don't have appropriate dating clothes. Move aside. I'll figure something out," Dawn said, elbowing Carly out of her own closet.

Carly sat down on the bed, shaking her head in bemusement. "You really think you're going to find something I can't," she said.

"It's all about layering, darling," Dawn said. "Ah, here we go." She pulled out a rather plain-looking light green sundress and a short, white, short-sleeved jacket.

"I'm wearing that?" Carly said.

"Yep," Dawn said. "And these." She laid the dress and jacket on the bed, and pulled out a pair of strappy white heeled sandals.

"But... I wore those to my cousin's wedding!" Carly said.

"And they're getting new life tonight," Dawn said. "Okay, go on, put it all on."

Carly slipped into the outfit, then looked at herself critically in the mirror. "You were right, it does look good."

"I'm always right," Dawn said. "You're just realizing that now?"

Carly laughed. "Okay, okay." She pulled a small pearl drop necklace out of the jewelry box on her dresser and fastened it around her neck.

"I see you do have some small sense of style," Dawn said. She went over to Carly and straightened her jacket. "Now, you go get you some of Mr. Tight Pants."

"Seriously? You think I'm going to have sex on the first date?" Carly said.

"A girl can dream," Dawn said.

"Ugh. You're impossible," Carly chuckled. She made a little twirl for the mirror, her long black hair left loose to her waist.

"That's what he said," Dawn said, and they both dissolved into laughter.

There was a knock on her door. "Boy here, wants to see sister before the big event," Matthew called through the door.

"Shh, Matt, Dad'll hear you!" Carly said, opening the door and dragging her brother inside.

"You do know you're twenty-three years old, right?" Dawn said.

"Tell that to Dad," the siblings said together.

"You're sure you don't want me to drop you off and, you know, hang out in the bar?" Matthew asked.

Carly slugged him in the arm. "Don't you even dare. He's not some crazy stalker. He's just a regular guy."

Dawn gave Carly an evil grin. "With very tight pants."

"Dawn!" Carly said.

"So much information I didn't need to know," Matthew chuckled. "Alright, so you're taking your car. What did you tell Dad?"

"That I'm going out with Dawn," Carly said.

Dawn rolled her eyes. "Headline: Grown ass woman scared of overprotective father..."

"Yeah, yeah." Matthew put a supportive arm around Carly. "You'd be scared of him, too, if he was your dad."

"Don't I know it," Dawn muttered.

"Okay, you two, fight's over. Dawn and I have to leave," Carly said, "or I'm going to be late."

Matthew winked. "Do everything I would do."

"You always say that," Carly protested.

"And I always mean it," Matthew said.

Kiernan

Patrick's Irish Pub was located in downtown Minneapolis, near the Target Center. Its dark wood decor interspersed with pictures of famous American Irishmen and lightly scuffed furniture gave it a kind of homey feel. Kiernan decided it was the perfect place for a first —or rather second—date.

Carly had been insistent that Kiernan not pick her up at her home, which was 45 minutes out of his way anyway. Kiernan was a bit relieved at that, not because he would have minded the drive so much, but because that subtle Hunter tang in her scent made him leery of going wherever this hamlet of Vermillion was.

They'd agreed to meet at 9 PM. Kiernan had arrived early to secure a table—it was Saturday night, after all—securing coveted street parking with his rented SUV. At 9:10, Kiernan began to worry he may have been stood up.

Then, through the crowd, he saw her. A server was pointing her in the direction of his table. She looked positively mouth-watering, and

Kiernan had to beg his wolf for patience as he stood to pull out her chair.

"Sorry," Carly said breathlessly. "Parking was interesting."

"No doubt," Kiernan said. He sat down and immediately took her hand, laying their hands together on the polished wood tabletop. "I was beginning to worry a little, but I should have realized." He rubbed his thumb on the back of her hand, taking the reward for his patience when her pulse quickened and color rose to her cheeks.

"I thought this would be a nice place. I've always liked the ambiance," Carly said. "Plus the food is good, too."

"How do you feel about black and tans?" Kiernan asked, subtly flagging over their waiter.

"We're at Patrick's. Of course, you at least have to try theirs," Carly said.

"My thoughts exactly," Kiernan said. "Two black and tans, please."

The server nodded, and left them alone once more.

"I was thinking the fish and chips, but they also have a fantastic corned beef Rueben," Carly said, without even bothering to look at the menu.

"I'll go with the Rueben, then," Kiernan said. "Best of both worlds." He looked up as the server returned with glasses of their duel-colored ale, Bass on the bottom, Guinness on the top. "Thank you, sir."

"You're welcome. Are you ready to order?" the server asked.

"Yes, one corned beef Rueben, and one fish and chips," Kiernan said. Then he turned back to Carly. "Too bad we can't go fishing after this. I promise, when we go, we'll have a great fish fry after. I'm a bit of a master fryer."

"Handsome and humble," Carly said.

Kiernan grinned. "You know it."

The conversation was easy between them that way, right up until the food came. Then Kiernan began cautiously quizzing Carly about her background. "So, I know what you do for a living. How about your family? I know you have a brother."

"They take care of the family farm. I help, of course," Carly said. "We're kind of isolated."

"Isolated, huh." Kiernan mulled that over. "So, no incidents there?"

"Incidents? What do you mean 'incidents'?" Carly asked, clearly confused.

"Oh, you know, strangers accidentally falling into farm equipment or anything like that," Kiernan said.

"Kiernan, that's creepy," Carly replied, frowning.

He'd gone too far. "You're right, sorry."

"Are you some kind of amateur detective or something? That's only happened the once," Carly said.

Once. Right. "Seriously?" Kiernan feigned surprise. If she was associated with Hunters, it was absolutely no surprise to him that a stranger—meaning werewolf—would have "mysteriously" fallen into a combine. It was one of the preferred methods of Hunters dealing with lone wolves.

"Yeah, seriously," Carly said. She looked down at her plate. "Right, okay, I get it now. You're trying to pump me for information. The police never figured out what happened, but you and Google, you're going to make a case out of it." She stood and began digging in her purse.

"No, wait, Carly," Kiernan said, rising as well. "That's not why I asked you out. I'm sorry."

Carly pulled out her wallet. "Yeah, right."

Kiernan stopped her. "No, I've got this."

"Fine," Carly said and headed for the door.

Kiernan cursed and dropped a hundred on the table, then quickly followed her out. "Carly."

"What?!" Carly rounded on him. "What do you want, Kiernan?!"

Kiernan's wolf growled at the challenge. "This," he said and pulled her to him, giving her a searing kiss.

6

TAKE ME HOME

CARLY

He tasted like woodsmoke and Guinness, and still had the lingering scent of cedar and cinnamon. Carly opened her mouth so she could pull back and tell him off but then went weak-kneed when his tongue pushed into her mouth, dancing with hers.

Kiernan's arms wrapped around her, holding her up, and as the kiss went on, she could feel him hardening. "I..." she whispered, not recognizing her own husky voice. "I think we may have a problem."

"I'm glad you're calling it a 'we' problem," Kiernan said, pressing his forehead against hers. "How do 'we' intend to take care of it?"

"I'm not the kind of girl who goes to bed with a man on the second date," Carly said, trying to sound prim but failing miserably. Her eyes dropped to his lips.

"How about the third?" Kiernan asked, fusing their lips together once more.

"Third? When did we go on three dates?" Carly asked.

"We'll call date one when you felt me up in your booth," Kiernan said.

"I did not feel you up!" Carly said.

"I wish you would have," Kiernan said.

Carly swatted his shoulder. "You're out of your mind. Plus I'm still a little pissed off at you over the whole farm equipment thing. I mean, who asks that?"

"Idiots who put their foots in their mouths," Kiernan said. "I really don't want to end the evening here. You sure you won't have coffee in my RV?"

"I'm not that kind of girl," Carly said again, but his puppy-dog look was cracking her resolve. She'd never gotten on so well with either of her previous boyfriends. She felt as though she'd known Kiernan forever. And oh, how desperately she wanted him. It was surprising and scary at the same time.

"I know you're not," Kiernan said. "And I'm not that kind of guy. But here we are."

Carly swallowed. "My friend and my brother keep encouraging me to do something impulsive. I must be out of my mind to even be considering this."

Kiernan nuzzled her neck, then her ear. She was still tight in his embrace. As usual, Kiernan drew her into a world that only he and she shared. "Carly," he whispered her name and the low rumble of it shot straight to her core. "Come home with me."

"I can't," Carly said with a little moan. "I drove separately. They'll tow my car."

Kiernan laughed at that. "Of all the reasons you could have had, that's the one you came up with?"

Carly blushed. "It's true."

"I tell you what," Kiernan said. "You follow me home, and if you change your mind on the way there, you just turn right back around and go to Vermillion."

It was an invitation. It was a challenge. It was dangerous. It was an adventure. It was nothing like anything she'd done before, and nothing Carly would have ever considered doing. Still, she found herself saying, "Okay."

Kiernan's smile tugged at Carly's heart, and he finally let her go. "Allow me to escort you to your car," he said, taking her hand.

"Okay," Carly said again. They walked in silence the short few blocks to where she had parked, though the air between them was thick with sensual tension. Carly unlocked the door of her silver Prius, and Kiernan stepped in to open it, ushering her inside.

"Don't change your mind," he pleaded. They kissed again, then Kiernan directed her to where he was parked.

There were thirty minutes of doubt between Minneapolis and an RV park in Shakopee, near the fairgrounds. But Carly still followed his taillights all the way there. It was fully night, but his RV still looked big, black, and imposing in the ambient light.

Kiernan was magically at her car door before she'd even turned off the engine. Carly decided she must have dazed off, because she could have sworn she was right behind him. Kiernan opened her door and offered her his hand. "You came," he said in a low, sexy tone.

"I came," Carly said breathlessly.

Kiernan pulled her up out of the car and into his arms, kissing her thoroughly. "I'm glad," he whispered in her ear, and it sent shivers down Carly's spine.

Carly barely remembered getting into the plush RV. She wasn't even sure her feet touched the ground. Once the door closed behind them, Kiernan pushed her back against it and treated her to their most passionate kiss yet. Carly wound her arms around the back of his neck and kissed him hungrily.

Kiernan's thigh pressed between hers, and she soon found herself rubbing against it, soaking her panties while he palmed her breasts through the thin fabric of her dress. She might have been embarrassed if his hard length wasn't pressed into her stomach, proving he was just as turned on as she was.

Then with an animalistic growl, Kiernan pulled off her jacket and whipped her dress right over her head, tossing them aside. "Bed," he said. It felt like an order, but this time, Carly was happy to follow it.

"Where—?" she began, but Kiernan simply scooped her up and took her to the back of the RV. There he deposited her on a soft, but firm queen-sized bed. He pulled his black polo shirt over his head, revealing all the mouth-watering muscles Carly had restrained herself from touching when she measured him. She didn't have to restrain herself now. When Kiernan descended to kiss her, Carly ran her hands over his chest. This elicited another growl.

Carly trailed her hands lower, going for the fly of his jeans. "Please, for the love of God and all that is holy, tell me you have protection," she said while her brain was still able to function.

Kiernan stretched above her, giving her a tantalizing view of his strong chest, and opened a drawer. He pulled out a condom, and laid it next to them. "It would be very impolite if I didn't, don't you think?" he said, voice gruff with desire.

"Thank God," Carly sighed and pressed a kiss to his chest while she continued to fiddle with his jeans.

Kiernan, meanwhile, undid the clasp of her bra and tossed that away as well. She heard his sharp intake of breath as he stared at her dark-tipped breasts.

Carly blushed, but finally freed Kiernan of his pants, his large erection standing out proudly, covered only by gray cotton boxers. Kiernan kicked off the jeans, then came back over her to feast on her nipples. Carly gasped and held the back of his head, her fingers spiking through his hair.

The sensation was second only to the long, slow stroke of Kiernan's finger over her soaked panties at her apex.

"Oh God," Carly said.

"You can call me Kiernan," Kiernan chuckled, which made Carly swat him.

"Cheeky bastard," she said. She got him back by slipping her hand inside his boxers and gripping his cock.

Carly gasped in surprise when Kiernan ripped her panties in half. "Hey, what if that was my favorite pair?" she said.

"I'll buy you new ones," Kiernan growled. He prowled down her body and latched onto her core, spearing her with his tongue.

Carly mewled at the sensation and her hands fisted in Kiernan's hair, holding him close to her. He was as skilled down there as he was with kissing, and he held her hips down when she threatened to dislodge him by bucking with need.

Kiernan sucked her clit, and Carly came hard, calling his name. He lapped up her juices while she panted, then shucked his boxers and prowled back up the bed. He ripped the condom wrapper open with his teeth and rolled the condom on.

"I like it when you call my name like that," he rumbled. "Let's hear you do it again."

7

ALL IN THE FAMILY

Kiernan

Kiernan sank slowly into Carly's warm depths, groaning at how amazing she felt. She tasted divine, and with her taste still on his lips, Kiernan kissed his mate. Their tongues met and tangled while Kiernan started to thrust, slowly. He fit perfectly inside her. Everything about her was perfect. And she was his, forever.

"Kiernan," Carly moaned, and he possessively kissed his name off her lips.

"Carly," he whispered in her ear in the way he knew she liked. He was enjoying learning these sorts of things about her body, and so was unhurried in his pace.

That was until she wrapped her legs around his waist and started to beg. "Please, Kiernan."

Kiernan felt a growl rise in his chest. His wolf was impatient to mark her, but Kiernan had sternly explained that tonight was not that night. They did not want to scare their mate away. Still, he thrust harder and faster, biting her gently where he would mark her later, forcing his wolf to be satisfied with that.

When she came around him this time, Kiernan almost lost his mind, her inner muscles trembling around his cock. He thrust twice more, then buried himself deep inside her while emptying his seed into the condom.

Kiernan was distantly aware that Carly was looking at him strangely, as though he'd suddenly grown a second head. "What?" he asked when his vision cleared a little, still intimately joined with her.

"You said 'mate,'" Carly said, wrinkling her nose up in confusion.

Kiernan wanted to kiss that cute, scrunched little nose. So he did. "Did I?" he said, inwardly kicking his wolf.

"You did," Carly said.

"Hmm, that's odd," Kiernan agreed, trying to distract her by nibbling up the side of her neck.

Mercifully, it worked. Carly wriggled underneath him, all flushed and beautiful. It made Kiernan want to go again.

So he did.

Carly

It was dawn by the time they stopped. Carly groaned, stretching muscles she didn't know she had. "We have to work today," she reminded Kiernan, who had started to doze.

"Ngh," Kiernan objected, grabbing her waist with one arm and pulling her back down when Carly made a move to get up.

"Kiernan, we have to be there by 8:30. It's 5 AM, and I still need to go home. Shower. Change into my RenFest clothes..."

"Ngh," Kiernan grunted again, burying his face in her neck. He licked the spot on her shoulder he'd nibbled several times the night before.

"Kiernan!" Carly laughed. "Ugh, you'll never sell a thing if you keep me in bed all day."

"Worth it," Kiernan said, getting cozy.

Carly rolled her eyes. "Alright you. Up. UP!"

Kiernan growled in that way that made Carly shiver, but finally released her and rolled to the other side of the bed, sitting up. "Spoil sport," he grumbled, retrieving his boxers. He took one look at her panties and winced. "Oh yeah, I did that, didn't I."

"Yes," Carly said. "Now I have to go home half naked because of you."

"What? You've still got the dress," Kiernan said. He took the panties and brought them to his nose, taking a deep breath.

Carly's mouth went dry. "I don't care what you do, mister. We're going to work today. It's the second day of the festival and I'll be damned if I leave Dawn wondering where I am."

"She'd adjust," Kiernan said, but pulled on his boxers just the same. Instead of throwing the ruined panties away, he put them in his bedside drawer next to the condoms. "Need to get more of those," he observed, pulling one single condom out of the box. He raised an eyebrow at Carly.

"No way, not a chance. I'm going home. I still have to lace myself into a bodice," Carly said.

"A very sexy bodice," Kiernan said. "I like the way your boobs..."

"Stop, stop!" Carly laughed. "How about I promise, if we do this during the week, I'll stay. I'll stay all day long. But today is Sunday and we need to work."

"So, tonight and tomorrow, then," Kiernan said, and Carly just stared.

"You want to see me again tonight?" she said.

"Is that a problem?" Kiernan asked.

"Well, no, it's not like I had plans, but—"

Kiernan kissed the rest of the sentence away. "Good. Pack a bag. You can stay right here."

Carly felt heat chase through her at his kiss. "Okay," she said, breathless.

"You really sure we don't need this right now?" Kiernan asked, twirling the condom between his fingers.

"You really are incorrigible," Carly said, giving him a little shove. She moved past him to pluck her bra off the floor, snapping it on while she hunted down her shoes and dress.

"I know what I am, but what are you?" Kiernan called after her.

"Late!" Carly called back before throwing on her dress, grabbing her purse and jacket, and walking out the door.

Forty-five minutes later, Carly snuck into her house. Or at least she tried to, but this was a farm and her parents and brother were already awake and having breakfast. Carly winced as the door creaked shut behind her.

"Did you and Dawn have a nice time?" her mother chirped before Carly even made it to the stairs.

"Oh, yeah, it was very nice," Carly said.

Her brother made a vulgar motion behind their parents' backs, knowing full well she was doing the walk of shame.

"It's unlike you to jeopardize your job by staying out all night," her father said from behind his newspaper. He snapped it shut disapprovingly. "Your mother and I were worried."

"S-Sorry," Carly said, though it grated on her. She was twenty-three, after all. But her father was, in a word, scary. He'd never struck his children or berated them, of course, but his expectations for them were high, and his demeanor was cold. Sometimes it was hard to remember he loved them at all.

"Well, I suppose you're an adult now," her father went on. "Though I'd expect more responsibility from an adult."

"Dad, come on, she went out for a night. When's the last time she did that?" Matthew asked, backing her up. "Don't you ever want us to have any fun?"

Her father grunted and picked up his paper again. "Fun," he muttered.

Carly gave Matthew a grateful smile, then took the stairs two at a time to get up to her bedroom. She showered and changed into her festival garb.

Matthew, clearly having waited as long as he was prepared to, knocked on her door just as Carly finished lacing her bodice. "Are you decent?" he asked.

"Yeah, come on in," Carly said. She sat down on her bed, preparing for a long conversation.

Grinning from ear to ear, Matthew came in her room and shut the door behind them. "So... all night, huh?" he asked.

Carly blushed. "You know, if it were you, Dad wouldn't have batted an eyelash. But me? I have to pretend to go out with my girlfriend—"

"In order to get some," Matthew said. "Yeah, I know, life's unfair. He does it out of love, though. I think."

"I hope so, otherwise our father is a psychopath," Carly said.

"... that is always a possibility, too," Matthew laughed. "I'm glad you had a nice night."

"Me, too," Carly said. Then her eyes got wide. "Oh no, what am I going to tell them about tonight?"

"Tonight?!" Matthew said. "Jesus, what kind of horn dog is he?"

Carly blushed. "Stop it, I'm serious. Kiernan asked me out again, and I said I'd stay over."

"Say it's some kind of RenFest thing," Matthew said. "Tell them you and Dawn are staying over at the fair for some kind of first weekend slumber party."

Carly rose and kissed his cheek. "Matt, you're a genius," she said and hugged him.

"If you'd gotten more practice sneaking around in high school, you'd be just as much of a genius as me," Matthew said. "Alright, I'm sure I'll see you later today. Mom'll be sending me with something else, maybe puppy chow."

"Oh come on, that's not fair and you know it," Carly said. "We'll get powdered sugar all over our costumes. YOU'RE the one who'd have to eat it."

"Now wouldn't that be a crying shame," Matthew grinned. "Can't wait to meet this Kiernan guy."

Carly groaned. "You promise to be nice."

"Hey, I'm always nice. I'm not Dad," Matthew said. "You wound me."

"A-huh," Carly said. "And Chris in college just happened to ghost me after three months?"

"He was seeing someone else on the side," Matthew grumbled. "That was a relationship mercy killing."

"You're impossible, you know that, right?" Carly sighed. "Just don't do a police investigation on this one, okay? If it doesn't work out, I want to decide that for myself."

"Okay, you got it," Matthew said with the wide smile that always told Carly he was lying.

"Gah!" Carly said, throwing up her hands. She picked up her overnight bag and stomped out of her room and back down the stairs. "Gotta go. RenFest. Staying out tonight. RenFest thing. By-ye!" Carly made her escape before her parents could comment.

Kiernan

Kiernan was showing a toy chest to a new grandmother when he scented him. He turned around slowly, watching the shorts-clad, t-shirt wearing, dark-haired Hunter approach. "Hello," Kiernan said, his nose wrinkling at the strong scent of wolfsbane. "Give me a moment, I'm almost finished here."

"Take your time," Matthew said, settling himself into one of the Adirondack chairs Kiernan and Carly had been sitting in just the day before.

"I love it," the woman said. "I'll have my son come pick it up later today. You have such fine craftsmanship." She squeezed Kiernan's bicep, and he smiled. It wasn't the first time, nor would it be the last that a woman bought something from him just because they liked his body.

"Thanks," Kiernan said, gently removing her hand and shaking it. "I look forward to it."

The woman gave him a coquettish look as she walked away. Then Kiernan turned to the problem at hand. "So," he said cautiously, "what brings you to my shop?"

"You kept my sister out all last night," Matthew said. "So I figured I'd come see what all the fuss is about. Though Dawn is right, you do have really tight pants."

Her family were Hunters, then. Kiernan didn't think Carly knew.

Hunters had a penchant for keeping their women in the dark, and his subtle questioning had brought out an honest answer—that the farm accident had simply been an accident, as far as she knew. He recognized the tang now that rose off her skin and offended his senses at times, it was the scent of wolfsbane.

"I guess I do," Kiernan said after a beat, looking down at his trousers. "I had the pleasure of meeting Dawn and Carly yesterday."

"And the pleasure of being with my sister all night," Matthew added. "Don't get offended, bro. I'm just here to find out your intentions. I mean, I'd be a little pissed off if you just see my sister as a RenFest stand, but as long as you're honest with her about it, I could respect that, too. She deserves to have fun as much as anybody. But if you're looking for more than that, then I have to see what kind of guy you are. So, which is it?"

Kiernan could hardly tell a Hunter that Carly was his mate. But as Carly's brother, he had to respect the man and respect the fact that he was looking out for his sister. "I'm looking for more than that," Kiernan said.

Matthew nodded. "I'd ask you how you can say that after one day, but my sister's incredible, and you're a man with taste if you can see that."

"I knew it the moment I met her," Kiernan said. He was still standing at a safe distance from Matthew. He didn't want to start itching or sneezing or worse.

Unfortunately, Matthew patted the chair next to him. "Let's sit and have a conversation."

Shit, Kiernan thought.

8

DISAPPROVAL

Kiernan

Trying to breathe as little as possible, Kiernan sat down next to Matthew. This close, he realized something else. Matthew was related in some way to the Hunter that killed his parents. His anger flared, and he saw red. If Matthew hadn't been Carly's brother, or had been old enough to have done it himself, the younger man would be dead by now.

Kiernan tamped down on his roiling emotions. It was best not to reveal himself, and to do that, he needed to carry on a conversation with Carly's brother. And hopefully not break out in hives from the wolfsbane. "Do you like Matt or Matthew better?" he asked.

"Matt," Matthew said. "You can call me Matt. You spend the night with my sister, I figure it's better if we're on familiar terms."

Kiernan wasn't sure if Matthew was being the "cool brother" or being a dick. "So, is this my interrogation?"

"Absolutely," Matthew said. "Glad you realize that off the bat. Parents, hometown, social security number?"

Kiernan had to laugh, despite his discomfort. "I don't have a criminal record. Not even a speeding ticket. I'm from a small town in Wisconsin. My parents... died when I was a teenager."

That, at least, made the tenacious Matthew pause. "Oh, man, sorry to hear that." But it was only a brief reprieve. "What's your last name?"

"Peters," Kiernan said. "What's yours?"

"Wow, sleeping with my sister and don't even know her last name," Matthew said, shaking his head.

"It didn't come up," Kiernan said.

"I'll just bet it didn't. Our last name is Waite," Matthew said.

Waite. He'd have to remember that for research later. Matthew wasn't the only one who was going to be doing a little background check. Kiernan wanted to know the name of the person who'd killed his parents. "And your parents are living, and you all live on a farm and grow corn," Kiernan said.

"Someone was good in school," Matthew said.

"Carly went to college at the U of M," Kiernan went on, "and studied literature. Do you go?"

"Nah," Matthew said. "I mean, I'd like to, out of state. But my dad needs my help around the farm."

I'll just bet he does, Kiernan thought. "It's good of you to stick around and help your family."

"Family's everything," Matthew said. "Do you have any siblings, at least?"

"No," Kiernan said, a pang in his chest. "It's just me." And the pack, but he hadn't seen them in years. He'd become more of a lone wolf, especially since he'd fled the Beta position the Alpha had been trying to put him in.

"Dang, man, I'm sorry," Matthew said. "That's... kind of really depressing."

"I have friends here and there, but I travel a lot," Kiernan said. "You know, going from fair to fair."

"You figure you're taking my sister with you from fair to fair?" Matthew asked.

Kiernan nodded. "If she'll let me, yeah."

"You're gonna butt heads with our dad, then," Matthew chuckled. "Can't wait to see it."

Kiernan was afraid he and Carly's father would do more than "butt heads," but he didn't say anything. The wolfsbane was becoming thicker in the air as Matthew sweated, and Kiernan coughed. His eyes had begun to water. "So, your father is more of the 'protect my daughter's virtue' type."

"Hell yes," Matthew said. "Though he has no idea that ship sailed back in college, and I'm not going to tell him." He regarded Kiernan with keen eyes. "Something wrong? Your eyes are watering."

"Hay fever," Kiernan said quickly. "It's a bitch."

"Doesn't that season end in July?" Matthew asked.

"Maybe not hay fever, then. I don't know, some sort of allergies," Kiernan said. Another group of people approached his tent and Kiernan sprang from his chair. "Sorry, I've got to go. Can we continue this later?"

Matthew frowned. "We sure will," he said, also rising. "Later."

⁂

Carly

Carly was at her spinning wheel when Matthew approached their booth. She was all smiles until he slammed the cooler from their mother down on the counter and beckoned her over.

"What's up?" Carly asked, coming from the counter. Dawn watched with curiosity behind them.

"Don't see him again," Matthew said without preamble.

"What?" Carly said. "Why not?"

"He's bad news," Matthew said.

"He's—Matt, you just met him. How can you say he's bad news?" Carly said.

Matthew shook his head. "I know he is. Just do this one thing for me, okay? Stop seeing him." He gripped Carly's hands. "Please."

"Matt, you're out of your mind," Carly said, her anger rising. "I know he's not seeing anybody else. He hasn't been here long enough. So why warn me off him?"

"Just... reasons," Matthew said. "Okay, I didn't want to do this, but I absolutely forbid you to see him."

"I'm sorry, you what? You forbid me?!" Carly said.

"Oh, this I've got to hear," Dawn said, stepping away from her loom and coming to the counter herself. "Did he actually say the word forbid? I thought I heard him say forbid."

"He did," Carly said. "Look, you asshat, I'm sorry if your conversation with Kiernan didn't go well, but I don't think you're giving him enough of a chance. I mean, how much time did you spend with him, anyway?"

"About twenty minutes, but that's not the point," Matthew said.

"TWENTY MINUTES?!! I'm getting this crap over a twenty-minute conversation?!" Carly said.

"I'm telling you he's not a good guy," Matthew said.

Carly folded her arms. "And you figured that out in twenty minutes."

Dawn had meanwhile dug in the cooler and was munching on an apple as all this went down. "I'm with her. Twenty minutes isn't long enough to call a person bad news. You should give him a chance."

"Because he wears tight pants?" Matthew snapped at her.

"Hey, you leave Dawn out of this. What's gotten into you?" Carly asked.

Matthew took several calming breaths. "Look, just let me do some research, okay? Just a little bit of research, and then I can tell you for sure whether or not he's good enough for you."

"Matt, you have gone and lost your damn mind," Carly reiterated. "I'm not going to stop seeing a guy just because you had one bad conversation with him."

"It's more than that," Matthew said.

"Oh? What else could you possibly have figured out in twenty minutes?" Carly asked.

Matthew's eyes shifted. "I... I can't tell you."

"You can't tell me," Carly said.

"Ooo, a mystery," Dawn grinned.

Matthew rounded on Dawn. "Shut up, Dawn, I'm serious!"

"Hey!" Dawn said.

"Don't you tell her to shut up!" Carly snapped.

"So you're not going to stop seeing him?" Matthew asked.

"Of course I'm not going to stop seeing him!" Carly said.

Matthew looked sad. "Even for me?"

"Matt, this is the first guy I've liked in a long time, and all you can tell me is you need to research him. Can't you and dad just let me be happy for five minutes?" Carly sighed.

"Fine," Matthew said, taking a deep breath. "But when I tell you I found something bad, you have to stop seeing him, okay?"

Carly worried her lower lip. "Depends on what it is. This 'I can't tell you' crap is not going to fly with me."

"Can't you just trust me because I'm your brother?" Matthew asked.

"Not after Chris, no," Carly said.

Matthew shook his head. "That's disappointing. But I'm going to prove it to you. Beyond a shadow of a doubt. And if you still won't listen to me, I'll tell Dad."

Carly's jaw dropped. "You wouldn't."

"That would be a real dick move, Matt," Dawn agreed.

"If he's as bad as I think he is, I'll tell Dad everything," Matthew said. "But for now, I'll give him the benefit of the doubt. Because you're asking me to. I just... I wish you wouldn't see him until I can find out more about him."

"Let me find out for myself," Carly pleaded. "Please, Matt. Just once, let me have a normal relationship with a guy. If there's something wrong, I'll figure it out on my own."

"You wouldn't even know to look for this," Matthew said sadly. He sighed and stepped away from the counter. "I'm going home. No, I won't say anything to Dad, yet. But just so you know, I think you're in danger."

9

SHOT IN THE DARK

CARLY

Just so you know, I think you're in danger. The words echoed in Carly's mind after Matthew left and for the rest of the day. Inwardly, she cursed him for casting seeds of doubt on her budding relationship with Kiernan. Not that you could really call it a relationship. It had only been two days.

Still, Carly felt Kiernan's absence keenly at lunch, and thought of going to see him at his tent, but decided he must be as busy as they were. A mother of two was standing beside Dawn's loom, letting her children watch as Dawn worked. The only problem was, the children were not big on keeping their hands to themselves, and Carly had to subtly help Dawn over lunch by keeping the kids from mussing her commissions.

At 7:30 PM, Kiernan showed up at their booth, wearing a thoughtful expression. It wasn't a good kind of thoughtful. Carly decided Matthew must have said something to scare him off, and wanted to strangle her brother.

"Hi," Carly said, hoping Kiernan wasn't coming to officially break up with her. He was a stand-up guy like that, she could tell. He wouldn't just ghost her out of his life.

"Hi," Kiernan said, suddenly smiling. "Are you ready to go?"

Carly could have died of relief, though Matthews words still niggled her brain. "Yeah, I am," she said.

"You kids do everything I wouldn't do," Dawn said. "Mr. Dangerous Man of Mystery Tight Pants."

Carly shot her friend A Look and grabbed her overnight bag, which Kiernan took from her to carry. He placed a hand at her back, and began escorting Carly away from the fairgrounds. "Mr. Dangerous Man of Mystery Tight Pants?" he asked. "What's that about?"

"Well, first it was just Mr. Tight Pants," Carly said, feeling heat rise to her cheeks. "Then my brother stopped by after seeing you today and said you were dangerous, but wouldn't say why. Honestly, I think he's just being ridiculous."

"Overprotective brothers are not a thing of the past," Kiernan said, though his smile didn't reach his eyes.

"Oh Jesus, he said something to you, didn't he?" Carly said, frustration building under her skin.

"Not in so many words," Kiernan said.

"Ugh, that bastard. And here I thought he was better than our father," Carly said. Then she winced. "No, I know he's better than our father, which makes this 'I think he's dangerous, let me research him' thing really weird."

"Do you think I'm dangerous?" Kiernan asked, stopping right beside his SUV.

Carly looked him up and down. Then she cupped his cheek. "I really don't," she said, wondering how it was she didn't. But she just knew, somehow, that Kiernan wasn't a danger. At least not to her.

Kiernan turned his head and kissed her palm. "Good," he said. He unlocked the SUV and put her bag in the back. Then he ran around the car and opened her door for her.

"You really are a gentleman," Carly observed, climbing into the passenger seat.

"It doesn't cost anything to be polite," Kiernan said with a shrug. "Besides, you're my m—date. A man should treat his woman right."

Carly giggled. "Now who's being all old-fashioned," she teased. "No, it's really nice. Thank you."

"You're welcome," Kiernan said with a smile. He got in and started the car, and then they were on their way.

Kiernan

Kiernan's wolf had been pacing all day, and now he knew it was justified. He hadn't hidden his true identity well enough, and Matthew now suspected Kiernan was a werewolf. Matthew wasn't wrong, of course, but having a Hunter on his tail while trying to court his mate was not an ideal situation. Had it been under any other circumstances, Kiernan would have cut and run—packed up his furniture and taken off in the middle of the night.

Carly was his mate, Matthew was her brother, and this had all the makings of a shitstorm, but he wasn't prepared to leave her behind. He knew Carly wouldn't just pack up and go with him. No, he still needed to woo her, and with deep roots in this Vermillion place, it would take some doing to get her on the road.

"Is it okay if we just go to my place tonight?" Kiernan asked, not wanting to be out in public with her. If Matthew alerted other hunters, it would not only be dangerous for him, but also for Carly. He didn't imagine dating, or mating, a werewolf would be high on their pardon list.

"Sure," Carly said. "As long as there's dinner. I'm starving."

Kiernan chuckled, causing his wolf to relax a bit. "There's dinner."

"Good," Carly said. Then she put a hand on his arm, and Kiernan glanced at her. "Don't let whatever my brother said get to you, okay? He scared off a college boyfriend of mine, once, and I wouldn't be surprised if he scared off my high school one, too. I mean, the college one especially was for the best, but it's still really hurtful and annoying, you know? I'm not going to stop seeing you just because my brother's being a dick."

"That's good," Kiernan said, "because I'm not going to stop seeing you just because your brother's being a dick."

Carly laughed, and it soothed Kiernan's soul. "He threatened to tell Dad, though, which will cause a whole heap of trouble. I just want you to be prepared."

Kiernan was sure she had no idea just how big that heap of trouble was going to be. "I understand your dad's a bit of a hardass."

"You have no idea," Carly sighed. "He's actually a bit scary, to be honest with you."

"I think I have some idea," Kiernan said.

"Matt must have warned you, then," Carly said. "My family, I swear."

"Can't live with 'em, can't shoot 'em," Kiernan said. At least he hoped not. He'd rather this situation not lead to bloodshed, but he also knew he needed to be ready for anything now.

"I know, right?" Carly said. Then she winced. "I'm sorry, this must be painful to talk about, since your family's gone. I should really be grateful for mine."

"It's alright. My parents have been gone a long time, and you need to vent," Kiernan said.

"I just wish I'd be left alone to make my own decisions. I mean, Christ, I'm twenty-three years old!" Carly said.

Kiernan looked over at her again. "Only twenty-three?"

"Yeah," Carly said. "Why, how old are you?"

Kiernan shifted uncomfortably. "Thirty-two."

"Wow, robbing the cradle," Carly said, and Kiernan burst out laughing.

"I suppose I am," Kiernan said. "Is that... okay?"

"I don't mind if you don't," Carly said.

Kiernan relaxed. "Good."

When they got to the RV camp, Kiernan could sense something was wrong. It was a smell on the air, a trick of the light. "Stay in the car a second," he said to Carly, then stepped out before she could protest. He looked around, then spotted him. "Matt."

"Werewolf," Matthew replied flatly. Then Matthew raised a gun and shot him.

10

TWO AND A HALF HOURS

Kiernan

Kiernan managed to duck to the side, but the bullet hit him in the shoulder just the same. The immediate burn told him it was silver. He wasn't surprised.

Matthew was taking aim again, but then Carly was there and standing front of Kiernan.

"Carly, go back in the car," Kiernan said, his voice pained.

Carly stood her ground. "The fuck I will! Matt? What the hell?! What the HELL are you doing here?! Why do you have a gun?!" She looked at Kiernan's shoulder. "Oh my God, did you just SHOOT Kieran?!"

"Get out of the way, Carly," Matthew demanded. "This is between me and him. He's a monster, and he needs to be put down."

"WHAT?! Matt, you've completely lost it!" Carly held her arms out as a shield while Kiernan was bent over slightly and cradling his shoulder.

"Carly. Get. In. The. Car." Kiernan's tone brooked no refusal.

The gunshot had drawn the attention of other RV-ers, and doors were opening and people were stepping out.

"Fuck," Matthew said. "This isn't over, asshole." He holstered the gun at his side under a jacket and retreated into the shadows.

"Matt!" Carly called. When her brother didn't answer, she turned to Kiernan. "Oh my God, Kiernan, oh my God!"

Pain lanced through Kiernan's whole body, emanating from his shoulder. "We have to go. Carly... you need to drive."

"I'll just call an ambulance." Carly turned towards the SUV.

Kiernan gripped her arm. "No. We need to go to MY doctor."

Carly frowned. "What do you mean YOUR doctor?"

People had begun to gather, and Kiernan shook his head. "Later. I'll explain... later. Just... we need to go now."

<hr>

CARLY

Carly was about to object again, but Kiernan's grip on her arm tightened, and people had already pulled out their phones, calling 911. Carly wanted to get Kiernan treated, and didn't know what the big deal was about going to a certain doctor. But then, her brain reminded her that her brother had done this. Her sweet, obviously confused baby brother. She didn't want the police hunting Matthew down. At least, not until she'd had time to think and they'd had time to talk.

"Where is this doctor?" Carly asked.

"Spooner," Kiernan said with a wince. "Wisconsin."

"WISCONSIN?!" Carly shook her head. "No, we've got to get you to a hospital now."

Kiernan grunted with pain, but remained adamant. "I'll be okay for the two and a half hours it takes to get there. Trust me. Please."

"Two and a half—!" Thoughts of Matthew being handcuffed were all that got Carly helping Kiernan into the SUV and sliding into the driver's seat herself. "I must be out of my mind."

"Thank you," Kiernan said. He was holding his shoulder, but very little blood was seeping out, and there was a burning smell on the air.

Carly didn't know what it all meant, but she was throwing the car into gear, and before she knew it, they were on the road in a spray of gravel.

"Don't speed too much. No more than five miles over," Kiernan instructed, his teeth gritted together.

Carly got them onto the highway, then reached back behind her and pulled her overnight bag to the front. She rummaged through it with one hand and pulled out a t-shirt. "Here. Use this on your shoulder. Keep pressure on. Two-and-a-half hours, Jesus."

"I'll be fine," Kiernan said again. He pulled his hand away for a second, and Carly saw that the edges of his wound were blackened as though charred.

Carly almost swerved over the line. "What the fuck, Kiernan?!"

"Just drive! Eyes on the road, not on me. I'll tell you where to exit and where to turn." Kiernan pressed the t-shirt to his shoulder.

It was a tense two-and-a-half hours, especially since they had to slow down to 25 miles per hour through several small towns. When a slow, laden truck pulled in front of them just before the final stretch of highway, Carly cursed roundly and fluently.

Kiernan chuckled. "You have a better vocabulary than a British sailor."

"Yeah, well, the situation calls for it," Carly said. "Two hours and now this fucker."

Kiernan put a hand on Carly's knee. "Breathe. Just breathe."

When the truck finally turned off in Spooner thirty minutes later, Carly gunned it.

"Slow down!" Kiernan protested.

Grumbling under her breath, Carly eased her foot off the gas pedal.

"Turn left by that gas station. It's just another twenty minutes," Kiernan said.

Carly whipped her head around to look at him. "You said two-and-a-half hours! That's more like three!"

"Two-and-a-half hours to Spooner. We still need to get to the lake."

"Lake?" Carly repeated.

"Dunn Lake. I'll tell you where to turn. He lives at a resort." Kiernan groaned in pain.

"Fuck," Carly said, and started taking county roads so insignificant that they were called "T" and "K." "We're having a really long conversation when this is over."

"I know," Kiernan sighed. "Just trust me for now."

"Hmph." Carly passed Dunn Lake Resort, looking at Kiernan for confirmation, but he shook his head.

"Not yet," he said.

They began to circle the lake. About halfway around, Kiernan stopped her and pointed at a sign. It was set back in the trees a bit, which made Carly wonder how anyone ever found the place to stay there. "Crescent Moon Path Resort?" she said, reading the worn wooden sign in the SUV's headlights.

"That's the one. Turn in here." Kiernan pointed.

Carly turned right down a dirt path. A dust cloud rose around them, and Carly thought she heard a wolf howl. "We're not going to be eaten by nature before I can get you to your doctor, are we?"

"I hope not," Kiernan said cryptically, and Carly stared at him. "SERIOUSLY?!"

Kiernan squeezed her knee. "It'll be fine. I'm sure they're coming out to meet us. They're not going to leave me untreated."

"They?" Carly said.

Indeed, "they" showed up. Just as cabins appeared in the darkness —along with a large lodge—a group of men, perhaps five or six of them, stood in the road with their arms folded.

Carly put on the brakes and rolled down her window. "Help! My— er—boyfriend needs a doctor!"

"You smell like Hunter," the one in front of the group said, his eyes narrowing in the light of the headlights.

Hunter? Carly shook her head. "No, his name is Kiernan. He said his doctor is here. He's been shot!"

"Kiernan?" the group leader said with a frown. He went over to the other side of the SUV and wrenched the door open.

"Hi Alec," Kiernan grunted. "Fancy meeting you here."

"Fuck. Who is she? Did you lead them here, you dumb fuck?!" Alec dragged Kiernan out of the SUV and threw him at the others.

"Hey!" Carly opened her door. One of the men kicked it back shut.

Kiernan

Two men held Kiernan while Alec, his Alpha, looked him over. "Did you lead them here?!" he asked Kiernan again.

"No. At least, I don't think so. It was just one Hunter. He ran away." Kiernan looked up at Carly, who was struggling between herself and the much stronger man on the other side to get her door open. "She's my mate."

Alec's eyes widened. "Fuck," he said, running a hand through his hair. "Alright, fine. We'll take you to Doc." He nodded to the men, who were, of course, actually werewolves, and they began carrying him off.

"Her, too," Kiernan demanded. "I want Carly with me."

Alec glanced back at Carly. "She smells like Hunter."

"She's still my mate. Kiernan actually grinned slightly as Carly finally rolled down the car window and made herself known.

"Look, motherfucker, I'm getting out of this car if I have to kick out the windshield to do it, so open the damn door!"

"Feisty," Alec said with a nod of approval. "It's okay, Sean, let her come, too."

Sean stood back from the door and Carly tumbled out. She stood up, dusted off her dress, and stalked towards them in a swish of skirts.

"You." Carly stabbed Alec in the chest with a finger. "You asshole..."

"I sure am, honey." Alec looked her up and down. Then he looked at Kiernan and took in his garb. "I don't even want to know. Guys, take him to see Doc."

"Yeah, you'd better take him to see Doc," Carly muttered, stomping after them.

With his wolf hearing, Kiernan caught more of what Alec said, once they were outside Carly's range of hearing. "Keep up the perimeter, double the guard. Sean, keep an eye on the Huntress. If she fucks anything up, I'm mounting your head in the lodge next to Kiernan's."

"Yes, my Alpha," Sean said.

Kiernan was annoyed, but he wasn't in a position to complain. First, he needed to get a bullet out of his shoulder. Next, he had to grovel to his Alpha to let them stay.

Lastly, he had to explain to Carly what the fuck was going on.

11

COLD RECEPTION

CARLY

"Do you think I'm going to steal something?" Carly asked, getting tired of the silent sentinel standing next to her as she sat, waiting for a gray-haired, grizzled-looking mountain man to tell her Kiernan was okay. She'd ask Kiernan, again, but he was just going to tell her something manly. What she wanted was the God's honest truth.

Sean grinned at her, and for some reason, it just made Carly more pissed off. "Haven't you already?"

"What? No," Carly said. "I haven't touched a damn thing."

"The way he looks at you? I doubt that," Sean replied.

Carly was already weirded out by everything around her. The strange doctor, the not-exactly-hoppin' resort, the guy who thought he was all big and bad who ran the place. And the people in it. "Is this some kind of cult?"

Sean choked on a laugh. "Oh, I like you," he said. "I can't wait to hear the conversation you're going to have with Kiernan. It's going to be a real treat."

Chalking that one up to a yes. "Religious?" Carly asked. "Earthy? Oh my God, is this some kind of sex cult?! Because I am so not doing your leader. I don't care how hot he is."

"Ouch," Kiernan said from the bed. "Carly, could you at least wait until I'm dead before you find another man hot?"

"Every man here is hot. It's not normal," Carly said. She realized now that was what bothered her the most. Every one of the men who'd accosted them could have walked off a magazine cover. Or rather a centerfold. Not that any of them could hold a candle to Kiernan.

Sean laughed harder. "If I weren't looking for my own mate—"

"You'd still be dead for even thinking about it," Kiernan growled.

"You're lucky to be alive yourself," Doc said. "A few inches down and to the right and we'd be burying you out in the woods."

A cemetery in the woods? Mated? "Kiernan, did you bring me to your cult because you didn't want a doctor to find out you haven't had all your immunizations or something?" Carly asked.

"He didn't bring you to his cult. He brought you to his pack, Hunter," Doc spat, looking over his shoulder at Carly. He'd been prickly to her since she walked in the room. Now he was being downright rude, and Carly had no idea why.

"Who peed in your bran flakes?" Carly shot back.

"Carly, please," Kiernan said. "I'll explain everything in a minute." Then he hissed as Doc began roughly sewing him up.

Carly marched over and swatted Doc's arm. "Don't be an asshole just because you don't like me. Sew him up nicely."

"I'm not being an asshole because I don't like you, though I don't. I'm being an asshole because I don't like HIM," Doc said.

"Carly, go sit down. I can take it," Kiernan said.

"Look you cantankerous old fart—" Carly began.

"Old fart?!" Doc said. He dropped the needle. "Fine. You and your medical degree can go ahead and sew him up yourself."

Sean started to object, then his eyebrows shot up when Carly replied, "Fine, I will." She plopped herself down on the edge of the bed, dabbed some lidocaine on the wound, then began gently sewing Kiernan up.

"This is a surprise," Kiernan said while Doc squawked.

"I have a very accident-prone brother," Carly said. "Mom taught me how."

"Nice of her." Kiernan put a hand over Carly's when she was finished. "I would like you to try to get along with my pack, though. At least as long as we're here."

"You're all sewn up. We can leave now," Carly sniffed, sliding off the bed and setting the medical supplies aside.

Doc snorted. "Not with Hunters on your tail, you can't."

"Hunters? Mates? Pack? Jesus, Kiernan, what are you into here?" Carly asked.

"Thanks, Doc. I've got this," Kiernan said. "Sean, you can go, too."

"You're welcome," Doc grunted, snatching up his equipment and lumbering off.

"Not a chance," Sean said. "Alec was really specific about what kind of punishment I'll be getting if I don't stick to her like white on rice."

Kiernan laid his head back and groaned. He scrubbed a hand over his face. "Fine. Just... fine. Carly, we're here because my pack is here. I can't go to a regular hospital, and there was no guarantee the Superior Pack would take us in if we'd driven to Grand Marais. You see... I'm a werewolf."

Kiernan

Kiernan was prepared for any number of responses from Carly. Or so he thought.

"Werewolf?! Are you JOKING?!" Carly yelled so loud that both he and Sean winced.

"No," Kiernan said.

"You're in some weird cosplaying cult?!" Carly went on, and that was when Sean had to sit down because he was howling with laughter, so much so that he was actually almost howling. "What is he, a vampire?!"

"No, Sean is a werewolf," Kiernan said patiently. "Just like me."

Carly rolled her eyes. "Do the 'vampires' have a 'coven' across the lake, and you play fang-y water polo on Sundays?" She used air quotes to punctuate her words.

Sean was now taking in great gasps of air, almost unable to breathe. "Fuck me, your mate is a stitch and a half!"

"Thanks," Carly said. "Mate? When did I ever agree to be anybody's mate? I'm not staying in a cult, I don't care how much I like you or how good the sex is."

"You stay with the Hunters," Sean pointed out.

Confusion clouded Carly's face. "The who?"

"The Who is a band. The Hunters are a pimple on the ass of humanity," Sean said.

Carly threw up her hands. "You aren't making any sense. You're crazy. BOTH of you are CRAZY." She started to leave.

Kiernan caught her wrist. "Where are you going?"

"Home. I'm going home. I don't even know how I got caught up in this to begin with," Carly said. Her eyes were brimming with tears, but her jaw had a determined set to it.

Sean, meanwhile, had moved to guard the door. "Sorry, can't let you do that."

Seeing Carly cry made Kiernan's soul hurt. "It's fine. She's fine. She can go home," he said. "I haven't marked her."

"She smells like us now," Sean said.

"That, and she knows where we live," a new voice added.

Kiernan tugged Carly so she was sitting on the bed again, then slid her behind him protectively while she protested and beat on his back. Kiernan winced, but did not loose his grip on her wrist. "What do you want, Alec?"

"Six million dollars and a lake home in the wilds of Canada, away from all the tourists," Alec said. "But it doesn't look like anybody's getting what they want today."

"If Carly wants to go home, she can just go home. Just let her go home, Alec. We'll work it out between ourselves—" Kiernan began.

"Let the Huntress go home to tell all her Hunter friends and family where the werewolves are? Yeah, not happening." Alec stalked over by Kiernan and leaned over to sniff Carly.

Kiernan growled and shoved him in the chest with his injured arm. "Leave her alone."

"Still smells like wolfsbane," Alec said with a grimace. "Huntress, you need to take a shower."

"Excuse me?!" Carly said. "What, now you're planning to keep me here?!"

"Sure am," Alec replied. "Unless you'd rather I... fed you to the wolves." He laughed at his own little joke.

Neither Kiernan nor Carly were laughing. In fact, Kiernan's fingers had begun to elongate and grow claws. He felt the change, and tried to force it back, but it was too late.

"Oh my God," Carly gasped, trying to twist away from him. "Oh my God, Kiernan, you weren't kidding!"

Alec gave Carly a fang-y smile. "I think your mate wants to challenge me."

"Are you going to let us stay?" Kiernan growled, a real growl this time.

Alec looked Kiernan up and down. Then he looked at Carly. "You can stay. But she's staying in the basement. As a prisoner."

Kiernan let out a roar. "You're not keeping her in any damned basement!" He tried to think of a way out. He never should have brought Carly here.

"What are you going to do about it?" Alec retorted.

Kiernan began to shift more, the seams of his pants ripping.

"Yeah, I thought those pants were too tight," Alec said. "Now you're going to go all wolfy on your mate. She's scared out of her mind, can't you tell?"

Kiernan whipped his head around to look at Carly.

That was all the opening Alec needed. His face contorted, and his head became that of an oversized wolf.

"Kiernan!" Carly said, tugging his arm, and it was all that kept Alec's jaws from snapping around the back of his neck.

SUBMIT, Kiernan heard the order in his head, his wolf picking it out of Alec's thundering growl.

NEVER, Kiernan snarled back. He shredded his clothes when he fully shifted, as did Alec. Kiernan stood protectively over Carly on the bed.

Kiernan knew he couldn't exactly challenge Alec for the Alpha spot—he'd left the pack, after all. That meant he'd have to fight all of them, which he was not capable of, but for Carly, he was sure as hell going to try. Kieran settled himself back for a pounce, then felt his heart beat double-time when Carly popped out from behind him.

"You asshole!" she yelled and punched Alec, Alpha of the Crescent Moon Pack, right in the furry face.

Startled, Alec sat back on his haunches, shaking his head and snorting.

Kiernan knew they were probably going to die in the next few seconds, but he couldn't help but be proud of his mate. He licked her cheek.

Carly touched the spot, frozen for a moment. Then she looked in Kiernan's eyes and took a deep breath. "You and me, we're having words later. But right now, I just want to smack that smug look right off that fucker's face."

She had certainly done that, Kiernan reflected. It might be the last thing she ever did, but Alec certainly no longer looked smug. He looked bewildered.

Confusion melted into anger, however, and Kiernan's back hair stood up.

"We're gonna die, aren't we," Carly whispered, seeing other men gathering just beyond the door where Sean stood.

Kiernan sighed.

And nodded.

12

MONSTERS AND MEN

CARLY

Carly had never imagined she'd die dressed as a Medieval peasant surrounded by werewolves, like out of some bad B movie, but she'd be damned if she was going down without a fight. She grabbed the nearest weapon, a discarded scalpel, and pointed the bloody instrument at the werewolves. "I hope you get wolfy Hepatitis," she said.

The wolf she'd identified as Sean made several barking, hacking sounds, which Carly interpreted to be a laugh.

Alec snapped his jaws at him, then turned back to Carly and Kiernan. His hackles went up, but just before the big brown wolf would have launched himself at them, a curly-haired blond woman ran into the room.

"Alec, stop it, stop!" the woman cried. "What the hell are you all doing?! That's my brother!"

The other wolves, except for Alec, bowed their heads and took a respectful step back. Alec growled loudly.

"Well I don't care what he's done, you haven't even given him a chance to explain!" the woman said.

The growl turned to a whine.

"You were seriously going to kill my brother without even CONSULTING me first?!" the woman shouted.

Alec laid down on the floor and dropped his head between his paws, looking positively pitiful.

"That's right. You'd better be sorry." The woman looked over at Kiernan and Carly. "I apologize for the rude welcome. My name is Jenny. I'm this loser's mate." She jabbed a thumb in Alec's direction.

Alec made a low rumble, but one icy look from Jenny silenced him.

"Um, hi. I'm Carly," Carly said.

"You must be this loser's mate," Jenny said, pointing at Kiernan.

Carly bristled. "I wouldn't exactly call him a loser."

"He ran out on his pack, then brought a Hunter home," Jenny said. "What do you call that?"

"Stupid," Alec contributed. He had shifted back into human form and was now standing buck naked behind Jenny.

Jenny sighed, and gave Alec a respectful nod. "Please just hear him out. Now, Kiernan, would you like to explain properly why in God's name you came here with your Hunter mate?"

Carly watched as her sandy-haired wolf turned back into a sandy-haired man. Also naked under the low-hanging, wrought iron lights. "There wasn't anywhere else to go," Kiernan said.

The other werewolves began shifting back as well. It was like Saturday night at a strip club, except there was nowhere to shove the dollar bills. Carly didn't know whether to stare or shield her eyes. The devil and angel on her shoulders hadn't quite worked that one out yet. And yet... Carly looked at Kiernan. Both angel and devil were agreed that he was the yummiest one of the bunch.

"You think there's Hunters on your trail?" Jenny asked.

"If there aren't, there will be," Alec grunted, "as long as he has her."

Jenny frowned at Alec. "Would you hand me back over to Hunters if we were in the same situation?"

Alec's snarl shook the floorboards, and the lights rattled in their fixtures.

"I didn't think so," Jenny said. "So, we've got a bit of a situation to resolve here. I can hardly blame Kiernan for coming home wounded. Sure, it wasn't the best plan to bring a Hunter with him, but what else was he going to do, honestly? The Hunters would have figured out she'd been with him—I mean, she smells to high heaven of him, if you take the wolfsbane out of the equation—and probably tortured and killed her. You'd never have left me to that. Why would you expect any other member of our pack to do anything different?"

"He's not a member of our pack." Alec's voice dripped contempt.

"That's debatable. He was never officially exiled, now was he?" Jenny said.

Alec grumbled under his breath. "Well, no..."

"Great, then we can move onto other problems," Jenny said.

"Are... are you a werewolf?" Carly asked.

Jenny gave a toothy grin, her fangs extending just enough to show that she was. "Absolutely."

"Is Kiernan going to make me into a werewolf?" Carly continued, looking at the man who was supposedly her mate.

"No," Jenny said with a laugh. "Dear God, no. He couldn't even if he wanted to. You're either born a werewolf or you're not. Biting is strictly for dominance and mating."

"Ahuh," Carly said. She looked at Kiernan. "Well, say something."

"I thought Jenny was doing a pretty good job," Kiernan replied. "But I'd never mate you without discussing it first. I didn't come here to force you to stay with the pack. I honestly just couldn't reveal our existence to a regular doctor. We have a completely different blood type. I'd have been wiped out by a Hunter before I made it out of surgery."

Carly just got more frustrated. "What is a Hunter, already?!"

"You are," Alec said.

Kiernan

"That isn't fair," Kiernan rumbled. "Her family is, but she isn't."

"Fuck fair," Alec said. "There are Hunters, and not Hunters. She's a Hunter, or at least one of their women."

"Personally, I've always found it terribly unfair that Hunters are always men," Jenny sniffed. "I think a woman as feisty as Carly here would be a great asset to them."

"You're saying my father is a Hunter?" Carly asked.

"I'm saying your brother is. That's why he shot me." Kiernan put a hand over Carly's. "I'm sorry."

Carly shook his hand off, and Kiernan's heart sank. "So what makes werewolves good and Hunters bad?" she asked, and Kiernan could hear the desperation in her tone. "I mean, aren't werewolves supposed to be monsters?"

"See, there she goes. Huntress," Alec said.

"Alec, you are being a bit unfair." Jenny put a hand on her mate's arm. "At least give her some time to process all this."

Alec grunted, but went silent.

Indeed, Carly was trying very, very hard to process everything. She was somewhere between numb and panicking, or both ends of the spectrum at once, she couldn't quite tell.

Kiernan, who had been quiet up to this point, finally said, "Do you think I'm a monster?"

13

SUCKER PUNCH

Kiernan

"Well, not you specifically, but I do want to remind you that we just almost got ripped to shreds by your pack," Carly said.

At least she didn't hate him. Kiernan thought he could work with that. "You do make a good point."

"It was to avoid being ripped to shreds by your family," Alec said. "Or rather shot to death. Doc just rooted a silver bullet out of Kiernan's shoulder. It's not like they don't know what he is. And now they're going to hunt him, and especially you, and he brought you here. We have pups here. We need to protect our families."

"Kiernan is our family," Jenny argued.

"He was. Then I said I wanted him to be my Beta and he took off." Alec glowered at Kiernan. "Some best friend you turned out to be."

It stung, but Kiernan was still going to defend himself. "I didn't want to be tied down. Besides, how else would I have met my mate?"

"You didn't want to be tied down, but you wanted to find your mate. Those are polar opposites of each other, you realize that, right?" Alec said.

Kiernan shifted uncomfortably under Alec, Jenny, Carly, and the whole pack's attention. "I didn't expect to ever find my mate. Things are different now."

"Yes, you have a mate. Who's a Hunter. Who's going to draw all the other Hunters down on our heads. Thanks for that," Alec said.

"Could you maybe stop catastrophizing for one minute? They don't even know she's here," Jenny sighed.

Alec muttered something under his breath.

"What? I didn't catch that," Jenny said.

"I said I offered to put her in the basement," Alec replied. "He's the one who rejected the offer."

Jenny smacked Alec on the back of the head. "You offered to put his mate in our dungeon?!"

Alec's growl made Jenny shy away this time. "I'm indulging you, woman, but don't cross the line. I'm still the Alpha of this pack."

Kiernan saw the way Jenny's eye ticked when Alec called her "woman." Someone was going to be sleeping on the floor tonight. He looked at Carly, who still had an air of frustration about her. Probably two someones. He just hoped wherever they put them had a rug or an extra blanket.

Carly

"Okay, Mr. Alpha," Carly said. "You all still haven't answered my question about werewolves being monsters."

"I thought Kiernan was example enough." Alec started to pace back and forth, growling at intervals. "We just want to live in peace. We don't hurt anybody. It's the Hunters who are hell bent on our extinction. Still trying to figure out what we ever did to them, but this has been going on for over a thousand years. You think if we didn't want peace, people in general wouldn't know about us?"

"I suppose," Carly conceded. "But my brother's not a bad man. I have a hard time believing he'd be mixed up in killing people."

Kiernan reached for her hand again. Carly gave in and didn't pull away this time. She needed something to hang onto while her world was falling apart.

"Hunters don't see werewolves as people," Jenny said.

Carly thought of her loving, funny, incorrigible brother and just couldn't get her head around him being one of these Hunters. They'd have never convinced her in a hundred years if she hadn't seen him shoot Kiernan herself. "I just don't understand all this." She felt Kiernan squeeze her hand and pressed her forehead against his shoulder. "I suppose I don't have to if we're dying tonight."

"You're not dying tonight," Jenny said. "Alec, please. Please. For me. For the pack. In the name of love and justice, please just... let them stay a while. We'll figure all this out. It's not like they won't be here in the morning if you still want to rip your best friend's throat out."

Alec bristled. Then he barked, an actual, real bark, at the men behind him and they took off. "We're going to regret this," he said to his mate.

"Any more than you'd regret killing him?" Jenny asked, looking soulfully into Alec's eyes.

Alec turned and walked away, muttering under his breath.

Carly relaxed, and felt Kiernan do the same under her forehead. She looked up at Jenny. "What now?"

Kiernan

"Now you get some sleep," Jenny said. She looked at Sean, who handed a pair of shorts to Kiernan. "I took the liberty of firing up your A/C when I heard you were here. If I thought Alec was going to be such an idiot, I would have come here first."

Kiernan's stomach roiled. He had no desire to go back to his childhood home. But, it wasn't as though they could stay in the lodge—not with Alec on the warpath.

"It's clean," Jenny added with an understanding expression. "Everything but the furniture is still in storage. New bedding, everything. I thought, well, I thought maybe you'd come back someday."

"I guess I did," Kiernan said. His voice was gruff, and he knew Carly had heard it because of the bemused expression she gave him.

"Kiernan hasn't been home since his parents were killed," Jenny explained when he didn't.

"Kiernan's parents? Aren't they your parents, too?" Carly asked.

"It's a long story," Jenny said. "He became my brother when he moved in with my family when he was thirteen."

Carly nodded. "Was it a car wreck or something?"

Jenny winced. "Kiernan's parents were killed by Hunters. It was pretty brutal."

"Oh God," Carly said, and Kiernan was surprised when she hugged him from behind. "I'm so sorry."

Her touch was balm for his soul. That was, until her next question. "Did you ever find them?"

Kiernan put his hands over her arms, holding her there. "Yes."

"You must have killed them, then. I mean, that's how it works, right?" Carly asked.

"I didn't know you'd found them," Jenny said. "It must have been during your travels."

Kiernan evaded Jenny's eyes. "I only found them recently."

"Are they dead, then?" Jenny pressed.

"No. I can't-I can't do that," Kiernan said.

"Why not?" the women asked together.

Kiernan heaved a sigh. "Because it was your family, Carly."

14

HOME SWEET HOME

CARLY

Carly would have preferred it if he'd slapped her. The gut punch of that revelation was so painful that she would have pulled away, except for his grip on her arms. "What?"

"It wasn't your brother," Kiernan said quickly. "It was probably your father. Or even your grandfather."

"Are you sure?" Jenny asked.

Kiernan nodded.

"This is my family you're talking about. We're farmers for God's sake." If it was true, and Kiernan clearly believed it was, Carly had to admit, she was glad Matthew hadn't had anything to do with it. But she still felt sick. "Oh my God. How-how can you even bear to touch me?"

"You're my mate," Kiernan said. "Whether you decide to accept me or not, you're still my mate. I could never hurt your family. I know you love them. Even if your father is an asshat."

Carly gave his collarbone a light slap. It was all she could do with his grip on her. Otherwise, she might have punched him in the arm. "How can you joke?! Oh my God, this is just... oh my God..."

"This is one of those laugh or cry situations," Kiernan said, bending his head and kissing her arm. "I prefer to laugh at Fate's little ironies today."

From the stinging behind her eyes, Carly decided her way of dealing with Fate's little ironies was going to be to cry.

As though he'd sensed it, or perhaps smelled it, Kiernan pulled Carly into his lap and wrapped his arms around her. "It's not your fault, and I don't want you to feel bad about it. And Matt had nothing to do with it. I'm not mad that he shot me. Okay, maybe a little peeved, but he was just doing it because he wanted to be a good brother to you. All this going on around you just means there are a lot of people in this world who care about you. Especially me."

Her family couldn't be involved. They just couldn't. But Carly also knew Kiernan wasn't lying. He truly believed her family were the—monsters. What was she supposed to think?

Carly was not a crier by nature, but this? This was just too much. She burst into the heavy sobs of one who only had a good cry once every half decade. "Jesus, what is happening to my life?"

"I'll get some tissues," Jenny said, and made herself scarce.

Kiernan spoke softly in her ear, little reassurances and sweet nothings. It was the rumbling in his chest that was truly comforting, though, and allowed Carly to pull it back together by the time Jenny returned. "Thanks," Carly said when Jenny handed her the box. She grabbed a couple and dabbed her eyes and face. "God..."

"I think maybe it's time to get dressed and get to bed," Jenny said, her voice soft and kind.

"I have an overnight bag in the car," Carly said. "Oh my God... this is all so surreal."

Jenny squeezed Carly's shoulder. "It'll feel better after a good sleep and some long talks."

Carly felt a little less miserable at her friendly touch.

"You don't have to take us there. I remember where it is," Kiernan said.

Jenny's eyes became unfocused for a moment. "Sean is already there. He's parked himself on your pullout sofa." Jenny winced at Kiernan's expression.

"He did say he was supposed to watch me," Carly pointed out, feeling bad for Jenny. "Don't shoot the messenger." She hadn't even noticed Sean had left during her crying jag.

Kiernan dropped his chin onto Carly's shoulder. "I'm not even in on the mindlink anymore?"

"You did leave," Jenny said. "Alec hasn't accepted you back."

"He's really pissing me off," Kiernan grumbled. "And I can watch my own mate in my own house, I don't need help with that."

"Which part of 'he hasn't accepted you back' didn't you understand?" Jenny asked. "You might as well be a lone wolf. You're going to have to work very hard to get back into his good graces, brother."

Carly didn't know that they ought to be putting much effort into getting in that asshole's good graces, but she didn't say so. She changed the subject. "So, the house we're going to, is it yours as well?"

"No, it's Kiernan's. I live here in the lodge, and my family home is where my mother currently lives," Jenny said. She gave Kiernan an apologetic look. "Alec says you can't stay there right now."

Carly blinked. "I thought your parents were dead."

"Oh," Jenny said. "No, Kiernan's parents are dead. He stayed with us from thirteen on up, until he left."

"It's complicated." Kiernan scooped Carly onto the floor. "Let's go get your bag."

"Rob moved your SUV into the parking lot," Jenny said.

Kiernan nodded and took Carly's hand. "Thank you. We'll take it from here."

Kiernan

Once they had Carly's things, Kiernan led her to his family home. Every step he took was weighted with dread. He hadn't been back there since his parents' funeral almost twenty years ago. Alec knew this. Kiernan decided this must be part of his punishment.

"You don't look so good," Carly said. She was holding his left hand as they walked down the path, his injured arm. His right arm was occupied by her bag, slung over his good shoulder, which he'd insisted on carrying.

"I'll be fine in a couple of days. Werewolf healing," Kiernan said. "It'll be like I was never shot at all."

"Even with the silver?" Carly asked.

Kiernan shrugged. "Maybe there'll be a scar, I'm not sure."

"What does silver do exactly?" Carly asked.

"It burns. It also keeps us from shifting." Kiernan fell silent again.

Carly was chewing her lip. He'd begun to understand it as a sign of indecision. If he were feeling better, he'd have thought it was cute, but right now, with his parents' home on the horizon, he wasn't in the mood. "Are you sure the bag's not too heavy?" she asked him at last.

Fighting the urge to roll his eyes, Kiernan looked down at her, expecting she meant to start the argument all over again. The genuine concern in her eyes, however, made him relent. "It's not the bag. It's where we're going." Realization dawned on her face. "You haven't been home since your parents died. Duh, she said that."

"And Alec won't let me go back to Jenny's family home," Kiernan said.

"Would it be better for you if we really did stay in this basement place?" Carly asked. "I mean, how bad can it be?"

"The basement is more of a dungeon," Kiernan explained.

"Oh." Carly chewed her lip again. "Well, I mean, as long as it has a mattress or cots or bunkbeds or something..."

It warmed Kiernan's heart that she'd be willing to endure the basement, whatever its accoutrements, to keep him from having to return to his childhood home. He squeezed her hand. "No. I needed to do this at some point, and I'm just glad I'm doing it with you."

Carly gave an honest reply. "I'm still pissed off at you, you know."

"I know," Kiernan said. "Doesn't change facts."

They arrived at the end of the path, where a cheerful log cabin already had warm lights on inside. Kiernan could see Sean in the kitchen, making himself a sandwich through the open shades. The interior had split log paneling on the walls, and the floors were wood as well. The furniture was rustic, and there was a stone fireplace opposite the sofa, which was now pulled out into a bed.

As far as Kiernan could see from the outside, everything was as he'd left it, minus the family curiosities and knickknacks. He wondered if his parents' room was the same. He'd emptied his own room when he left, and the pack had graciously stripped the rest and put it in storage for him. Now, it might as well be a real resort cabin, empty of anything identifying except the people in it.

"It looks nice," Carly said, and Kiernan realized he'd been standing, frozen, for some time.

"Thank you. I've always thought so." Kiernan took a deep breath, then led Carly to the front door.

The door opened before Kiernan even put his hand on the knob. "Oh good, you're here," Sean said. "You hungry? They stocked the fridge."

Kiernan looked at Carly. "Are you hungry?"

"Mostly tired." Carly had a point. It was now past 3 AM after all.

"I'll get you set up in my parents' room," Kiernan said. He turned to Sean. "There's still furniture in my room, right?"

"Dunno, man, didn't check," Sean said. "I kind of figured with her being your mate and all..."

Carly's hand tightened in his, and Kiernan turned his attention back to her. "You okay?"

"You're just asking that now?" Carly said, and her laugh was a little hysterical.

Oh crap. "We'll talk in the morning. Or whenever you wake up. I promise," Kiernan said.

Carly shook her head.

"You want to talk now?" Kiernan hazarded.

"Stop putting words in my mouth!" Carly said. "I was going to say I want you to stay with me. But don't think you're getting lucky, Mister. I just trust you more than... all this other crazy shit going on around me right now."

"Fair enough," Kiernan said. "Want me to take the floor?"

Carly sighed. "No. I just... feel better when you're close to me, okay?"

For the first time since he'd been shot, Kiernan's wolf perked up a bit. "That's hopeful," he rumbled with a slight smile.

"Don't get any ideas," Carly warned again.

"I won't," Kiernan said. "We've got too much we need to talk about. And we're both wrecked anyway. Just sleep."

"Just sleep," Carly repeated, cementing the idea. Then she frowned and looked at Sean. "Hey, if there's another bedroom, why are you taking the pullout?"

"It's between you and the door," Kiernan said before Sean could answer.

Carly threw up her hands in disgust. "Honestly." She started stomping off in the direction of the kitchen.

"Hallway to the left," Kiernan called after her.

Carly changed direction, muttering under her breath about werewolves being assholes.

"You know we can hear you with that werewolf hearing of ours, right?" Sean chuckled.

"In that case, fuck you!" came the shout down the hall.

Sean clapped Kiernan on the shoulder. "She says the sweetest things. You're a lucky man."

"Don't I know it," Kiernan said with no irony at all.

15

JUST A KISS

CARLY

It was hot. Only this time, she wasn't standing at a booth at RenFest. This time, she was curled on her side with a werewolf spooning her, his bad arm slung over her waist. Kiernan's breath was warm on the back of her neck, feathering strands of black hair that had escaped her braid. He was in boxers and a t-shirt that Sean had lent him, in deference to their agreement. She remembered from sleeping with him in the RV that he preferred to sleep naked.

Carly was in a matching t-shirt and shorts with a Hello Kitty pattern on them. She remembered her conversation with Dawn about getting a cat instead of a man. At this moment, she rather wished she had.

"Hey," Kiernan breathed against her shoulder.

Of course. Being a werewolf, he could probably hear or feel or see or maybe even smell she was awake. Carly wiped her eyes, realizing she'd started crying again.

"Oh, Carly," Kiernan sighed, and then she was in his lap.

Carly wanted to push him away, but she was just too numb. Plus, if she were honest with herself, his embrace felt comforting and good. She leaned her cheek against his good shoulder.

"It's going to be okay," Kiernan said, stroking her hair.

"How?" Carly asked.

"Hmm?"

"HOW is it going to be okay? My family are probably worried sick about me. Oh, and according to you, they're murderers. Dawn and Matt are going to go nuts. Plus, you know, the fact that my brother shot you, I'm being held captive by a pack of werewolves I didn't know existed until last night..." Carly said. She realized, as she rattled on, she was starting to hyperventilate.

Kiernan rubbed her back gently. "Breathe," he said. "I'm going to make it okay. I don't care what it takes. If you want to go home, I'll find a way to get you there. The last thing I want is for you to be unhappy."

Carly laughed bitterly. "How can I go back to my old life now?"

"I-I don't know," Kiernan admitted, and he sounded genuinely sad about it.

"Well, at least you're honest," Carly said. She slid out of his lap, and he let her go. "Can I use the bathroom first?"

"Sure. Sean's in the other one, so I'll just wait." Kiernan got out of the bed and started making it.

Carly paused at the door of the ensuite bathroom. "How's your shoulder?"

"Better. It'll be even better tomorrow, too," Kiernan said, giving her a reassuring smile.

Carly nodded and went into the bathroom. She cried in the shower, and was sure the two werewolves could hear it, but there was nothing she could do to stop herself.

By the time she got out, Kiernan and Sean were having a very animated conversation in the kitchen. Sean was cooking breakfast, and Kiernan was slamming plates onto the counter. "I'm just saying she should see some of the sights while she's here," Kiernan said.

"Yeah, right. You want to take her to Hayward so she can call her family," Sean said. "Don't even try lying to me."

Kiernan began slamming down the silverware. "Look. She's been crying since last night. She's alone, and confused, and those people deserve to know their daughter's okay just as much as she deserves to talk to them."

"You do remember they killed your family, right?" Sean asked. "I wouldn't say they deserve anything."

A glass cracked in Kiernan's hand, and he swore, tossing it in the trash before grabbing another one. "Shit, is there anything people keep private anymore?"

"We're a pack. Jenny told Alec, Alec told the rest of us, you know how it works," Sean said.

"I'm not even done discussing that with Carly yet," Kiernan said. "And maybe her family don't deserve to hear from her, but she deserves to hear from them."

"They're just going to tell her that we're evil and she needs to get the fuck away from us." Sean started plating eggs and bacon. "Isn't that right, Carly?"

Carly blushed, realizing she'd been caught eavesdropping. Though it wasn't as though she'd snuck up on them. They were werewolves, after all. "Maybe they will. It doesn't mean I have to believe them."

"Right. You're going to believe us instead," Sean snorted.

"Hey man, you don't know her," Kiernan said. He sounded plenty pissed off, and Carly was secretly happy he was in her corner.

"And you do?" Sean asked. "Just how long have you known her?"

Kiernan coughed. "Three days."

"THREE DAYS?!! Oh hell no. We're not having her call home," Sean said.

"She's my mate. I trust her," Kiernan insisted. "I trusted her with my life, didn't I? She got me here, didn't she?"

"Whatever," Sean said. "Alec's never going to allow it anyway." He started bringing plates to the table, balancing one on his arm.

Carly was confused by Kiernan's sudden silence, until Sean groaned. "You're not planning to tell him."

"I thought he might have some strong objections, and I'm just not in the mood for his bullshit right now," Kiernan said.

"I just want to talk to my brother," Carly begged Sean as she moved into the kitchen and began pouring them orange juice. "Just for a minute."

"And what possible reason would I have to let you do that? Especially without telling Alec," Sean said.

Carly decided to appeal to his sense of fairness. "It's the right thing to do."

Sean's brown eyes became unfocused. Then he looked at the two of them. "The answer is no."

"Of course you told him," Kiernan growled. He stabbed his eggs hard enough to crack the plate.

Carly's heart felt a lot like that poor plate. "Oh."

They ate in silence for a while, then Carly asked, "Are you really sure I can't contact my family, Sean? Would it be so bad?"

"Alec said no," Sean said.

Carly looked around them, half expecting him to pop out of the furniture. "When?"

"When I contacted him," Sean replied.

"I don't remember you doing that," Carly said, frowning.

Sean shrugged at her. "We can do it telepathically, because we're in the same pack. That's what I was doing before when I was quiet."

"Oh," Carly said. "And he said no—"

Kiernan shoved his plate away, hard enough that it skidded across the table and shattered on the floor. "Ask Jenny."

"Hey!" Sean said. "Careful with the dinnerware!"

"Ask. Jenny." Kiernan's eyes were fiery enough that even Carly wanted to scoot away.

"She's not the Alpha," Sean argued.

"I don't care," Kiernan said.

"You should," Sean muttered, but his eyes went vague again. Emotions played across his face, and Carly began to understand some kind of argument was going on.

Finally, Sean's vision cleared. "Apparently we're going to Hayward."

"Good," Kiernan said, and got up to clean up his mess.

"I'm driving," Sean warned him.

"And you're keeping an eye on us. Yeah, I know," Kiernan said. He swept the remains of the plate off the floor and dumped them in the trash.

Carly's mood lifted for the first time since Matthew had shot Kiernan. She ran around the table and gave Sean a hug and a kiss on the cheek. "Thank you."

Sean cleared his throat self-consciously while Kiernan let out a low growl. "You're welcome," Sean said.

Kiernan

The ride to Hayward was fraught with tension. Carly was nervous, Kiernan could feel it in her pulse. But the most friction was in the silent war between himself and Sean. He didn't like that his mate had kissed Sean, no matter how innocently, and Sean knew it. The bastard had been smiling to himself the entire thirty-five minutes it took to get there.

Kiernan knew he was sulking, and tried to remember he was the one holding Carly's hand, not Sean.

"Are you okay?" Carly asked as Sean parked their SUV.

"I'm fine," Kiernan said.

"You don't seem fine," Carly replied.

Kiernan raked his hand through his hair. "I don't like you kissing other men."

"Other... you mean Sean?" Carly asked, sounding incredulous.

"Yes, I mean Sean," Kiernan grumped.

Carly laughed at that, and Kiernan felt his braincells sizzle. "Kiernan, it's Sean. He's doing something nice for me, that's all."

"I still don't like it," Kiernan rumbled.

Then, Kiernan's eyebrows shot up in surprise as Carly kissed him on the lips. "There," she said. "Feel better?"

He did. "I do. Just... don't go around kissing Sean anymore. Next thing you know, you'll be kissing Alec."

"Now that's never gonna happen," Carly vowed. "Asshat."

Kiernan couldn't help it. He laughed, his dark mood dissipating. "Try not to say that to his face."

"That's going to take some effort," she said.

16

BAD CALL

Hayward was quite a charming small town. It had a candy store where they were pulling taffy from scratch, and other little shops on Main Street, from clothing to a bait shop. There was even a nearby brewery. Hayward also hosted the Freshwater Fishing Hall of Fame, which had a small park attached that was overseen by a large musky and sunfish sculpture.

Carly barely registered any of it. She was rather annoyed Sean insisted on going on a sightseeing tour before she called Matthew. By the time they stopped at the gas station off of Highway 63, it was 11:30 AM. "You're trying to punish them, aren't you," Carly accused Sean.

"Maybe," Sean said. "But we're here now, aren't we?"

"Fucker," Carly muttered and went to the pay phone. Sean and Kiernan stood close by, Sean to make sure she didn't reveal any identifying information, no doubt. Kiernan? Carly got the feeling he was worried about her. He worried about her a lot. It was both annoying and adorable.

It took three rings before Matthew answered his phone. "Hello?" he said, sounding confused.

"Matt!" Carly cried. "Are you okay?"

"What do you mean, am I okay? Of course I'm not okay! You ran off with that... that..."

"Werewolf?" Carly supplied.

There was a long silence on the other end of the line. "Carly," Matthew said, his voice dropping to a whisper. "Where are you? Can you talk?"

"No and no," Carly said. "You shot Kiernan. You think I'm going to tell you where he is?"

"Yeah I shot the fucker. He's a werewolf!" Matthew all but shouted.

"So... we really do kill people?" Carly asked, her heart dropping.

Matthew was about to answer, when Carly heard a voice in the background that made her blood run cold. "Is that your sister?" her father asked.

"Er... it's a wrong number," Matthew said, his voice becoming distant as though he'd pulled the phone away from his mouth or hidden it behind his back.

"Liar," her father said, his tone promising nothing but dire consequences. "Hand me the phone."

"Dad, I was just talking her out of a fit of insanity," Matthew said. "Give me another minute—"

"Hand. Me. The. Phone." Carly had never heard her father sound so scary.

Matthew probably hadn't either, because the next thing Carly knew, Jamison Waite Jr., her father, was on the phone. "Caroline Noelle Waite, you get your ass straight home this instant."

"I can't do that, Dad," Carly said. "I'm not exactly alone here. Plus, I have it on good authority that you and Matthew kill people."

Her father tsked. "I'm not going to discuss this with you over an open line. Did you tell them where the farm is?"

"Just that it's in Vermillion," Carly said. "I don't want you to be killed, either. I don't want anybody killed. This whole thing is crazy."

"I can see where you'd think that, but as long as you're with them, you're in terrible danger." Her father sighed. "Now, I am willing to forgive you for helping that creature find his way back to his RV last night. And I suppose you also took him somewhere to get treated. I will forgive that as well. But I will not forgive you if you side with them against us."

Carly made an exasperated sound. "I'm not siding with anybody! Dad, Matthew shot a man, doesn't that bother you at all?"

"He shot a monster. That's his job. That's my job. That was your grandfather's job, and his father before him," her father said. "We can discuss all that at length when you are safely home. Right now, you will simply do as I say and try to escape. Or find a way to tell me where you are so we can come get you."

"I'm not going to let you kill them, Dad," Carly said. "Sure, the Alpha is an asshole, but there are good people there. They're people, just like me and you."

The silence that followed was dark and dangerous. "I'm sorry you feel that way." Her father's voice was positively bone-chilling. Carly shivered.

Kiernan put his arm around her.

"Dad, please try to understand. I'm trying very hard to navigate all this," Carly said.

"There is nothing to navigate," her father replied harshly. "Why are you being so disobedient? What, are you fucking him or something?!"

"Dad!" Matthew said in the background, at the same time Carly yelled it over the phone.

Sean made a "quiet down" motion as gas station patrons began looking at them curiously.

"Are you?" her father asked.

"I don't see where that's any of your business," Carly said, lowering her voice.

"I assure you, it is," her father replied. "I will not have my daughter be some wolf's bitch."

Carly's jaw dropped. She heard Matthew protesting, but was too shocked to resist when Kiernan pulled the phone from her fingers.

"Listen you murdering, soulless asshole," Kiernan seethed. "You watch your mouth. I will not let you talk to my mate that way."

"Kiernan!" Carly gasped.

She was surprised the phone didn't explode when her father responded. "WHAT?!!!"

"You heard me," Kiernan said.

"You are dead, do you understand me? You are DEAD!!!" her father screamed. "The both of you!!!"

"Dad!" Matthew said in the background.

Kiernan's voice went low. "Not if I get you first."

Kiernan

As he slammed the phone back into its cradle, Kiernan felt Carly begin beating her fists on his chest. He caught her wrists. "Not here," he said.

By now, they'd gotten the attention of several people. One kid was even filming them on his phone.

"Shit," Sean said. He went over to the kid, yanked his phone away, and stomped it on the ground. "We've got to go."

While the kid threatened to call the police, and some people actually started to, Kiernan took Carly by the wrist and dragged her towards the SUV.

"Let me go!" Carly said. "Let me go!"

Kiernan did—after he got her in the back seat. He slid in next to her while Sean hopped in the driver's seat and locked the doors.

"Sorry, Carly, but I can't have you jumping out," Sean said.

Carly's shriek of rage could rival any wolf howl. "Why did you do that?!" she said, beating on Kiernan's chest again. "Why?!"

Kiernan let her, feeling his heart break a little when a tear rolled down her cheek. "He was disrespecting you."

"Yeah, he does that," Carly said. "Especially when he's angry. I had it under control."

"Um, word from the peanut gallery, you didn't have it under control," Sean piped up from the front seat.

"Sean," Kiernan said. "Let her say her peace."

"I protected you!" Carly said, slugging him in the shoulder. At least it was his good shoulder. "How could you out me like that?! Now he hates me!"

"Peanut gallery again," Sean said. "He was going to hate you anyway, whenever he found out."

"How the hell was he going to find out?!" Carly raged.

Kiernan stopped her from punching him again. "That's enough punching for now, Rocky. If you want to have a conversation, let's have a conversation. But stop hitting me."

"Augh!" Carly exclaimed. "Just... argh! And you threatened him!"

"He threatened me first," Kiernan said.

"That's not the point! Did you really have to stoop to his level?" Carly said.

Kiernan gave that some reflection. "On second thought, I may have overreacted."

"Ya' think?" Carly said.

Kiernan mulled it over some more, then shook his head. "Actually, no. I think I gave him less than what he deserved. He insulted you. He probably killed my parents. All in all, I think I was pretty civil."

Carly's angry scowl burned right through him. "By threatening to kill him."

"I'm with Kiernan on this one. I think, given the circumstances, he was pretty chill," Sean said.

Carly went silent, but Kiernan could feel the steam coming off her all the way back to the resort. She sprang out of the SUV once they got there and went fuming down the path.

"Right at the fork, not left!" Sean called after her.

Kiernan sighed and scrubbed his face with his hands.

Sean came around the side of the car. "Dude, you are so fucked."

"Tell me about it," Kiernan said.

17

BETA

CARLY

When they got back to Kiernan's cabin, Sean made himself scarce, which Carly appreciated. She'd ignored his presence all the way there, but aside from looming over her, he'd not said or done anything. Sean sat down and turned on the television, a surprisingly newer model, considering how long Kiernan had been away from the place. This left Carly to her own devices.

Carly went to the bedroom and threw herself on the bed. She was livid at Kiernan, but she also felt rather foolish about throwing a public tantrum. No matter how much pain she was in, Carly had thought she had better self-control than that.

She screamed into a pillow, fairly certain Sean could hear her, even with the TV going. She didn't care. Carly needed to get it out somehow.

Carly wasn't even aware she'd fallen asleep until she woke up and looked at the clock. It had been an hour since she and Kiernan had parted ways. Was he also so steamed that he couldn't face her?

Fuck that, Carly thought, and walked out of the bedroom. "Hey, Sean? Where's Kiernan?"

"In a meeting," Sean said, flipping between channels.

"A meeting?" Carly frowned at Sean. "A meeting with who?"

"The council," Sean replied.

The council? Carly went over, grabbed the remote, and turned the TV off. "I wasn't invited?"

"You're not the one in trouble," Sean said, trying to snatch the remote back.

Carly held it out of his reach. "Now Kiernan's in trouble?"

"Well, you knew that already," Sean said. With an inhuman lunge of speed, he retrieved the remote from her and turned the TV back on.

"What are they doing to him?" Carly demanded, trying to get the remote back.

"Nothing you need to be concerned about," Sean replied.

Carly marched over to the wall and ripped the plug out of the socket. The TV went black. "Don't you tell me what I should or should need to be concerned about! Are they waterboarding him or something?"

"Pfft," Sean chuckled. "God, you're funny. They're just talking to him."

"About what?"

"Well, you know our help has a cost," Sean said.

"What do you mean? What cost?" Carly asked.

When Sean didn't answer right away, she waved the plug in the air. "What cost?"

"Ugh. I don't know why people are so excited to find their mates. You can be a headache and a half, you know that?" Sean said. "He's just being told he has to stick around here, and take his rightful place in the pack."

"You're planning to trap him here?!" Carly gasped.

San sighed. "It's not like we'd completely stop him from doing his furniture... thing."

"His furniture 'thing'?" Carly was beginning to understand why she and Kiernan agreed so easily about what constituted 'real' work. His furniture was not a 'thing' any more than her yarn and commissions business was a 'thing.' Though, she had to admit, her father had referred to it that way more than once. It made Carly see red. "I'll have you know he makes fantastic furniture, and it's not a 'thing.' It's his passion!"

"Yeah, whatever," Sean said.

Carly rammed the plug back into the wall. "You people. I swear to God."

"That's Fate, baby," Sean said with a shrug, going through the streaming services until he found ESPN.

"Yeah, well, I have a few words for Fate. And don't call me 'baby.'" Carly walked to the door.

Sean turned off the TV. "Where do you think you're going?"

"The lodge. You coming or not?" Carly snapped.

Sean got to his feet, grumbling under his breath about Fate and mates and something to do with bullshit. "You are such a pain in the ass."

"You haven't seen pain in the ass yet. But I promise you, you're about to."

Kiernan

Kiernan had started after Carly when they left the SUV, keeping a bit behind as Sean jogged to catch up. He wanted to give Carly her space. Sean, on the other hand, was taking his job of guardian very seriously, and wasn't giving her any space at all. Kiernan growled. He was going to have to have a word with him.

The path was blocked by a wall of muscle when Kiernan turned at a bend in the path. "What the—"

Strong hands grabbed Kiernan by the arms and duck marched him back in the direction of the lodge. "What the fuck?!" Kiernan said, but no one would answer him.

They dragged him into the lodge and into the conference room, then dumped him on the floor. Kiernan winced as his bad shoulder hit the hardwood. Alec was standing at the head of the table, with six grim-faced elders lining the sides.

"Alec, what the fuck?" Kiernan asked.

"So," Alec said, coming around the side of the polished wood conference table. "Imagine my surprise when I saw this on the internet." He shoved a tablet in Kiernan's face.

Kiernan didn't need to see the video to know what it was. The frozen preview image of Carly beating on his chest was enough. "I can explain."

"Let's watch, shall we?" Alec continued, starting the video.

It was thirty-six damning seconds of fighting. Thirty-six seconds of making a big scene. Thirty-six seconds where they might have been exposed.

Thankfully, they weren't.

"You can see where I'd be a mite concerned," Alec said. "We don't make scenes like this. Causing this kind of ruckus among the public makes people start asking questions. Then cops show up. Then, we have problems."

"Did the cops show up?" Kiernan asked.

"Thankfully, no," Alec said.

"Then what's the problem?" Kiernan asked.

Alec put the tablet on the table and crouched down next to Kiernan. "The problem," he said in his ear, "is that you have absolutely no control over your mate."

Kiernan choked on a laugh. "Tell me sometime how that 'controlling your mate' thing is working with Jenny, then we'll talk."

"You think this is funny?" Alec gripped his hair and forced Kiernan to look at him. "I don't think it's funny."

"Her father disowned her because I was a bastard. What would you have done? I'm surprised she didn't cut off my dick," Kiernan said.

"You're making being a bastard into a habit," Alec grumbled. He let go of Kiernan's hair. "Jenny said it was selfish of you to bring her here, and I agree. Now, she doesn't have any options."

Kiernan's stomach roiled. Alec wasn't wrong. Still... "She doesn't have any options because you're not giving her any. And I had no idea at the time whether or not she was in danger from her brother or other Hunters."

"And you couldn't drive yourself," Alec said.

Kiernan grimaced. "And I couldn't drive myself."

"You make a good point about the Hunters, though," Alec conceded. "All the more reason you should have left her there."

"Are we really going to go round and round this again?!"

"No. We're not." Alec pulled Kiernan to his feet and planted him in a chair. He himself leaned on the edge of the table. "We've discussed it. Jenny vouched for you, so you're here. And we've decided not to kill you."

"Do you want a parade?" Kiernan asked.

"No," Alec said. "I want a Beta."

1 8

SUCCESSION

Kiernan

"What does you wanting a Beta have to do with me?" Kiernan asked, though he had a sinking feeling he already knew.

"Don't play dumb," Alec said. "It's your rightful place, just like your father was my father's Beta and your grandpa was my grandpa's Beta and back on down the line. I've wanted you as my Beta ever since I took over the pack. And now, if you want to stay here, you're going to do it." He leaned over Kiernan, putting his hands on the arms of Kiernan's chair.

Back in the day, Kiernan had made these chairs. He didn't remember them being so confining.

"You think you'll last five seconds out there on your own? What about your mate?" Alec asked in a low tone.

"You're not going to let us go anyway, so what does it matter?" Kiernan said.

"True," Alec said. "But I don't know that you want to be a prisoner here for the rest of your life. If you were my Beta, there wouldn't be a problem."

Kiernan grit his teeth. "If I were your Beta, you'd be nattering in my head all the time. And I'd have to submit to your rule."

"Funny that," Alec said. Then he sniffed the air and looked up. "What fresh hell...? She really needs to wash her clothes."

Kiernan scented his mate and turned to the door just in time to watch her march in, Sean trailing in her wake.

"Are you completely incompetent?" Alec asked Sean.

"Well, aside from locking her in her room—" Sean began.

"Then you should have locked her in her room!" Alec growled.

"I'm right here," Carly said, her arms folded. "And you're an asshole."

Alec let out a snarl. "Yes, I am. We've been over that. But I'm the asshole who's in charge, so it might do you some good to watch your tongue for once."

Kiernan got out of the chair, now that Alec had freed him, and went over to Carly. "Carly." He took her by the shoulders. "You really shouldn't be here."

"I disagree," Carly said.

"Of course you do," Alec grunted.

"Hey, lay off my mate. She's had a rough day, and this whole situation isn't helping," Kiernan snarled.

"That's why I'm here. I want to figure out this whole situation, and tell you not to do... whatever it is you're planning to do," Carly said.

"He wants to make Kiernan his Beta," Sean supplied.

Alec scowled at Sean. "Did I make the right choice in selecting you to be in charge of her?"

Sean shrugged. "You try it sometime."

"What's a Beta?" Carly whispered to Kiernan.

"It's sort of like an assistant and second in command," Kiernan said.

"Wait, does that mean you'd be stuck here?!" Carly gaped. "That's not fair!"

Alec let out a roar. "Enough! Ever since you got here, there's been nothing but insubordination all around! You..." He prowled closer to Carly and Kiernan, but his eyes were focused on Carly.

Kiernan did not see this as okay. "Are you threatening my mate?" he rumbled.

"Shouldn't I? She's been nothing but trouble since she got here," Alec said.

Kiernan began shifting in his anger, his body breaking out in fur, his fangs starting to drop.

Carly put a hand on his arm, however, and it stopped him. The hair receded and the fangs retracted.

Alec, who had begun to do the same, stopped shifting as well. "It's you become Beta or we kill your mate and you're out in the cold. That's the council's decision."

Kiernan's jaw worked. He felt his freedom slipping away. But it was a small thing in comparison to losing Carly. "Since you asked so nicely," he spat.

"Good," Alec said. "The ceremony will happen tonight. Now, to other business."

"Wait, I'm not done—" Carly began.

Kiernan hugged Carly to him, putting her face in his chest so she couldn't say anything else. "We're done."

Carly

Alec seemed to be waiting for something, then let out an exasperated sound. "Get out."

Sean and Kiernan each put a hand on one of Carly's shoulders and steered her out of the conference room.

"What was that?!" Carly objected once the door slammed shut behind them.

"He can still hear you," Sean said.

Carly opened her mouth to shout something so Alec could hear it even better, but thought better of it. She contented herself with a simple, soft, "Motherfucker."

"Please," Kiernan said tiredly. "Please, stop antagonizing him."

"He's being a dick," Carly said.

"He's being a dick," Kiernan agreed. "But he's the dick in charge of this place, and we have nowhere else to go where we'd be protected."

"You mean you have nowhere else to go. He's going to kill me," Carly said.

Kiernan growled. "Over my dead body."

"Pretty sure he knows that, which is why he threatened to kill her," Sean said. "I doubt he has any intention of letting you go, either."

"Yeah, I got that impression." Kiernan looked out over the lake, a caged animal.

Carly put a hand on Kiernan's chest. "It's not fair." She looked Sean up and down. "Do you suppose you could, I don't know, overpower Sean and we could get the fuck out of here?"

Sean and Kiernan both laughed at that, though Kiernan's laugh was bitter.

"What? What's so funny? Is he stronger than you or something?" Carly asked.

"No," Kiernan sighed. "But we can't outrun the pack. Even in the SUV. No matter how far we drove. They have our scent, yours and mine. They'll communicate it to every pack from the North Pole to Cape Horn. There's nowhere to go. Besides, your family is coming for you. We need the pack to protect us."

"They don't even know where I am," Carly said.

"They will," Kiernan said. "They always do."

Carly wasn't so worried about Matthew finding them. Him, she was sure she could talk down.

The idea of her father finding her with Kiernan, however, scared her down to her toes.

19

MAKING UP

Kiernan

Kiernan swished and spat several times in their ensuite bathroom, but it was no use. He couldn't get the taste of vomit out of his mouth. Or maybe it was just the taste of being trapped. He'd been sick once they returned to the cabin, feeling his freedom slip away.

"Feeling better?" Carly called from the bedroom.

No, he thought to himself. Everything had gone spectacularly to hell. Worse, he'd dragged Carly down with him. "I'm feeling better," he called back.

Carly came into the bathroom and locked eyes with him in the mirror. "Liar."

"That, too," Kiernan said. He turned around, leaning against the sink and pulling Carly between his legs. "I'm sorry," he said, pressing his forehead to hers. "I fucked up."

Kiernan stared at the floor for what felt like forever, then he felt Carly's hands on his cheeks. He looked up into her beautiful green eyes.

"You know," she said. "Between getting stuck here and seeing you as a rug on our living room floor, I'd choose here. I think Matt really would have killed you. That would have broken my heart."

Kiernan's own heart pounded. "That's-that's good to hear." He wondered if he could kiss her.

Carly made the decision for him, placing a soft kiss on his lips. "This doesn't mean I'm agreeing to be your mate."

"I understand," Kiernan said.

"And we're probably not going to have sex," Carly added.

Kiernan grinned. "Probably?"

"Oh shut up," Carly grumbled. But she kissed him again just the same.

C ARLY

ESPN got louder and louder over the next few hours, but then, so did they. Make up sex really was fantastic, Carly decided. She also sent a short blessing in the direction of whomever had stocked them up on condoms.

Kiernan trailed his fingertips down her arm, raising goosebumps in their wake. "Will you come to the ceremony tonight?"

Carly heard the hopeful uncertainty in his tone, and rolled so she could prop her chin on his chest. "If you'll be there, I'll be there."

"Good," Kiernan said. He relaxed underneath her.

"Are you worried?" Carly asked. "What happens during the ceremony?"

Kiernan's gaze evaded hers for a moment. "Well... Alec bites the back of my neck."

Now Carly was worried. "What if he hurts you?"

"It's mostly ceremonial. He probably won't sink his teeth in too much, just enough to leave a scar," Kiernan said. "They put silver powder over it so the mark gets burned into my skin. I wash it out in the morning."

"By morning?! Isn't that going to hurt?!" Carly asked.

"Like hell," Kiernan confirmed. He stroked his hands down Carly's back. "It'll be okay, though. It's not like it'll kill me."

Carly rolled her eyes. "Whatever doesn't kill you makes you stronger?"

"Something like that," Kiernan said. "Anyway, you don't need to worry about it. Just you being there makes me stronger."

"Like, literally? Is that like a wolfy mate thing?" Carly was curious.

Kiernan's rumbling laugh rolled through her, almost making her want to see if there were more condoms in the dresser. But she was tired, and so was he, and he was going to need his strength for tonight, if the ceremony was like he said. "No, no wolfy superpowers from getting a mate. Just a deep sense of... contentment."

"Contentment?" Carly asked.

Kiernan blushed, and Carly thought it looked good on him. She wondered if he felt the same when she did it. "It's like something missing sliding into place. Something you didn't even know you were missing until it's there."

"Oh." That was deep. It was Carly's turn to blush.

Kiernan ran a thumb over her cheek. "I'm not going to pressure you into becoming my mate, you know, officially. I don't want to do that to you. You can make up your own mind. There's no rush."

Carly snuggled him. This was why she loved him.

She froze suddenly at the errant thought. Oh my God, do I love him? she asked herself.

The answer was a complex snarl of emotions, and Carly decided to let it go for the time being. As he said, there was going to be plenty of time.

"What are you thinking about?" Kiernan asked, combing his fingers through her hair, which she had left long today.

"Nothing much," Carly said quickly. "Just worried about the ceremony tonight."

"I'll be fine," Kiernan said. "Don't worry. Besides, I'll have you to take care of me."

Carly chewed her lip. "How am I going to resist the urge to wash the silver out early?"

Kiernan thumbed her lip out from between her teeth and kissed her. "I'll stop you. I won't be so weak that I can't."

"Well, that's a relief. Not that you'll stop me, just that you won't be so weak that you still could if you need to," Carly said. She played her fingers over his chest, and felt the thump thumping of his heart pick up under her hand.

"Don't do that," Kiernan said.

"Or what?" Carly teased.

Kiernan rolled her underneath him. "Or we're going to need another condom."

Kiernan

They were interrupted by a knock on the door. "Hey, Kiernan, don't you know Jenny's here?" Sean said.

Kiernan sighed and rolled back off Carly. "I've been a little distracted."

"Yeah, I noticed," Sean said. "Anyway, she's in the kitchen."

Kiernan grumbled and got up to hunt down some pants and a shirt.

Carly had her hand over her mouth. The way her eyes danced gave Kiernan the distinct impression she was trying not to giggle.

"You can get up, too. I'm sure I'm not the only one she's here to see," Kiernan said.

Carly wriggled out of bed, and Kiernan stopped dressing long enough to appreciate her very fine backside. "Do you suppose she's here to talk about the ceremony?" she asked.

"Hmm?" Kiernan said. "Oh, sure. Probably."

"You were looking at my butt, weren't you," Carly said, folding her arms over her breasts.

That was a shame. "Maybe."

"You and my brother, Matt. You're both incorrigible," Carly sighed, and began pulling on pants and a t-shirt.

"We'll continue this later," Kiernan purred, and Carly frowned.

"Are you even going to want to after the ceremony?" she asked.

Kiernan gave her a slow grin. "You'd be surprised."

"Ugh, men," Carly said, putting on some socks. "I swear I should have gotten a cat."

"Sorry, babe. I'm not that kind of shifter," Kiernan said.

Carly blinked at him. "You mean there are others?"

Kiernan nodded. "But we can talk about that later. Right now, Jenny's here."

"Right," Carly said. "Jenny's here. Jenny's here and you're going to get bitten and then burned by silver powder. Only one of those sounds appealing."

"Welcome to my world," Kiernan said.

20

LOVE WOES

CARLY

Jenny was sitting at the table, graceful in shorts and a halter top. She had her legs crossed, one tennis shoed foot bouncing idly in the air. Sean had gotten her some cold pink lemonade, and she sipped it as she waited for Carly and Kiernan to sit as well. ESPN told Carly where Sean was. He must not have been invited to this conversation.

"I'm glad you two made up," Jenny said.

Werewolf senses. Carly was never going to get used to them. "Er... yeah, we did." Carly blushed.

"It's awful when mates are at odds with each other," Jenny said.

"How's it been going with you and Alec?" Kiernan asked.

Jenny winced. "About as well as can be expected."

"Sorry to hear it," Kiernan said.

"Life happens." Jenny looked down at the table, though. "Honestly, I don't know how we're going to get through this one."

Carly wanted to offer some words of comfort, but she had none. Alec, in Carly's eyes, was completely irredeemable.

"I'm sure you will. Alec's not completely irredeemable," Kiernan said, sitting down and putting a hand over Jenny's.

Carly choked on her lemonade in surprise.

"Are you okay, babe?" Kiernan asked. He patted Carly on the back.

"Yeah, fine," Carly coughed. "Wrong tube."

"Figured that much," Kiernan said. He turned back to Jenny as Carly's coughs quieted down. "He loves you and he's your mate. Just hang onto that."

Jenny shook her head. "What if love isn't enough?"

Kiernan

Kiernan wanted to rip Alec's balls off more than ever for making his sister so sad. What the fuck was wrong with Alec, anyway? He also felt bad for creating this impossible situation for his sister and his best friend. It hadn't been avoidable, but it still sucked. "Love has to be enough, Jenny. If it's not, what's the point of having a mate?"

"Some days, I just don't know," Jenny said miserably.

"Your mate's being a dick," Carly said, and Kiernan frowned at her.

But Jenny nodded her head in agreement. "Yeah, he is."

"Did you tell him he's being a dick?" Carly asked.

"Many times," Jenny said with a laugh.

"Maybe you should try understanding his situation...?" Kiernan said. That got two women staring daggers at him, and Kiernan swallowed. "Maybe not?"

"You haven't been here, Kiernan. He's getting worse every year. He doesn't have a Beta, and there's all this stress coming down on him," Jenny said.

Kiernan couldn't hide his confusion. "Why didn't he choose a Beta?"

Jenny stared him straight in the eye as though he were terminally stupid. "He was waiting for you, duh."

"I said I wasn't coming back. I meant it," Kiernan said.

"Yet, here you are," Jenny replied.

"Not exactly by choice, Jenny," Kiernan said.

Jenny shrugged. "That's one of the things we're fighting about. I told him it was wrong of him to force you to be his Beta. But he's adamant, and the council has spoken. There's nothing I can do."

"Jenny." Kiernan squeezed her hand. "You don't need to apologize for not being able to do anything. You kept us from being killed. That's plenty."

"I'm kind of happy to be alive, yeah," Carly said.

Jenny gave a wet laugh, and Kiernan realized she was going to start crying. He felt like a heel. "Hey, I'll do all my Beta duties, Alec will—"

"Get the stick out of his ass," Carly provided.

"—and things will get better, okay? I can't say I'm sorry I left, but I'm sorry I left you to deal with this. I didn't know," Kiernan said.

"Kiernan, you made it very clear what your priorities were. You never hid your intentions from anybody. This is not your fault." Jenny patted his hand with her free one. Then her eyes went blank. "Oh. I guess it's time to start preparing for the ceremony. I'll send someone over with your outfits." She slid her hands out of Kiernan's. "Thanks for listening."

"Anytime," Kiernan said.

Carly looked from Kiernan to Jenny and back again. "Outfits?"

"You're not expected to wear the mate's robes," Jenny said. "You're not officially Kiernan's mate yet, as he hasn't marked you. But it is a formal occasion, so I thought I'd get you a dress."

"Tradition," Kiernan said, giving Carly's knee a squeeze. Her pulse took off, and his groin tightened. Maybe there'd be just enough time to get in one more round.

"Yeah, okay. I don't want to schlep in there," Carly said, blushing. "I'll look good for you."

Kiernan gave her his sexiest smile. "You always look good to me."

Carly

She should have known he was a werewolf from the beginning. Only a wolf could perfect that I'm-going-to-eat-you-up smile. Carly shifted uncomfortably in her seat. She knew he could smell her arousal. He'd told her as much before.

What was most embarrassing was that Jenny and even Sean probably smelled it, too. Jenny just smiled and rose from her chair in one lithe movement. "I'll see you two later," Jenny said. "Don't be late."

"I make no promises," Kiernan rumbled, setting the table to vibrating.

The gravelly rumbles also traveled up Carly's knee, and she blushed. "You don't fight fair."

"Are we still fighting?" Kiernan asked, sliding closer to her.

Carly swallowed. She could already feel the heat from his body. "No. Not right now."

"Then there's no reason for me not to do this." Kiernan swept Carly up in a fireman's carry, planting her over his good shoulder.

"Hey! Hey!" Carly laughed in surprise. "What are you, some kind of caveman? Put me down."

Sean ignored them, but already turned up ESPN.

"No babe," Kiernan said, depositing Carly on the bed and peeling his shirt over his head. "I'm a wolf."

"Are you sure we have time for this?" Carly gasped as Kiernan removed his pants. Her eyes went to his dick and she saw he was already hard.

"We're gonna make time," Kiernan said and began divesting Carly of her pants.

Carly pulled her shirt over her head and tossed it over the side of the bed. "You're addictive, you know that, right? And having a body like that doesn't help matters."

The condom wrapper crinkled as Kiernan tore it open with his teeth. "My body? Look at yours. If you walked around naked all day like some of the she-wolves, I'd always have a hard-on."

Carly tugged Kiernan down by his arm so they were nose to nose. "Don't you dare go ogling some naked she-wolves."

"Babe, the only woman I want to ogle is you." Then Kiernan thrust into her, hard.

Carly squealed with astonishment, but not with pain. She was still ready for him from before. It was just a shock to have Kiernan be so forceful.

"Are you okay?" Kiernan breathed in her ear.

Carly nodded against his cheek. "Yeah." She pulled his head back a little so she could search his amber eyes. There was need in them, but also unease. "You're nervous about the ceremony."

"I'm nervous about what comes after," Kiernan admitted, brushing her cheek with the back of his hand.

Carly wound her arms around the back of his neck, and her legs around his waist. "Take what you need," she said.

Kiernan groaned, and then Carly was hanging on for dear life as he thrust hard and fast. His lips captured her moans, while his hand gripped the headboard and used it as leverage.

Carly worried they might break the bed, it creaked so ominously. Then, Carly wasn't worried about anything at all as she felt delightful little fireworks all over her body. She cried out against Kiernan's mouth.

Kiernan groaned and gave two more deep thrusts before burying himself deep inside her and finding his own release. He held Carly against him as they both shivered in the aftermath. "Thank you, Carly."

Carly nodded, stroking the back of his neck. Soon, stupid Alec was going to bite him there, and his life would be changed forever. Hers, too. "It's not fair," she said softly.

"No," Kiernan agreed, "it's not. But it's necessary."

There was a knock on the door and Kiernan growled. Because he was still inside her, Carly felt the growl right in her core.

"Sorry to interrupt," Sean called through the door, "but your clothes are here."

"You have the world's worst timing," Kieran said, pulling as gently out of Carly as he had been rough earlier and discarding the condom in the trash. Carly pulled up a sheet before Kiernan opened the door.

"Here," Sean said, handing over a white robe and something in a garment bag. "You've got thirty minutes."

Thirty minutes? That was hardly enough time to get showered and changed, let alone apply make-up.

As though sensing her distress, Kiernan shut the door in Sean's face. "You shower first," he said. "If we get in together, we'll never get out again."

There was truth to that. Carly got out of bed and kissed him, then raced for the shower. The last thing she wanted was to be late on top of riling Alec up today. It wouldn't be fair to Jenny.

Kiernan handed her a towel when she got out, then there was a changing of the guard, Kiernan showering while Carly struggled to do her make-up and hair. She was almost able to keep herself from being distracted by his yumminess when Kiernan stepped out of the shower again. Almost.

She poked herself in the eye with her liner. "Ouch."

"I'll just go get dressed," Kiernan chuckled.

Carly finished her make-up, fluffed her hair, and trotted back into the bedroom. Kiernan was wrapped up in a white robe with a wolf howling at the crescent moon on one lapel. He held a delicate green, sleeveless, floor-length dress out to Carly. "Here's what was in the bag."

"Wow," Carly said. She wished she had more time to admire it, but the clock told her they now only had five minutes to get to the lodge. She stepped into the dress as he held it open for her, the open back making it impossible to wear a bra. Matching heels were on the floor.

"I'd suggest putting those on when we get there," Kiernan said. "They're not exactly something you want to wear for a walk in the woods."

Carly nodded and put on some flats, taking the heels up in her hand. "Are we ready?"

"No," Kiernan said. "But we're going."

Carly looked at the clock again and groaned. "Crap. We're going to be late!"

THE BITE

Kiernan

The main hall of the lodge was dark, lit only by thick, white candles. Pack members stood at either side of a path, that ran down the middle from the doors to a small raised platform at the front. The elders had been provided chairs on the platform, arching behind Alec in a kind of choir formation. Alec stood at the center in a black robe with the same crescent moon and wolf patch that decorated Kiernan's robe. Everyone else wore formal attire—suits and dresses.

"You sure you wouldn't rather we live in the basement?" Carly whispered, looking around at all the serious faces.

Kiernan chuckled, even as her words inspired Sean to close the heavy wooden doors behind them and subtly stand to block them. "Babe, even if we could go back and do that at this point, I wouldn't let you stay in the basement."

Carly chewed her lip, her pulse picking up. Kiernan would rather her pulse had picked up because of something he did rather than nerves. He rubbed his thumb against her wrist to comfort her.

Jenny was gesturing for Carly to stand next to her at the front. Carly looked up at him, and Kiernan gave her a reassuring smile. "Go on," he murmured. "Everything's going to be fine."

Carly moved over next to Jenny, standing between her and one of the elders' mates. Kiernan continued up onto the platform and stopped before Alec.

"Well, brother, here I am," Kiernan said, spreading his arms out briefly in a kind of "ta-da" motion.

"As you always should have been," Alec replied. His voice was gruff, angry. It gave Kiernan a bad feeling.

Alec turned to the rest of the room. "Today, we welcome our brother home, and into his predestined position as Beta of this pack. Anyone who has any objections, voice them now or forever remain silent."

Much to Kiernan's surprise, no one said a word. He'd expected at least one or two of the stronger werewolves to share their displeasure that a near-outsider was being named Beta. Instead, there was nothing but the chirp of crickets and the wind through the trees through the open windows.

They must have worked all this out earlier, Kiernan reasoned. There went his last hope.

Alec nodded and turned to Kiernan. "As there are no objections, you will remove your robe and assume a submissive position before me."

Kiernan heard Carly give a little squeak of protest as Kiernan dropped his robe, leaving him naked, and knelt before Alec, bowing his head to expose the back of his neck.

"You should have done this when I told you to." Alec's harsh words were his only warning. Then he struck, long werewolf teeth ripping into Kiernan's muscle.

Kiernan grunted. It was more than was necessary to complete the ceremony. A lot more.

As Alec tore his teeth back out, Kiernan could feel blood rushing down his neck and over his shoulders, chest, and back. He heard Carly's abortive scream and jerked his head that way, the pain making a white wooziness flicker over his body. Sean was standing behind Carly now and had a hand over her mouth.

Despite his pain, Kiernan growled menacingly.

That growl turned to a whimper of pain as an elder came over and dusted his wound with silver powder. It burned even worse than Matthew's silver bullet.

The only good thing about the silver was that it cauterized his flesh, and the bleeding slowed, then stopped.

Kiernan opened his eyes again, not having realized he'd shut them.

"Who is your Alpha?" Alec demanded.

Kiernan licked his lips. At some point, he must have screamed. "You are, my Alpha."

"Who do you serve?" Alec continued.

"I... serve you, my Alpha," Kiernan said.

A commotion caught his attention. Kiernan looked over and saw that Sean now had Carly completely restrained. From the scent of blood in the air, other than his, Carly must have bitten him. Carly was kicking Sean's shins with her heels, and Sean grunted as a few kicks hit home.

To say Kiernan was displeased by the sight of his mate being manhandled by Sean was an understatement. He bared his fangs at Sean.

Alec ignored the situation. "Swear fealty to me and to this pack as my Beta," he said, tipping Kiernan's chin up to look at him. His expression was smug.

Kiernan wasn't sure if he'd ever hated anyone in his life as much as he hated Alec in that moment. "I do so swear."

"Rise and meet your pack," Alec said.

Everyone but Alec, Sean, and Carly pressed their right fists to their left shoulders. "Beta Kiernan," they said.

"Now, will you get down there and control your mate before she gives Sean some permanent damage?" Alec murmured in his ear.

Kiernan's teeth ground against each other hard enough to be heard by the people in the front three rows, without the need of werewolf enhancement. "Yes, my Alpha." He pulled his robe up, which quickly soaked through with blood, and went down by Carly. He snarled at Sean, who was more than happy to let her go.

Carly threw herself into his arms. Her tears soon mixed with his blood at his collarbone.

"I'm okay," Kiernan said, stroking her back. "I'm just fine. Everything is just fine."

He hoped it was true.

C ARLY

When blood began gushing over Kiernan's body, it snapped the last of Carly's resolve. She'd screamed and made a start for the platform. Then Sean had been there with his hand over her mouth. Once they added the silver to the equation, Sean had to lift her off the floor. Kiernan's scream rent her heart in two.

Hate did not begin to describe how Carly was feeling towards everyone in that room except Kiernan. She even hated Jenny, who was trying to take her hand, but Carly slapped it away. She kicked Sean's shins all the way through the sick fealty swearing. She only stopped when Kiernan finally descended from the platform and came over to her.

Carly grabbed onto Kiernan, pressing herself to him. She could feel blood seeping through his robe in the warm stickiness on her hands and arms. Her temple and cheek did not escape staining, either.

She'd intended to be cool and collected. She'd intended not to make a scene, or cry, or do anything that might embarrass Kiernan. But then that monster had done a lot more than a little nibble, and Carly was now past caring about appearances.

"... I'm just fine. Everything is just fine." Kiernan's deep voice soothed Carly, but they made very little sense.

"How can you possibly be fine?!" Carly croaked, wiping her tears away with bloody hands. Then she saw her hands. "Oh my God."

"Careful, or you'll get it on your dress," Kiernan said.

"What do I care about a dress?!" Carly tugged his shoulder so she could see the wound.

Kiernan tugged back. "Werewolf healing. It looks worse than it is."

"The hell you say!" Carly stared at his open, angry red wound. She could smell the burning from the silver powder.

Kiernan grasped her upper arms. "Carly. You need to be calm right now. Okay? Just be calm."

"Are you done yet?" Alec asked, appearing beside Kiernan.

Kiernan growled. "Alec, I've got this handled. Please just step away."

Carly lunged at Alec, Kiernan's grip on her arms the only thing keeping her from gouging his eyes out. "Let go! Let me go!"

Alec chuckled. "I think your mate wants to challenge me."

"Don't tempt her," Kiernan muttered. He wrapped his arms around Carly, hugging her tight. "Carly... Carly... come on, Babe. Let's go home."

"You were just supposed to bite him a little! What was that all about?!" Carly glared at Alec over Kiernan's shoulder.

Alec shrugged. "Some people need more of a reminder."

"Asshole," Carly snapped. "I hope my father kills you!"

Alec reeled back as though he'd been slapped. "You dare-"

"Kiernan, take her home," Jenny said, stepping forward and putting a hand on Alec's shoulder. "Let's send everyone home. The ceremony's over."

"We still have dinner and drinks to go," Alec said.

"Dinner and drinks?! Are you seri-" The rest of Carly's protest was muffled by Kiernan's hand.

Jenny's eyes narrowed. "Someone put paid to that. Kiernan won't be able to stand upright through the whole thing." She turned and faced the crowd. "Everyone, please go home. We will do a proper welcome dinner for Kiernan when he is healed. Thank you all for coming."

Murmurs spread through the crowd, but one-by-one they began filtering out.

"I'll send Doc to your house," Jenny added to Kiernan, Carly, and Sean. "Go now."

Carly eyeballed Alec as she turned with Kiernan towards the door. About halfway down the walkway, Kiernan stumbled.

"I hope you're proud of yourself," Carly heard Jenny say to Alec.

Carly ducked under one of Kiernan's arms to try to help, but it turned out he was too heavy when he leaned on her. Sean took his other side, and Carly gave Sean a grudging look of gratitude.

"It's fine," Kiernan said, his voice losing its strength. "Just... I'll lay down for a bit and everything will be..."

Kiernan collapsed before he could finish his sentence.

2 2

SEEING DOC AGAIN

CARLY

Sean and Jenny carried Kiernan between them all the way back to Kiernan's home. They laid him on the bed in the master bedroom, the one that he and Carly shared. Alec had tried to help at first, but Jenny had snarled something wolfy at him, and he'd reluctantly retreated.

"Doc is on his way," Jenny said as she helped Carly take off the bloody white robe.

Carly kicked off her shoes. A glance in the dresser mirror showed she looked as though she'd murdered someone. "Is he going to be nicer this time?" Carly asked.

"He will be if I'm here. Help me roll him on his side. Doc's going to need access to the wound." Jenny began rolling Kiernan, and Carly moved to help her.

"Everyone just stood there," Carly said, putting a hand on Kiernan's back. She hoped it would let him know she was with him. "Everyone just... watched."

"That's not how the ceremony usually goes. I'm sorry." Deep sadness and anger tinged Jenny's voice.

"Why didn't anyone stop him?" Carly asked.

Jenny sat on the edge of the bed and put her head in her hands.

115

"Well, for one thing, Alec is the Alpha. For another... I think people were just shocked. It's certainly not anything the elders would have approved of."

"How is Alec still Alpha if he pulls crap like that?" Carly rubbed Kiernan's back gently, and he rumbled a little. It gave her hope.

"He won't be much longer if he keeps pulling crap like that," Jenny said. "If someone doesn't challenge him, the elders will get rid of him. I wouldn't be surprised if he gets a hell of a talking to tonight yet. Though not from me. I'm-I'm not going home."

"You're not in danger from him, are you?" Carly asked.

Jenny shook her head. "No, never. Alec's usually much nicer. You've just seen the wounded side of him, I guess. No, he hurt my brother. And he's been an ass since the moment you two arrived. I understand it's stressful and it's brought up a lot of bad emotions in him, but honestly, I've had it. If he's going to be this way, I'm not going home." She fidgeted her hands in her lap. "I don't suppose Kiernan's old room is free."

"Sean's taken the couch pullout. I haven't looked, but if there's a bed in there, have at it," Carly said.

"Thanks," Jenny said.

There was a knock on the doorframe, and Sean ushered Doc in.

"I knew that ceremonial bite was far too intense," Doc grumbled, opening his bag and starting to lay out supplies. He handed Carly a bottle with a nozzle on it. "That's distilled water. Could you warm it up in a bath on the stove for me? We've got to flush the silver out."

"I thought it had to stay in for like twelve hours?" Carly said.

Doc snorted. "That was before Hannibal Lecter showed up. Go ahead and heat it up." He began ripping open bags of sterilized instruments and setting them on a tray.

Eight agonizing minutes later, Carly returned to the room and handed Doc the bottle.

"Thank you," Doc said. He tested the water on his wrist. Satisfied, he began flushing out Kiernan's wound.

Jenny held a basin by the bedside and caught most of the silver-and-blood clouded water.

"Stitch girl, did you wash your hands?" Doc asked after a moment.

"Yes," Carly said. "I thought maybe I could help."

"You can. Thread a needle for me," Doc said as he finished flushing out Kiernan's bite.

Carly threaded a needle and handed it to Doc when he reached a hand towards her.

"Disinfect the wound, please," Doc said.

Carly soaked a cotton ball in disinfectant and placed it in a set of forceps before dabbing it over Kiernan's ravaged flesh.

Kiernan hissed.

"Good sign," Doc said, though hurting Kiernan more felt like a punch in the gut to Carly. "At least he's not unconscious. Kiernan, I'm going to be stitching you up now. Then it's rest and fluids for you." He turned to Carly. "I'd leave pain medication, but werewolves tend to metabolize that too quickly for it to be worth the trouble."

"Okay," Carly said. She put her hand on the small of Kiernan's back while Doc worked.

Kiernan groaned after a while. "Fucking Alec."

"Hey." Carly moved to Kiernan's other side and took his hand. "Doc's still working on you. You need to stay still, okay?"

"Figured," Kiernan grunted. He closed his eyes again.

"Oh, and Jenny's going to stay with us for a while," Carly added.

Kiernan's eyes flew open. "What?"

"She's pissed off at Alec. I said she could use your old room. I hope that's okay." Carly pressed her cheek against their joined hands.

"No, that's fine," Kiernan said. He grazed Carly's cheek with his finger. "You've got blood on you."

"Not as much as you." Carly kissed the back of his hand, then his lips.

"Stop moving your head. I remember what it was like to be mated, but right now this has to take precedence," Doc said.

Kiernan grumbled and Carly smiled. "I'm glad you're going to be okay. He's going to be okay, right?"

"He'll be fine." Doc finished sewing, smeared some Bacitracin over his stitches, and finished up by taping a gauze pad over the entire area. "It'll be a few days. The stitches will dissolve on their own, just like the ones in his shoulder."

"See? Werewolf healing," Kiernan said.

Carly let out a breath she didn't know she'd been holding and pressed her forehead to the mattress, feeling tears threatening at the corners of her eyes.

"I'll come and check on Kiernan tomorrow," Doc said. "You both get some rest. It's been a long day." He gathered up his tools and put them in his bag, snapping it shut before heading out.

"Thank you, Doc," Jenny said as she showed him out.

If Doc responded, Carly didn't hear it. For what felt like the millionth time in three days, she burst into tears.

Kiernan

Kiernan reached out and stroked Carly's hair. "It's okay, Babe."

Carly's head shot up. "Stop saying that!" Tears streaked down her cheeks, cutting paths through remnants of his blood.

Kiernan thumbed at her tears, then just gave up and completely wiped her cheeks with his palm. "What do you want me to say? Tell me, I'll say it."

"None of this is okay!" Carly said. "He ripped you apart like a piece of meat! It's bad enough he trapped you here. Both of us. But he had to treat you like raw steak, too?" She held his palm against her cheek. Her eyes closed, and fresh tears rolled down her cheeks.

Kiernan pulled Carly down for a wet kiss, then patted the bed next to him. "Come here."

Carly got on the bed, ruined green dress and all, and snuggled into his chest. She pressed her face into the crook of his neck, and sobbed. Kiernan's heart broke. He wasn't sure there was anything he could say to put the situation back to rights.

"Listen. The hard part's over now," Kiernan said.

"No, it's not," Carly replied. "The hard part's just starting."

It was difficult to argue that point. He'd have liked to have said that they at least had each other, but she hadn't accepted him yet, and he wasn't sure if that would put pressure on her. Instead, he slipped his hand under Carly's hair and stroked the back of her neck in silence.

"When do you start your duties as Beta?" Carly asked after a while.

"Not until Doc clears me, I'm sure," Kiernan said.

Carly traced her fingers up and down his arm. Kiernan wished he were feeling better—as it was, his wolf was grumping about being wounded and unable to pounce his mate, per doctor's orders. "Do you know what those duties are?" Carly asked.

"I do," Kiernan said. "Mostly secretarial, though I do oversee the patrols as well. A lot of paperwork. A LOT of paperwork."

"Do you help run the resort, then? Or... is this really a resort? I mean, to people actually come here and stay during the summer?" Carly asked. "Or is it just a resort on paper?"

"People come and stay here, but just werewolf families," Kiernan said. "Even werewolves like having places to vacation, you know. It's hard to go on family vacations alone, what with the threat of Hunters. That and a lot of werewolf families have teenagers, and you have to be careful with them accidentally shifting if they get overexcited or it's a full moon."

"How do they go to school?" Carly asked.

"Very, very carefully. Many are homeschooled during that time, until they get better control," Kiernan said. "Normal people are surprisingly breakable, if you don't know your own strength."

Carly nodded and kissed him.

Kiernan knew he shouldn't, but he deepened the kiss, his arm tight around Carly's waist, his naked body leaving her unable to deny his hardening length through her dress.

Carly pulled back and gave his shoulder a warning shove. "Nuh-uh, mister. Doc said rest. That isn't resting."

"It's exercise," Kiernan grinned. "Exercise is good for you."

"Yeah, well, we'll 'exercise' when you're feeling better," Carly said.

Kiernan gave her puppy eyes. "Promise?"

Carly laughed, her tears drying up. "Promise."

23

EARTH SHATTERING

Kiernan

'Where is my mate?' Alec's voice in his head woke Kiernan from a dead sleep. He groaned and looked at the clock—4:27 AM. Carly was sleeping against him, still in her green dress. He decided it had to be uncomfortable, and sat up with a wince. It was a testament to how tired and wrung out she was that she didn't wake up as he slowly peeled it off her.

'Where is my mate?' came the demand again.

'In my room,' Kiernan responded testily. 'Do you have any fucking idea what time it is?'

'She's not answering me,' Alec whined. 'And what do you mean she's in your room?!'

Kiernan sighed and got back into bed after dropping Carly's stained dress over a chair. She mumbled in her sleep and flopped back into him, making him smile.

'What do you mean she's in your room?!!' Alec said again.

'Jealous much?' Kiernan needled. But he was tired and just wanted to end the conversation as soon as possible. 'She's in my old room. Keep your shirt on.'

There was a blessed quiet, and Kiernan hoped that was the end of the conversation, but then Alec continued. 'I'm sorry.'

'For what? For trapping me here, threatening to kill my mate, ripping out the back of my neck, or pissing off your mate?' Kiernan asked, his roiling emotions backing up the questions. Now that they were linked, Alec couldn't avoid feeling the hurt he'd caused any more than Kiernan could hide it.

'Ripping out the back of your neck,' Alec said. 'And pissing off my mate.'

'At least you're honest.' Kiernan slowly put an arm around Carly as not to wake her and cuddled her to him.

'Is she eating?' Alec asked.

Kiernan stifled a groan. 'Alec. As far as I know, she's been asleep. It's 4:30 in the morning.'

'She's awake. I can feel it. She's been awake all night, but she won't talk to me,' Alec said.

'You want me to check on her,' Kiernan inferred.

'Yes,' Alec said.

Kiernan growled, then wished he hadn't. Carly started shifting. But the little smile on her face told him she liked it, and Kiernan gave her a besotted look. 'Is that an order?'

'Does it have to be?' Alec asked.

Kiernan sighed and gently wiggled away from Carly, pulling a sheet up over her as he got out of bed. There was a tantalizing view of bare breasts and lacy underwear, and Kiernan wanted to murder Alec for taking that away from him, but if Jenny had been up all night, he wanted to assure himself just as much as Alec that his sister was okay. 'No, it doesn't have to be an order.'

"Mphf?" Carly said, her eyes blinking open.

Kiernan kissed her forehead. "Go back to sleep. I'll be back in a bit. Just checking on Jenny."

"Ngh." Carly clumsily reached for his wrist, but Kiernan laughed softly and pulled away.

"Later. I promise," he said. 'You owe me big time, brother.'

Carly made cute little grumbly noises, then passed out again.

Kiernan could hear her breathing even out as he pulled on a pair of boxers. He padded out of the room, then down the hall a bit to a wooden door on the left. Kiernan sniffed the air. Jenny was, indeed, awake. But then again, so was Sean.

Sean gave Kiernan a thumbs up from the living room. Out of deference to the rest of the household, he'd shut off ESPN and was doing a Word Find instead. Kiernan imagined it had been left there one day by Jenny's mother. She was a Word Find fiend.

Kiernan knocked softly on Jenny's door. "Jenny?"

"You can tell him to go to hell," Jenny said through the closed door.

Kiernan sighed. "Can I come in? I don't want to wake up Carly by yelling back and forth through the door."

There was a pause. Then, the door opened and Jenny went back to sit on Kiernan's old bed. It was old now, and a twin. Kiernan wondered if it was even at all comfortable to sleep on. "That asshole told me to 'get it together.' Can you believe that?" Jenny hissed.

Kiernan sat down next to her. "It's Alec. Of course I can believe it."

"If anyone should be getting it together..." Jenny said.

"No argument here." Kiernan took one of Jenny's hands and held it. "Much as I'd like for him to suffer, I don't want you to. So I will tell you he apologized."

"Just for the bite?" Jenny asked.

"It's a start," Kiernan said.

"Not enough of one." Jenny rubbed her toe over a varnished knot in the hardwood floor. "Kiernan, I'm sorry. This is all terribly unfair to you and your mate. And now he has you doing his dirty work."

Kiernan bumped shoulders with her, grinning. "Isn't that what being Beta is all about?"

Jenny did not share his smile.

Kiernan's face fell. "It's too late now, Jenny. It's done. I guess we all just have to learn to live with it."

"Oh I'll live with it," Jenny said. "I might also be living with you. Hope you like kids."

"Like fuck, Jenny, are you pregnant?!" Kiernan gasped.

Jenny nodded, though she didn't seem happy about it. "I'm not bringing up a child in some man-child's dictatorship. If he won't leave me alone here, then I'm leaving. Maybe I'll go pick up your RV for you. I know you had to leave it behind. And your furniture."

Kiernan winced. "It should be fine until next weekend. I put everything away before I got shot, and the fair is only open on weekends. I'm paid at the RV camp until October, when the fair ends."

"I'll take you," Sean volunteered from the next room.

"Thanks, Sean," Jenny said. "Maybe I can sell your furniture on the road for you for a while. Give Alec some time to think. Me, too."

"I am booked for Camelot Days in Florida in November," Kiernan said.

"Florida in November sounds nice!" Sean called.

Jenny laughed, though it was a sad laugh. "You know, it does."

"What about being away from your mate? I mean, obviously he knows you're pregnant," Kiernan said. Alec would have smelled the change in her.

"It'll be hard. But I think it's the right thing to do," Jenny said.

"What happened between the two of you, anyway? If I can ask." Kiernan patted her knee.

Jenny sighed. "Lots of little things that added up to big things. I'd like to blame it on his stress of doing the whole running of the pack thing alone, but then I think of you and know you would never let things get so out of hand with Carly. I guess seeing you with her reminds me of how Alec and I used to be, and how that just... faded away. We don't talk, and when we do, it's either us fighting or him barking orders. I just... I can't take it anymore."

"Jenny, I'm sorry," Kiernan sighed. "Hey, on the bright side, Alec has a Beta now, so when he goes chasing you around the country..."

"You'd let me do it?" Jenny asked, brightening.

"Let you? How could I stop you? Besides, I did make commitments and I was hoping to sell some more of my stuff," Kiernan said.

Jenny hugged Kiernan tightly. "Thank you, Kiernan. I knew I could count on you."

"I'll pack a bag. I can leave just as soon as you mark your mate, you know, so she's officially 'one of us' and Alec can stop the babysitting guard," Sean said, his large frame now dominating the doorway.

"Why do you think you're going?" Kiernan frowned.

Sean shrugged. "Somebody has to. Might as well be me. Get your mate marked and we're good to go."

"You think that's going to happen this week yet, do you?" Kiernan asked with a nervous laugh.

"I do," Jenny said.

CARLY

Carly whuffled the pillow, then reached out blindly to her right, trying to find Kiernan. When he wasn't there, she frowned. Sometime during the night, he'd removed her dress, but all secondary indications confirmed they hadn't had sex. Though she was fairly certain she'd have remembered that.

She got out of bed and hunted down a t-shirt and shorts. When she got out into the hall, Carly saw Sean. From the way his lips were moving, she was sure he was talking to somebody in Kiernan's old room, though it was beyond her hearing range.

"Hi," Carly said. "It's like 5:30. What is everyone doing up?" She peeked onto Kiernan's—now Jenny's—room and saw them sitting together on the bed. Though she knew she had no reason to be, Carly felt a bit jealous of the way they were just sitting there easily, holding hands. She didn't like herself for feeling that way.

"Jenny was just offering to take my furniture on the road while we're here," Kiernan said. He said it so quickly that Carly knew that wasn't all Jenny had said.

"And?" Carly prompted.

"And... we can talk about the rest later," Kiernan said. He got up and Sean stood aside so Kiernan could pull Carly into the room. He sat back down on the bed, but with Carly on his knee this time.

"How are you feeling?" Carly asked, pressing the back of her hand to his forehead. Satisfied he didn't have a high or low temperature, she then went on to poke and prod him elsewhere.

Kiernan chuckled and stilled her hands with his. "I'm feeling much better." He kissed her nose.

Jenny was looking at them with longing in her eyes, and Carly blushed, feeling bad for her situation with Alec, and also feeling bad for her unwarranted jealousy. "Is Alec going with you?" Carly asked. "Kind of a, you know, well-deserved vacation?"

"I wish," Jenny said. "No, I don't, actually. We need some time apart."

"I'm sorry," Carly said.

"I'm taking Sean." Jenny nodded in Sean's direction. "If other things fall into place. Otherwise, I'll take someone else, so it's nothing you need to worry about."

Carly was confused. "What am I worrying about now-oh. Sean can't leave until I'm mated, right?"

"There's no rush," Kiernan said quickly.

Carly gave him a peck on the lips. "I know. You haven't rushed me and I appreciate that."

"It's been less than a week," Kiernan added.

That made Carly giggle. "But it's been an eventful week already. Why, you getting cold feet?"

Kiernan groaned and kissed her in a way that could get them cited for public indecency. "Never. Werewolves mate for life."

"So, even if I rejected you, you'd never have another mate?" Carly asked.

Kiernan paled a little, and Carly added, "I'm not saying I ever would reject you, I'm just curious."

"It's very unlikely I would be granted another mate. I mean, it's happened before, but it's extremely rare," Kiernan said.

"Plus it would hurt like a sonofabitch, or so I've been told," Sean said.

Kiernan glowered at Sean. "Gee, thanks. Just when I was going for the 'no pressure' approach."

Carly hugged Kiernan. "Don't be mad at Sean. I feel better knowing the truth."

"Having your mate isn't sunshine and flowers all the time, though. We all still have normal relationship problems," Jenny said sadly.

It was Carly's turn to take Jenny's hand. "I really hate Alec. But I hope you work things out for your sake, not his. It must be truly awful to be fighting like this. I mean, this isn't a small fight. This is like major, earth-shattering stuff."

"Tell me about it," Jenny whispered.

24

BREAKFAST TIME

Kiernan

Like clockwork, Alec contacted Kiernan again as soon as the conversation ended, just as he was walking into the kitchen with Carly. 'Is she eating?'

'She will be once we get breakfast ready. I think she'll force herself to, at least for the pup,' Kiernan replied.

"Your eyes did that thing," Carly said.

His mate was an observant little thing. Kiernan nodded and put a hand at the small of her back, ushering her into the kitchen. "I'm talking to Alec."

"You tell him what I'm going to do!" Jenny said.

How had he known he was going to be playing telephone between these two. "Fine," Kiernan said. 'Jenny's taking a vacation from you. She said she'd finish out my Minnesota commitment, then do the one in Florida. It'll be a few months.'

'What the fuck are you talking about?! Months?! FLORIDA?!!!' Alec said.

'Minnesota first. That one's open until the beginning of October. Then Camelot Days are open three weekends in November. She'll be back by Thanksgiving. Probably,' Kiernan said.

'THANKSGIVING?!!!!' Alec's distress crackled over their connection, and it made Kiernan wince.

'Play stupid games, win stupid prizes, brother,' Kiernan shrugged.

Kiernan didn't notice he'd stopped moving until Carly started making noise in the kitchen. She was trying not to interrupt him, but the sound of bacon on the frypan wasn't exactly easy to mask. 'Listen, if you want your mate fed, I gotta go.'

'I forbid it! I absolutely forbid it! She's with pup for God's sake!' Alec shouted.

Kiernan wiped a hand over his face, trying very hard not to telegraph to Alec that he was an idiot, but failing miserably. 'Try that one on your mate. See how that goes down.'

'I'm not letting her go to Minnesota alone! Especially after the Hunter incident!' Alec said.

'She's going with Sean,' Kiernan said.

Kiernan had to grip the counter at the roll of emotions that followed that revelation. 'Sean isn't mated!!!' Alec argued.

'Sounds like you have problems then, brother, if you don't have enough faith in your mate and one of your most trusted packmates,' Kiernan said.

Alec sulked over their connection. 'That's hardly my biggest concern.'

'If you're going to chase her around the country, I suggest getting your own RV,' Kiernan said. 'She's not going to let you crash on the floor.'

'She'd at least give me the sofa,' Alec argued.

'If you're lucky, Sean's taking the sofa,' Kiernan laughed.

Alec didn't find it funny at all. 'You are such an asshole.'

'Right back atcha,' Kiernan said. 'Now fuck off, I'm trying to feed your mate. You can try and have a screaming match with her over breakfast, but my money's on Jenny.'

Kiernan felt Alec's gloomy sigh all the way down to his toes. 'Mine, too,' the Alpha said. Then the connection closed and Kiernan went into the kitchen. "Sorry about that. Wolf problems."

"I am so totally going to be jealous of that mind connection thing when we're mated," Carly said. "Then I'd always know what you were thinking instead of trying to guess. I thought maybe pancakes today. I found some mix in the lazy Susan—what?"

Kiernan was standing, frozen, with a goofy smile on his face. "You said 'when' we're mates, not 'if' this time."

Carly blushed, and Kiernan heard her pulse quicken. "Just shut up and help me cook."

<hr>

CARLY

Carly wondered if it was just a slip of the tongue, or her subconscious making the decision for her. As she examined her emotions, she nearly burned the bacon.

Kiernan bumped his hip against hers just in time. He was mixing pancake batter, whisking it up in a large bowl.

Carly squeaked and took the bacon off the burner, taking a tongs to quickly put it on a plate.

"What smells like bacon burning?" Sean asked from the sofa.

"Bacon burning," Kiernan said. "Don't worry, we saved it."

"Good, because baby wants bacon," Jenny said. She was sitting next to Sean. Carly thought it was sweet that ESPN-loving Sean had given up the remote to Jenny, and was sitting through a Lifetime movie with her.

"Baby?" Carly echoed. "Oh, Jenny, are you pregnant?!"

Jenny nodded. "That I am." She didn't sound too happy about it.

"I'll go set the table," Carly said, after an awkward pause. She picked up the bacon and set it in the middle of the table before going to get more plates.

Sean stood up. "Nah, Carly, you and Kiernan are cooking. I should at least do something."

Carly shook her head. "You are doing something. Sit. Setting the table isn't gonna kill me."

Sean sat back down with a muttered, "Okay."

Kiernan poured pancake batter on a griddle he'd pulled out. "Movie any good?"

"It's a Lifetime movie, man. She killed her husband," Sean said.

"One sympathizes," Jenny grumbled.

Carly choked on a laugh. "I'm sorry, that's not funny."

"You either laugh or you cry," Jenny said. Carly realized then where Kiernan had gotten the phrase from.

Kiernan came to the table several minutes later with a massive mound of pancakes on a tray. "Time to eat!"

Conversation began to flow more easily after everyone sat down, with Kiernan describing the Minnesota and Florida fairs for Jenny's benefit. She smiled and seemed to get more and more excited about her planned vacation as they ate.

Then, just as they were finishing up, Kiernan's eyes went unfocused again. "Fuck," he said.

The front door rattled on its hinges, threatening to crack down the middle, heavy oak though it was, as someone banged on it. Carly's attention jumped to the door. Through the window, she could see Alec standing there, his hair standing at angles, his chin scruffy, and his shirt only half tucked.

"I'll... clear the dishes," Sean said, and began cleaning up with inhuman speed.

Jenny folded her arms, gave Alec the most scathing look Carly had ever seen, and retreated to her bedroom.

"Oh come on, Jenny, we need to talk!" Alec yelled through the door.

Carly was thinking of running interference—she was still livid over the way he'd treated Kiernan, and now the bastard wasn't giving Jenny her space—but Kiernan got to the door too quickly. "Alec," Kiernan said, "she doesn't want to talk to you."

"Yeah, well, I want to talk to her," Alec said, muscling his way into the cabin.

Kiernan sighed. "It doesn't work that way, Alec."

"I'm not going to yell at her through the window of your SUV while she's taking off," Alec said. "We need to discuss this!"

"Go away!" Jenny called back.

"Brother, give her some space. It's only been since last night," Kiernan said. "I'd also suggest, you know, not yelling at her."

"It was a figure of speech." Alec went around Kiernan to go knock on Jenny's door.

Carly was surprised at how quiet the knock was, given how he'd nearly splintered the front door a moment ago.

"Jenny, love," Alec begged through the door. "Please, let's talk about this."

"Alec, go away. I need a break," Jenny said through the door.

"Please," Alec said again. Carly almost felt bad for him as he pressed his forehead against the door. Almost.

"I think we should take a walk," Sean murmured.

Kiernan frowned critically at the situation, but anyone could see Jenny wasn't in any danger and Alec wasn't going to break down the door. Now they were just invading their privacy. "Yeah, sure," Kiernan said. He put an arm around Carly's shoulders and directed her towards the door.

Carly remembered Jenny's words, and they rattled around her head again. What if love isn't enough? She chewed her lip, thinking.

Sean jogged ahead of them down a path, which seemed to be slowly winding itself down towards the lake. Carly knew he was still within earshot, but was trying to give them at least the illusion of privacy. She appreciated that.

"Penny for your thoughts," Kiernan said, rubbing a thumb over her lower lip.

Oh boy howdy. Her thoughts. Carly looked up at Kiernan. Sure, she could tell him her thoughts.

But he wasn't going to like them.

25

MATED

Kiernan

Kiernan could see the wheels in Carly's head turning, and not driving in a good direction. He figured he'd head it off at the pass. The way she looked down at his question just confirmed his suspicions.

"You remember Dawn, right? My friend who was weaving next to me in the booth at RenFest?" Carly said.

"I do," Kiernan said, thinking back.

Carly chewed her lip again. "She had a really, really messy divorce a couple of years ago."

"Mates don't divorce," Kiernan assured her. "I've only heard of it happening three times in the entire history of any pack."

"But are they always happy?" Carly asked.

Kiernan kissed Carly's temple. "Nobody's ever always happy, Carly."

"Right," Carly said. "My parents..."

"Your father doesn't sound like the kind of guy who makes a warm, fuzzy marriage, if that's where you're going with this," Kiernan said.

Carly snorted. "That's the understatement of the century. But you're right, that's where I was going with this. I don't know what Mom is thinking, but they're just two people cohabitating. She does domestic things. He works on the farm and reads the paper. It's like watching June and Ward Cleaver most of the time, only they barely talk to each other. And, you know, apparently my dad kills people in his spare time."

"Now now, it's not that bad," Kiernan said. "I think he probably kills people, and then farms in his spare time."

Carly's shoulders drooped under his arm, and Kiernan felt like an ass. "It was a joke," Kiernan added lamely.

"I know," Carly said. "But it wasn't funny ."

"It wasn't. I'm sorry," Kiernan said.

"Thanks for trying, though." Carly leaned her head against his shoulder. "I promised myself I'd never end up in a marriage like that."

Kiernan kissed the top of her head. "I promise you on my life, I will do everything in my power to make you happy. I'd die before making you live the kind of life you're describing."

"I believe you," Carly said. "But what if, someday, you change your mind?"

"Do you love me?" Kiernan asked.

Carly ducked her head. "That's not the point."

"That's the whole point," Kiernan said.

"It's only been four days." Carly kept looking at the ground.

Kiernan tipped her head up gently. "I know," he said, looking into her eyes. "But do you love me, anyway?"

Carly teared up, and Kiernan couldn't take it. He pushed Carly back against a birch tree and kissed her. "Babe, forget I said anything. You're right, it's too soon-"

"Yes," Carly said, tears rolling down her cheeks. "Yes. Yes I do love you."

Kiernan's heart pounded. "I love you, too."

MATE! his wolf howled.

Kiernan's fangs started to elongate, but at the same time he was telling his wolf to calm down, Carly put a hand over his mouth.

"What if love isn't enough?" she asked, searching his eyes.

"Then nothing ever will be, Babe," Kiernan said, forcing his fangs back. He licked her hand, and Carly finally smiled.

"Dawn said I should probably get a cat. But I guess I'm more of a dog girl at heart," she said.

Kiernan stumbled back dramatically, putting a hand over his chest. "Wolf. Wolf! You wound me."

Carly followed him, and was about to wrap her arms around the back of his neck, then felt the bandage and stopped at his shoulders. "So... about this mating thing..."

The look in her eyes had Kiernan cursing Alec for having taken over his house.

<hr>

CARLY

They didn't make it to the lake. Kiernan took Carly by the hand and hurried her down the path, then past the lodge and into the thick of the woods. Carly knew Sean was following somewhere, but she was starting to get used to his omnipresence. "I know what you're thinking," Carly panted as she fought to keep up, "and I'm pretty sure Doc would not count it as rest."

"We'll rest after," Kiernan grunted.

"Are we really going to have sex in the woods?" Carly asked.

"God, I hope so," Kiernan said. He stopped and pressed her back against another tree, smashing his lips to hers.

It was alright, because Carly was just as hungry for him. When he grabbed the waistband of her shorts, however, Carly stopped him. "Don't rip them. I have to walk back home, remember?"

Kiernan growled, but took the point and stripped her shorts off instead. He unzipped his shorts, his cock bulging out of his open fly. Miraculously, Kiernan produced a condom from his back pocket.

"Do you just carry those everywhere?" Carly giggled.

"Be prepared, that's my motto," Kiernan said with a grin.

Once the condom was on, he hiked her thighs up over his hips. Carly locked her ankles behind his back.

Carly moaned as Kiernan sank into her.

"Yes-s-s," Kiernan hissed. "God, Babe, you feel so good."

"So do you," Carly said. She clung to Kiernan's shoulders, minding the gauze and his bite.

Kiernan started to thrust, rocking her against the tree. The bark bit into her back and butt, but it wasn't painful enough for Carly to care. "Do you want me to?" Kiernan asked, nibbling a spot on Carly's left shoulder.

Carly chewed her lip. "Yes," she decided. "Yes, I want you to."

"Okay."

Expecting the bite right away, Carly squinted her eyes shut. She peeked one open when no bite came.

Kiernan was grinning at her. "I'll bite you when you come."

"Ohhh," Carly said. Of course, knowing what was ahead didn't make that particularly easy.

Kiernan was skilled and determined, however, and soon Carly was coming around him. "Kiernan!" she shouted.

Then he sank his teeth in.

2 6

STUPID IS

CARLY

It wasn't just a love bite, but he didn't go ripping through her flesh, either. Carly cried out in shock and pain.

"Sorry, Babe. Sorry," Kiernan said after he released her shoulder. He didn't move in her, just held her tight.

Carly shivered, but the pain quickly dulled to a throb. She even laughed when Kiernan began lapping at the blood. "Yeah?"

"Just trying to keep you from bleeding all over creation," Kiernan said. "There isn't a whole lot anyway."

"Really, Dracula?" Carly teased. She rolled her shoulder and found she was no worse for the wear. "That's what your bite was really supposed to be like, wasn't it."

"Maybe a tinge harder. It takes a bit more to scar a werewolf than a, well, normal person," Kiernan said.

Carly then noticed Kiernan still had a bit of a problem. "Didn't you come?"

Kiernan chuckled and gave Carly a kiss. "Funnily enough, causing my mate pain isn't that much of a turn-on for me."

Carly smiled and wiggled her hips. "I'm not in pain now. Well, not much, anyway."

"I will take that as an invitation, my mate," Kiernan rumbled. He kissed Carly and gripped her thighs, thrusting until he, too, found fulfillment.

Something warm and fuzzy unfurled in Carly at being called "mate."

"Don't look at me that way," Kiernan murmured, leaning an arm against the tree trunk after lowering her to the ground, his muscular frame looming over her.

"What way?" Carly asked.

"That way. Like I'm the only person in the world. If you keep looking at me that way, we're never going to make it to a bed, and your ass is going to be all scratched up," Kiernan said.

"Ah, but won't it be worth it?" Carly grinned.

Kiernan booped her on the nose. "Not when you're trying to sit at the breakfast table tomorrow, no."

"Spoilsport," Carly said, gripping the front of Kiernan's shirt and kissing him again.

Kiernan finally had to set Carly aside, taking several deep breaths. "You're gonna kill me, Babe." He did up his pants, then picked up her shorts from the brush and held them out to her for her to put her legs in. Kiernan eased them up her body, his knuckles brushing her skin.

"You are being completely unfair," Carly pouted.

"I know," Kiernan said. He held out his hand to her.

Carly took it. "Do you think they're done at the house yet? Or do you still want to see the lake."

"I've seen the lake," Kiernan said.

"You've seen me," Carly pointed out.

"Yeah," Kiernan said, "but I'm only ever going to get tired of one of you."

Last year's dead leaves made soft rustling noises under their feet as they walked out of the woods and onto the path. "So?" Carly asked.

"So... what?"

"Which aren't you going to get tired of, me or the lake?" Carly raised her eyebrows at him.

Kiernan pretended to think about it.

Carly swatted him on the arm. "Maybe I do want to see this lake now, if it's so spectacular."

Kiernan caught her wrist and pulled Carly to him. "Jenny said Alec was gone about fifteen minutes ago. And I don't give a damn about the lake."

"Good, I don't either," Carly said.

Kiernan

Kiernan left Carly blissfully asleep several hours later. He wandered out to his father's old woodworking shed down a different fork in the path. The old equipment that Kiernan used to use was still there, along with enough of his father's old woodworking tools to get Kiernan started on his planned project. He'd ask Sean to pick up the rest of his things in Eau Claire later. It was still in Wisconsin, just an hour and a half's drive south of Spooner, and where he'd set himself up years ago.

Several nice cuts of wood were left in the back of the shed, and Kiernan could still remember each one of them. He ran a hand over the rough length of oak he planned to use, smiling to himself. Carly was going to love it.

Kiernan had just hefted the oak over his shoulder, and was bringing it towards two saw benches he'd set up, when Alec arrived.

"You marked her, then. It's official?" Alec asked. He stood, still looking disheveled, with his hands in his pockets.

"I told you I did," Kiernan answered. "That can't be why you're here."

"Jenny told me apologies don't count if you don't do them in person, mindlink or not. So, this is me, apologizing," Alec said.

"Good for you." Kieran began measuring and making marks on the wood.

Alec scuffed his foot on the cement floor. "I am sorry, Kiernan."

"Great. Anything else I can do for you, my Alpha?" Kiernan asked.

"Yeah, actually. I need you to forgive me." Alec folded his arms over his chest.

"Really? How'd that go with Jenny?" Kiernan asked.

Alec let out a low, vibrating growl.

"That good, huh?" Kiernan said.

"I'm starting here because that's where she said I needed to start," Alec said. "Are you really going to bust my balls over this while my pregnant mate is threatening to go on a road trip to Hunter land with an un-mated werewolf?!"

"First, Hunter land is about 45 minutes away from the fair, I checked. Second, Sean is a loyal packmate. You trust him around my mate but not around yours? Third, hell yes I'm going to bust your balls. After what you did to me? What you threatened to do to my mate?" Kiernan poked Alec in the chest. "You keep saying you thought we were friends. Well, right back at'cha, asshole."

Alec's chin jutted out. "Correct me if I'm wrong, but didn't you bring a Hunter—"

"Hunter's daughter," Kiernan said.

"Whatever."

"You said to correct you if you're wrong." Kiernan went back to marking the wood for cutting.

"Fine. Hunter's daughter. You brought her here. You showed her where we live. She might have the purest of intentions, and I mean that, but her family doesn't. Do you think the same Hunters that tortured your parents and then left them to die would even hesitate to pull out a couple of fingernails if it meant Carly could tell them where they could find a whole pack of werewolves? I have to think about the whole pack here," Alec said.

Kiernan stopped marking the wood and leaned his hip against a heavy bandsaw. "Are we back to the kill me or kill me not question again?"

"No," Alec said. "I'm trying to explain to you where I'm coming from."

"You think I'm selfish for brining my mate here?" Kiernan asked.

"A little, yeah. But I can't say any one of us wouldn't have done the same," Alec said. "I just... wish you'd understand the kind of position you put me in."

"Seems like I now have the rest of my life to do that," Kiernan grumbled. Then he relented. "I get it, I do. But you threatened to kill my mate, or, at the very least, keep her in that godawful basement. How exactly am I supposed to forgive you for that?"

Alec's face lit with hope. "Then you'll at least forgive me for the Beta ceremony?"

"I'm working on it," Kiernan said.

"Could you work a little faster?" Alec wheedled.

"Nope. Plus, Jenny deserves a vacation. She's had to put up with your dumb ass for the last however many years." Kiernan waved Alec away from the oak slab. "Now, if you don't mind, I'm trying to score brownie points with my mate."

"Why, did you do something wrong?" Alec asked.

Kiernan sighed. "Alec, sometimes, I really think you were dropped on your head as a child."

2 7

MISADVENTURE

Carly padded out of the bedroom in shorts and a tank top, looking for Kiernan. Sean had, once again, been roped into a Lifetime movie with Jenny.

"Oh no he didn't," Sean was muttering.

"He sure did," Jenny said. "That asshole's going to die."

"No doubt," Sean replied. He looked up at Carly. "He's in his work-shop, but he doesn't want you to come down. He's in The Zone."

Carly understood being in The Zone while working and nodded. She plopped down on the sofa next to Jenny, all three of them crammed in their like sardines with Sean's bulk. "I wish I could get some more yarn," Carly said. "I was so ding-donged out the last time we were in Hayward that I didn't hit any of the lovely quilt shops."

"If I'd known you wanted yarn, we could have stopped," Sean said. "Why, you have a specific project in mind?"

"I brought some of my scarlet yarn with me to work on Kiernan's sweater, but I didn't bring enough for a whole sweater. I suppose I'll have to make him some slippers instead. It's not as though the dye lot will match, even if I do somehow get ahold of more scarlet yarn, and

145

as far as I know, I'm not supposed to be going out anyway." Carly was a bit sad about this. She really had wanted to make Kiernan a sweater.

Sean squeezed himself out of his spot. "I can take you to Hayward."

"But... I thought I wasn't supposed to go-" Carly began.

"You're not supposed to go alone. You're the Beta's mate now. You can go pretty much anywhere you want, with protection," Sean said. "Besides, Kiernan's going to be busy for hours. We'll be there and back before he even knows you're gone."

"I'd like to go to Hayward. Maybe find some cute little outfits for the baby," Jenny said.

"Do you know if it's a boy or a girl?" Carly asked.

"Boy. Alec's excited about having a successor, of course, but I'll just be happy with healthy," Jenny said.

Sean was about to turn off the TV, then thought better of it and set it to record the rest of the show instead. "I want to see how that asshole dies."

"Me, too," Jenny grinned.

The three of them got up and headed to Sean's car this time, a menacing black thick-grilled Jeep.

"Is it an unwritten rule that werewolf males have big, menacing SUVs?" Carly asked as she and Jenny slid into the back seat.

"Nope. Just one of the perks," Sean said. "Buckle up." He put the Jeep in gear.

They chatted this way the whole trip, Jenny and Carly mercilessly teasing Sean, who shot back with good-natured banter. Carly thought it was terribly unfortunate that Sean wasn't Jenny's mate . He sure seemed like much less of an asshat.

Hayward was sunny and it was a lazy Tuesday afternoon. Carly and Jenny flitted from shop to shop while Sean munched on freshly-pulled saltwater taffy. Jenny found several cute outfits for Baby Alpha, and Carly hit up a few quilt shops, combing them for just the right yarn. When she found it, she nearly squealed. "This is great! Good quality, right color. And there's even enough of it! Damn, but it's going to be expensive." She pulled out her debit card.

Jenny shook her head and pulled out her own black Amex. "Just in case they're tracking you," she explained. "If you really feel you need to, you can pay me back later. But that's not necessary." Then she sneezed.

Sean had stopped eating taffy as soon as the door to the shop opened. Two leather-clad bikers had walked in, sticking out in the quilt shop like bees at a picnic. "Wolfsbane," he whispered to Carly and Jenny as he moved over to the two women.

"Fuck," Jenny said. "Can you hold these for us? Jennifer Lane." She held out a fifty-dollar bill.

The shop owner nodded, the gray-haired proprietress also eyeballing the bikers. "Sure thing, honey." The woman scooped the yarn behind the counter. "Back's that way," she added, dropping her voice and pointing subtly.

"Thank you," Sean said. He herded Jenny and Carly out to the strip of a parking lot behind the building. Carly had taken a tourist map of Hayward off the counter to hide her face.

Sean began moving in a roundabout way in the direction of his car. He had Carly and Jenny wait behind a dumpster, then tiptoed down an alley to see how bad the situation was on Main Street where he'd parked. He was swearing roundly when he returned to them. "It's like a biker gang's descended on the place, and all of them smelling to high heaven of wolfsbane. I can't get us to the car."

Carly shook her head. "No, you can't get me to the car. Get Jenny out of here. I'll-I'll distract them."

Jenny balked. "Carly, that's suicide! They're going to take you!"

"Better me than the Luna and the future Alpha," Carly said, squeezing her hand.

"No, I won't allow it. Sean, don't listen to her!" Jenny said.

Sean looked from Carly to Jenny, and back again. "We're coming for you. You know that, right?"

Carly quickly rattled off the address to her family's farm in Vermillion, Minnesota, then stepped away from the dumpster. "Take her home."

"Carly!" Jenny protested, but Sean had her by the arm.

"Shhh," Sean said. "We'll go get her. You know we will."

Tears slid down Jenny's cheeks, but she reluctantly went with Sean.

Carly circled around to the other side of the strip of buildings, taking a different alley back onto Main Street. She kept her head down, walking away from the Jeep with her face stuck in the Hayward tourist map. When the Jeep's engine turned over, several eyes flicked Sean and Jenny's way, but as Carly was not in the cab, the Jeep was left to go on its way.

Once Sean's Jeep rounded a corner and was lost from sight, Carly sidled into a bar. She folded the tourist map and set it next to her on the counter, ordering a rum and Coke.

It didn't take long. Matthew, wearing jeans and a leather jacket, sat down on the barstool next to her. "Did you really think we wouldn't come looking for you?"

"I really hoped you wouldn't," Carly said. She sipped her rum and Coke. "So, what happens now?"

"Now we go home, Carly. You're safe now." Matthew put his hand over hers.

"Matt, I was never in any danger," Carly murmured, seeking his green eyes, identical to hers.

Matthew, however, was occupied with other things. He looked at the strap of Carly's tank-top, then pulled it aside as though the thin piece of fabric was somehow obscuring the truth. Carly's angry red mating mark was unmistakable.

"Oh Carly," Matthew whispered. "What have you done?"

2 8

———

HOME IN THE REARVIEW

Kiernan

Kiernan returned to the cabin, feeling he'd made good progress on the project he was working on for Carly. Today he'd smell of oak, rather than cedar. He wondered if Carly would like that. Kieran grinned at the idea of them finding out.

When he got to the cabin, everyone was gone. A mindlinked message from Sean a few hours ago had told him they were heading into Hayward so the women could go shopping. Kiernan figured they must not be back yet.

Kiernan felt Sean and Jenny's distress before wheels even hit gravel, and Sean was shouting to the pack the moment they were in range.

'Hunters in Hayward. I think they took Carly!'

Blood going cold, Kiernan loped the short distance from the cabin to the carpark. He arrived first, and had Sean out by his shirt before the man could even turn the engine off. 'What the fuck do you mean they took Carly?!'

'I don't know for sure,' Sean said, grabbing Kiernan's wrist. 'We left before we could see what happened.'

149

'You left her there?!!!' Kiernan roared, causing the gathering were-wolves to wince.

Sean looked sad. 'There were too many of them. I had to get the Luna out. I'm sorry. I'm so sorry, Kiernan.'

'It was her idea,' Jenny added miserably. 'She told Sean he had to get me out and that she'd lead them off.'

Of course, it was. Of course, it was Carly's idea. If he wasn't so damned proud, Kiernan would have vowed to throttle his mate.

'Do we know where she is?' Alec asked, coming through the crowd.

'They probably took her back home. Some farm in or around Vermillion, Minnesota,' Kiernan said.

Alec put his hand on Kiernan's arm, and Kiernan realized he still had Sean nearly hoisted by his shirtfront. Kiernan released Sean.

'Is that all we've got? Some farm in rural Minnesota?' Alec asked.

Sean rattled off the address. 'Carly gave it to me before she left.'

Good girl, Kiernan thought. 'Okay, let's go fuck some shit up.'

Alec shook his head. 'They're going to see your mating mark. They're going to know we're coming.'

Kiernan howled with rage. Several of the other werewolves joined him. 'What, are you suggesting we just leave her there?!!! Fuck that, I'll go on my own if I have to—'

'Of course, we're not leaving her there. But we're going to need help. If you want to get her out, you need to give me time,' Alec said. 'What good is it going to do her if you get yourself killed?'

Alec really was a good Alpha in a crisis, Kiernan had to admit. He'd been halfway to his SUV before reason dawned. 'But they're going to have seen the mating mark. What do you think they're going to do to her in the meantime? What do you mean "help"? How long is that going to take?'

'I'm calling the Superior Pack right now. We're going to need the numbers, and I know Alpha Edward has been itching to wipe the upper Midwest Hunters' out wholesale since that incident with his Luna,' Alec said, turning back towards the lodge. He looked over his shoulder at Kiernan. 'You coming?'

Kiernan jogged after him. Every footfall on the ground matched the beat of his heart.

Mate, his wolf lamented.

Kiernan tried to reassure his wolf that they were going to get their mate, he just needed to be patient.

He hoped that was the truth.

CARLY

"I don't even know what we're going to tell Dad about this," Matthew said, talking through his helmet intercom.

Carly had her arms wrapped around her brother from behind as they sped down the highway towards Minnesota. They were surrounded by what looked like a biker gang, but was really an entire contingent of Hunters on motorcycles. Most of them favored Harleys, including her brother, so it was a noisy convoy going down the road.

"He's my mate. What was I supposed to do?" Carly asked.

"I don't know, not let the fucker bite you?!" Matthew shouted, making the connection crackle. He'd been in a foul mood ever since he'd seen the mark. "Mate my ass. That's just werewolf speak for brainwashed prisoner. Honestly, Carly, what were they using on you? It's only been four days since you met him!"

Four days? Carly supposed that did sound a bit rushed. But everything with Kiernan just felt... right.

"Dad's going to kill you. I mean he might, actually, literally kill you," Matthew went on.

Carly didn't doubt it. Not after the phone call they'd had. "Could you maybe ask him not to?"

"Should I?" Matthew spat.

"I'm still your sister," Carly said softly.

"Are you?!" Matthew said. "Are you really? Because the Carly I know wouldn't be this blind stupid, I can tell you that right now!"

Carly was silent a while. "I'm sorry I disappointed you, but he really is the man I love and my mate."

Matthew was also quiet. "I'll try to keep dad from killing you," he finally seethed.

"Much appreciated," Carly said. "It'd kind of suck to be a newlywed and then..."

"Put through a combine?" Matthew supplied glumly.

Carly's breath caught. She remembered Kiernan's probing questions when they had their date at Patrick's Irish Pub, and she felt sick now that she knew the reason. "Is that what we do with them?"

"That's what we do with them. Had a nosy neighbor come by once so we had to call one an accident, but otherwise the combine's been modified for that use, yeah," Matthew said.

"You'd let Dad put me through a combine?!" Carly gasped.

"Hell no. Like I said, you're my sister. And you're brainwashed," Matthew said. "They can probably do some, I don't know, laser surgery on that bite mark once you come back to your senses."

"You're the one who's brainwashed! All of you! They're people, Matt, just like you and me. They aren't hurting anybody," Carly argued.

Matthew sighed. "Let's just get you home."

Home. In Carly's mind, Kiernan was home, and home was getting further and further behind them.

29

WHAT'S COMING TO THEM

Kiernan

"Those motherfuckers." Alpha Edward's booming disapproval shook the conference phone. "They're going to get what's coming to them, mark my word."

Alpha Edward's prompt support for a raid on the Vermillion farm had been a welcome relief. The Superior Pack, though named for the lake they lived on, was also superior in numbers. It boasted two or three times the strength of Alec's pack. Alpha Edward had dispatched scouts to Vermillion almost the moment Alec said the word "Hunter." It was a journey from the north of Minnesota to the south, and would take about four and a half hours to complete. That would leave Carly in Hunter hands without eyes on her for at least two hours.

Then they would need to wait to hear about numbers. Depending on how many Hunters there were at the farm, and in Vermillion proper, they might not even have enough werewolves between the two packs. That would lead to another call between Alpha Edward and some Canadian pack contacts.

Time was ticking, Kiernan was restless, and Alec was now leaning a bit protectively over the speaker phone. It was prudent—Kiernan did have the overwhelming urge to crush it.

"Hopefully it will just take our combined forces and we won't have to wait for the Canadians," Alec said.

"Damn skippy. I barely want to wait for the scouts," Alpha Edward said. "But we can't have senseless loss of life, either. You said their preferred method of disposal was a wood chipper?"

"Combine." Kiernan's teeth hurt from clenching them so hard.

"Bastards," Alpha Edward said. "I hope they have it on site. It'll help."

Kiernan rubbed his temples. "Please keep in mind that some of these people are my mate's family. I'm not saying we should let them live. I'm just saying we might want to give them a decent burial."

"Depends on who comes looking and how fast," Alec said while Alpha Edward muttered to himself.

"I still have no idea why Fate would pair you with a Hunter's daughter," Alpha Edward said.

"Fate has a sense of humor." Sean ducked his head after saying it, since Kiernan turned his glower on the other werewolf again. He'd been beyond pissed off at Sean since he'd come back from Hayward without Carly.

Alpha Edward did laugh at Sean's statement, though. "As if there wasn't enough evidence before. Right then, we'll see what the scouts say. I'm worried this Vermillion place is so small that a passel of black SUVs running through it is going to set off alarms."

"From what Carly's said of the place, I think a passel of any cars coming in, all in a row, is going to set off alarm bells," Kiernan sighed.

All he could do now was hope Carly would be alright until they got there.

CARLY

Carly dismounted the motorcycle after Matthew turned it off, careful not to burn herself on the tailpipe, as she was only wearing shorts. The farmhouse she called home had never looked so foreboding.

She began taking steps towards it when Matthew took off his jacket and wrapped it around her, putting her arms through the sleeves. "What are you doing?" Carly asked as he flipped the collar up around her neck and she drowned in the leather.

"What I can," Matthew said. Then he put an arm around Carly's shoulders and brought her into the house.

Jamison Waite, their father, was waiting inside, standing in the living room with his arms folded. Their mother, Rose, was sitting in a chair, holding an embroidery hoop and doing counted cross-stitch. When she saw her children, she smiled and put the hoop away in a crafting basket. "Matthew, Caroline-"

"Matt. Why did you even bother. Did you think they wouldn't call me?" Jamison asked, walking over and tearing Matthew's jacket off of Carly.

Carly's puffy, healing mating mark was now there for all to see.

Their mother gasped, while Jamison curled his lip. "I guess you were doing more than fucking him. Are you pregnant?"

"Jamison, language!" Rose said, but Jamison just snapped his fingers at her.

"Go make dinner," Jamison said.

"What? Carly's been bitten, surely there's something I should-" Rose began.

Jamison rounded on her. "Woman! Get your ass in the kitchen and make dinner!"

Rose stood stiffly and went to the kitchen.

"Dad, you can't treat Mom that way," Matthew said.

"Do you want some of this can of whoop-ass? Because there is plenty to go around!" Jamison put himself nose-to-nose with his son.

Matthew backed down. "I just think-"

"Nobody asked you to think," Jamison said. "If you'd been thinking, Carly would never have gone off with that werewolf bastard. Now we've got to deal with her."

"We've got to deprogram her," Matthew said.

Jamison shrugged. "Depends on how she answers my questions."

Carly's eyes widened. "You'd really put me in the combine, wouldn't you."

"I don't intend to be the grandfather of a 'pup.' Now, are you pregnant?" Jamison asked.

"That's none of your business, but no. I'm not yet," Carly said.

"There's always the Plan B pill, Dad, this is the 21st century." Matthew moved slightly, more protectively, in front of Carly.

Jamison nodded. "Yes, we'll get one of those."

"I'm not taking any damn pill," Carly objected. "You can't just start forcing medication down my throat!"

"Watch me. Matt, call Mr. Schmidt at the pharmacy. Tell him we need Plan B and some sleeping pills," Jamison said.

"How are we supposed to deprogram her if she's asleep?" Matthew asked.

Jamison smiled. It was a chilling thing to behold. "Deprogramming comes later. First, we're going to need to deal with a wolf problem, aren't we, Carly?"

Matthew blinked, then looked at Carly. "Did you tell them where we live?"

"Of course, I did," Carly said. "Why, you planning on taking me away to some super secret serial killers' base?"

"No, this is actually the ideal outcome of a bad situation. You might actually prove useful to me, Carly. You went to, what, the Crescent Moon Pack? They don't have enough forces to overcome us. Especially now that we've got more Hunters coming. They're call, who now, the Superior Pack? I can get enough people here to deal with however many they'd want to send from there, too. It's been at least a hundred years since we've been able to wipe out a pack wholesale. Two in one blow? That will make history." Jamison's eyes gleamed with the promise of glory.

"You're keeping me as bait," Carly said.

Jamison nodded. "Matthew, take her to her room and lock her in. Then make the call to Mr. Schmidt."

"Y-Yes, sir," Matthew sighed and began pushing Carly up the stairs.

"I can't believe you're helping him, Matt. I just can't believe it."
Carly sat on her bed and hugged an old teddy bear to her chest.

"I can't believe you let a werewolf bite you and are calling him
your mate, but here we are." Matthew began checking Carly's bathroom for potential weapons. He took her knitting bag and dumped a
razor, a scissor, and her sets of crochet and knitting needles into it, as
well as her entire sewing kit.

Carly scowled at him. "What do you expect me to do while I'm
waiting to be drugged out of my mind?"

"Read a book," Matthew said.

Carly crossed her legs up under her and played with the teddy
bear's arm. "Are you really going to kill my... husband?"

Matthew's expression turned dark. "I can only pray it's me.
Because I want that asshole to know exactly who he was fucking
with."

3 0

FOOLED OR FOOLISH?

Kiernan

The news was not good. Alpha Edward's scouts had been clocked almost immediately in Vermillion. Strangers in a small town? Once they weren't headed to the discount gas station, the bar, or to the church, the locals' eyes had stuck to them like glue.

But the town's eyes had also been on the number of cars and motorcycles passing through into the country. With the original estimate of how many had been in Hayward, plus the number of outsiders the scouts saw coming through, the numbers were not in their favor. They were going to have to call packs in Ontario.

That was more time Carly was in the Hunters' hands, without the scouts being able to get close enough to even see the farm, much less get eyes on her. It was Wednesday. Kiernan had only met Carly on Saturday. And still he felt he would die without her.

"You've got to keep up your strength," Jenny said at breakfast, laying scrambled eggs and sausage in front of him at the table. "When it's time to go, Carly's going to need you to be strong."

"You should be with Alec," Kiernan mumbled, shoveling food in his mouth without tasting a thing.

"No, I should be here." Jenny looked over at Sean, who was flipping channels, not seeing a one of them. "You going to come eat?"

Sean turned off the television. "Is he gonna let me?"

"If you pass out during the raid, I'll never forgive you," Kiernan grunted.

Sean took that as an invitation and came to the table. Both men looked scruffy and unkempt. Jenny just shook her head and plated up food for Sean, then herself.

"You're doing the dishes," Kiernan said to Sean, taking another tasteless forkful of food.

"Deal," Sean said.

And that was how the storm passed.

CARLY

Carly had choked down the Plan B with the sleeping pills the night before. She wasn't worried at all that she had been pregnant—Kiernan had used protection even when they'd mated, after all. She'd woken up in the late afternoon, and was staring out the window at all the activity abuzz below in the farmyard.

Much to Carly's surprise, Dawn alighted from a car and Matthew ushered her inside. Shortly after, the lock on Carly's door rattled, and Dawn poked her head in. "Hi, sleepyhead," she said.

"Are you one of them?" Carly asked, inclining her head towards the window.

"My dad is. Hunter women don't really do that kind of thing. So much for feminism," Dawn said.

"And here I always thought your dad was so nice," Carly said bitterly.

Dawn sat on the edge of her bed. "Hey, I get it. I liked him, too. I had absolutely no frikken' clue Mr. Tight Pants was a werewolf."

"He's my mate," Carly said, hugging her bear.

Dawn winced. "I know you think that now..."

"I don't think it. I know it. Just like I know you should go out with

Matthew and put both of you out of each other's misery." Carly sighed and looked out the window again. "All of you think I'm brainwashed. But I think you all are insane."

"Insane for wanting to keep our families safe from monsters? That's harsh, Carly. And now you won't even look at me? I'm your oldest friend," Dawn said.

Carly looked down at her bear. "That only makes it worse."

"Ugh, I can't believe you! Come on, snap out of it already. Were-wolves are actual monsters. They turn into wolves, for God's sake!" Dawn began gesturing with her hands. "They eat livestock. They eat people!"

"When's the last time you heard of even a rank-and-file wolf eating a person?" Carly asked.

Dawn cast about for an answer. "I don't know!" she said, exasperated. "I just know it happens!"

"You know what they tell you," Carly said.

"You're killing me here, Carly." Dawn's voice was pained. "How can you believe them and not me? Not us? Your dad, your brother..."

"I'm not saying you all don't believe it, or that you're lying to me. I'm saying it isn't true," Carly said. "I've been with them."

Dawn rolled her eyes. "You were with them three whole days. You really think that was long enough to see their dark side?"

"Yeah, they almost killed me a couple of times," Carly replied. "But that's because they were afraid of you guys."

"Good. They should be afraid." Dawn went to door when there was a knock. Matthew came in with a tray set for three.

"We having a sleepover?" Carly asked, her voice dripping sarcasm.

"We're eating together. Like people who love each other. Dad wanted you to come downstairs and eat with the whole family, but I thought you two would just be at each other's throats," Matthew said. He set the large tray down in the middle of Carly's bed.

Dawn started eating. "Mmm, chicken salad. Your mom makes the best. Don't tell Dad, though. He still thinks his grandma's recipe tops everybody's."

Matthew cut a hunk of banana bread off for each of them. Carly noticed the knife was plastic. "Come on," he said, dangling Carly's piece in front of her. "You know you want it."

Carly sighed and took the slice of banana bread, munching on it mutinously. "You two are such a pain in the ass, you know that, right? Is it really that hard for all of us to just get along? I mean, when's the last time a werewolf's needed to hunt a person, or livestock, for that matter. Werewolves eat Doritos, for God's sake."

Dawn choked on her chicken salad and Matthew patted her on the back. "Werewolves eat Doritos?"

"Yeah," Carly said. "If you'd caught him in Hayward, you'd have even seen Sean eating saltwater taffy."

"Caught him in-you were there with werewolves and you threw us off the scent." Matthew stabbed an accusing finger at her.

"Not just a pretty face." Carly finished her banana bread and, with a sigh, accepted the chicken salad Dawn was holding out to her.

"Damn, you're lucky Dad's never going to know that," Matthew said.

Carly raised an eyebrow at him. "You don't tell him everything?"

"I don't tell him half the shit that goes down." Matthew poured them each some root beer. "I mean, they only become werewolves when they hit puberty, right? So why not just figure out a way for them not to become werewolves? I'm not going to go slaughtering little kids who aren't even werewolves yet."

"So, you've let some go," Carly said.

"Damn skippy," Matthew replied.

"Oooo." Dawn plucked a Honeycrisp apple slice out of a shared bowl. "My dad's not even going to hear about that."

Matthew stared at Dawn. "Your dad's really okay with killing little kids?"

"I'm still trying to get over the fact that either you are okay with killing, period," Carly said.

"I mean, it's not ideal," Matthew said. "But it's not like there's a cure."

Carly frowned at both of them. "I don't think they'd call it a disease."

"What would you call it?" Matthew asked.

"I don't know, like how people used to think being left-handed was evil," Carly said.

"Isn't it?" Dawn asked with a grin.

Carly groaned and dropped her head into her hands. "You're both hopeless."

"Right back at'cha," Matthew said.

3 1

THE CALL

CARLY

On Thursday, Jamison Waite, Jr. finally came for her.

"Hello, Dad," Carly said when he opened the door.

"Carly." Jamison stepped in, Dawn's father Henry at his side.

"So, red hot pokers? Bamboo splinters? Water torture?" Carly asked, watching as the door closed behind them.

Jamison held out a cell phone. "Phone call."

"I'm not calling him so you can track the signal to his phone. I'm not an idiot," Carly said.

Jamison shook his head. "For you, not from you."

Carly gawked at Jamison and Henry. "Are you serious?"

"Carly?" Kiernan's voice came over the phone.

Carly snatched the phone. "Kiernan!"

Before she could say anything else, Jamison took the phone back. "There, she's alive. Now I want to talk to the Alpha."

Henry sat down on the bed next to Carly and put a hand over her mouth. Carly squealed in protest, but realized why when her father put the call on speaker.

"How do you know I'm not the Alpha?" Kiernan asked.

"Pfft. Please," Jamison said. "Even my daughter isn't that unlucky. But you've got power in that pack, I can tell. Beta?"

Jamison smiled, taking the silence that followed as confirmation. "Don't feel bad, Kiernan. I've been doing this for a while."

"I know. Did you kill my parents?" Kiernan asked.

"If you're talking about the former Beta of the Crescent Moon Pack and his wife, then I guess you could say that's debatable. Let's just say I helped. And I enjoyed it."

Carly let out an angry screech at that from behind Henry's hand.

"So it was your father," Kiernan said.

"That would be correct," Jamison confirmed. "Now, if your little trip down memory lane is over, the Alpha?"

There was a pause, then, "This is Alec."

"Alec, how nice to meet you. I suppose you're calling because you're under the mistaken impression that I'd be willing to negotiate for the release of my daughter?" Jamison said.

"I'm calling as a favor to a friend. Release Carly and surrender, so we can end this now before it gets worse." Alec's tone was hard.

"Oh? And why are you giving me such a generous offer?" Jamison asked.

"Because Carly is my Beta's mate, and he would rather we not slaughter her family," Alec said.

It was the first time Carly thought she might like the autocratic Alpha. She looked at her father, hoping he would take the deal.

"So you're not even going to try to lie to me and tell me you're not coming. I respect that," Jamison said with a smile. "I suppose you think you stand a chance."

Alec growled. "I suppose you think you do."

"Alec, Alpha of the Crescent Moon Pack, I don't think you keep as good of track of our numbers as we keep of yours. You don't have the juice to go up against us," Jamison grinned. "Though I am hoping against hope that you're still going to try."

"We're going to do more than try. Which is why I was calling. Since you refused my offer, then here's my warning. We're coming.

Put your women and children in your bunkers because we're coming in force," Alec said.

Jamison laughed aloud. "I look forward to meeting you on the field of battle, Alpha Alec. Oh, and Kiernan? When I find you, I'm going to capture you and torture you to death, slowly, in front of Carly. Only then, when you're begging to die and my Carly has seen what a monster you really are, will I put you through the combine."

———

Kiernan

Kiernan wondered how an asshole like Jamison Waite had ever produced a daughter like Carly. He snarled at the phone. "I'm going to lock you in a basement for the rest of your natural life."

"Funny, that doesn't sound quite as threatening," Jamison said.

"I have a vested interest in keeping you alive." Kiernan was pacing back and forth. So was Alec. Sean was leaning against the conference room door, watching them both. Alpha Edward, Alpha Jean Pierre, and Alpha Trevor were sitting at the conference table, listening silently, each with their Betas standing behind them.

"That's almost sweet. If I thought you were capable of the emotion, I'd say you loved Carly enough not to hurt her. But then, if that were the truth, you wouldn't have kidnapped and bitten her in the first place." Jamison was the loudest, but Kiernan could hear there were two other people in the room with him, one of them Carly.

"You're about to find out what I'm capable of," Kiernan rumbled.

"I'm sure. Anyway, say goodbye now. Just in case you get killed on the battlefield," Jamison said.

Kiernan, surrounded by the Alphas of four packs, said without hesitation, "I love you, Babe. I love you, and I'm coming."

Jamison snorted, then the line cut.

Kiernan leaned on the table and closed his eyes.

"You're sure you don't want to kill him?" Alpha Edwards asked.

"Getting less sure by the minute, but yes. I'd like to keep him alive if we can," Kiernan said.

"Hmph." Alpha Edward clearly disliked this idea.

Alpha Jean Pierre held up a hand. "Actually, zis man is clearly in a high-ranking position. I zink he may be an asset."

Alpha Trevor nodded. "Yes, he's got to have juice if he doesn't have to hand the phone off to anybody. He's calling in all these Hunters himself."

"I suppose we don't absolutely have to kill him," Alpha Edward decided.

"Please also leave her brother, Matt, alone," Alec said.

"And how will we know who zis person is?" Alpha Jean Pierre asked.

"Black hair, ear-length. Green eyes. About 6'1". Shit-eating grin," Kiernan supplied. "Slim build, but strong."

The Betas were taking down notes as Kiernan spoke.

"I don't know what Jamison Waite looks like," Kiernan said with an apologetic look at the Alphas.

"Gee, he didn't invite you over for family dinner? Color me surprised," Alpha Trevor said.

"Doesn't matter," Alec added. "He'll be the one giving the orders."

Jean Pierre raised a hand again. "Do you suppose zat zey are expecting us to come in head-on?"

"I'd hate to disappoint them," Alpha Edward said, rubbing his hands together.

"They might expect us to come in head-on, but we're not going to," Alec said. "We're parking about eight miles away at a nature park called Schaar's Bluff. Apparently they do a lot of weddings and events there, as well as hiking activities and things. There's ample parking. Then we're going there in teams, based on the information the scouts give us." He gave Alpha Edward a frustrated look. "Like we agreed."

"Zis is a good plan," Jean Pierre said with a nod.

"I'll tell the men to be ready." Kiernan turned towards the door.

Alec put a hand on his shoulder and stopped him. "I'll tell the men to be ready. They should hear it from their field commander, after all."

"You're-you're going to be on the ground yourself?" Kiernan gaped.

"You're my best friend. Of course I'm going to be there," Alec said. "Besides, like Alpha Edward said, it'd be a shame to disappoint Jamison Waite."

3 2

—————

LOGGERHEADS

Kiernan

It was only mere hours until everyone was on the road, but it seemed like forever. Kiernan had paced the parking lot like a mad thing, wearing down the loose gravel into a beaten path. When everyone was finally assembling, he sprang into Sean's Jeep, soon joined by Alec, who took shotgun, and Liam, another wolf of their pack.

"Okay, go go go!" Kiernan said.

Sean looked behind him. "Aren't you the one who was making me drive the speed limit all the way to Hayward the other day?"

Kiernan glowered at him. "Just go."

At least Sean didn't laugh this time. He put his foot to the floor, gravel pinging off other vehicles in the lot, and roared out of the resort.

"We should still try for the speed limit," Alec said. "We don't want to be pulled over. That would just waste more time."

Kiernan grit his teeth, but finally nodded. "You're right."

"I'm always right." Alec turned his attention out the window.

"Modesty, thy name is Alpha Alec," Sean chuckled.

171

Alec gave him a sharp look and Sean stopped. "Shouldn't you be concentrating on driving?"

"Yes, my Alpha," Sean agreed, sounding a bit peeved..

Kiernan knew Sean was just trying to make the trip to Minnesota a bit lighter and easier, but he'd have much preferred to have the two-and-a-half hours in silence. As it was, Sean kept chatting animatedly about this subject and that, with Alec grunting responses and Kiernan not responding at all.

Finally, Kiernan couldn't take it anymore. "Sean, just shut up will you?!"

Sean glanced back at Kiernan in the rearview mirror. "Sorry," Sean said. "Just trying to lighten the mood a bit."

"His mate's being held captive by Hunters. How are you planning to lighten the mood?" Alec asked, sitting up straighter in his seat.

"I... don't know." Sean raked a hand through his hair.

"Have you been making nice with his mate the way you've been making nice with mine?" Alec suddenly spat.

Kiernan grimaced. This could go south very quickly. "Alec..."

"I've been a friend to your mate. I don't know what else you're implying, my Alpha, but I haven't said or done anything that was outside of being a good friend." Sean's eyes were fixed to the road. He was stiff now, though from feeling insulted or worrying about his Alpha's wrath, it was difficult to tell.

"She won't even talk to me, but she's got plans to go gallivanting around the country with you." Alec's accusing look should have started Sean's hair on fire, but Sean didn't take his eyes off the road.

"You'd rather she go alone, my Alpha?" Sean asked.

Alec slammed a fist into the dashboard, denting it and making everyone in the car jump. "I'd rather she didn't go at all!"

Sean looked at the damage, but didn't say a word about it. "She's rather determined, my Alpha."

"So? You should be discouraging her, not volunteering to travel with her! You're unmated, for fuck's sake!" Alec said.

"Is it so difficult to believe I might want to find my own mate? Because clearly, she's not among our pack." Sean's tone was measured.

Kiernan wouldn't want to upset Alec either, if he were in Sean's position. "Alec, please just let it go. Please. You can talk to Jenny about it after we're done, but Sean really is just trying to be a good packmate to you and to Jenny. Like he said, you wouldn't want her going alone."

Alec turned to glare into the back seat. "You're the one who put the stupid idea in her head of selling your furniture all over the place."

"I did," Kiernan said. "But that was only after she said she needed to get away. Would you rather she run off and not tell you where she's going? At least this way you'll know where she is."

"Yeah. Florida." Alec stared mutinously out the windshield again. "Florida."

"Not a bad place to visit," Liam suggested, finally adding his own two cents.

The only response was a grumbled, "Florida."

Everyone fell back into silence. It was broken this time by Alec.

"Kiernan," he said. "Where did you get your RV?"

<hr>

Carly

Carly was reading "Pride and Prejudice." Or at least pretending to. What she was really doing was glancing through her window, over and over again, watching Hunters keep showing up. Weapons of various types were being unloaded from any number of vehicles. The Hunters also liked black SUVs, so it seemed. Carly wondered if they'd talked to the werewolves they hunted about this thing they had in common. She doubted it.

The weapons ranged from sniper-rifles to silver netting (or at least Carly assumed the glinting metal was silver). She even saw some old school crossbows, along with more than one modern compound hunting bow. Guns of all shapes and sizes seemed the order of the day, however. Carly's stomach twisted at the idea of Kiernan being blasted with sterling silver buckshot.

Matthew was usually in the farmyard, following Jamison and

Henry around. Today, however, it was just Jamison and Henry barking orders and directing the movement of men and equipment with gestures and finger-pointing.

When there was a knock on her door, Carly set her book aside. She knew who it was.

"Hi," Matthew said, poking his head in. "Sorry to disturb your reading."

"You're not." Carly tucked her legs up under her and faced him.

Matthew stepped into her room. "I just wanted to let you know that Dawn's gone to a safe house, along with Mom, so you don't need to worry about them. I also... wanted to try to convince you to go, too."

"You're going to try to sneak me out while Dad's not watching," Carly said.

"I'm going to try to sneak you out while Dad's not watching," Matthew confirmed. "He thinks you need to be here, but I don't."

Carly shrugged. "What if they don't smell me here? What then?"

"You gave them our address. They're going to start here first, anyway. And we're going to be ready for them, so... there's no need for you to be here. We'll kill them all before they ever think of trying to find you someplace else." Matthew sat on the edge of her bed and took her hands. "I don't want you to get caught up in this."

"I'm already caught up in this." Carly tugged her hands away. "And I'm not going anywhere. You're going to see, when they get here, that they're just people like you and me. And you're going to think you're one hell of an asshole for thinking any differently all these years."

Matthew's face screwed up with concern. "Please, Carly. Please go to the safe house. If you're right, then you being here isn't going to change my mind one way or another, it'll be meeting the bastards. If you're wrong, well, then you're safe just the same. I don't want you to die because Dad insists on dangling you as bait. He thinks you're a traitor. But you're just brainwashed—"

"You're the one who's brainwashed. Ugh, we can't keep having this conversation. You're never going to agree with me and I'm never going to agree with you. And I'm not going anywhere. Kiernan will find me here." Carly searched Matthew's eyes. "I don't want you to die. Please, you go to the safe house. Tell Dad someone needs to guard it."

"He already has guards for it. This is my time, Carly. I'm gonna show the old man what I'm really made of," Matthew said.

"You're gonna get killed." A tear rolled down Carly's cheek.

Matthew sighed and stood. "Then I'll get killed doing the right thing. I'm sorry I couldn't convince you to go to the safe house. But no matter what happens, I'm going to protect you." He walked out of her bedroom, shaking his head.

As the door closed, Carly looked back out the window and froze.

Through the open barn doors, she could see a series of men firing up the combine.

MELEE

Kiernan

Schaar's Bluff had a beautiful view of rounded limestone cliffs, green trees, and expensive homes all overlooking the mighty Mississippi. It boasted a playground, gathering spaces, and several trails. These would all be of interest to an intrepid traveler.

Kiernan was not an intrepid traveler. He alighted from Sean's SUV with one goal in mind.

MATE.

Alec was second out of the vehicle, followed by Sean and Liam. There were large, separate parking lots with the capacity to hold several vehicles, but their convoy of black SUVs still drew attention from park-goers.

"Marathon," Alpha Trevor said to those who seemed the most curious. It had been the best cover they could come up with on short notice and, indeed, most of the force was quickly going in and out of bathrooms and Schaar's Gathering Center to change into running shorts and tank tops with numbers plastered to their chests.

They'd rented out Schaar's Gathering Center, a large gray building often reserved for weddings, as a kind of base of operations for the

Alphas and team support. The Betas would be on-the-ground commanders overseen by Alec.

In that capacity, Alec began barking orders, getting the warriors ready for the eight-mile hike they'd be undertaking. For werewolves, it was hardly a stretch of the legs, but it was still time wasted between Kiernan and his mate. He paced this lot as well as the others assembled.

"You're going to wear your shoes right off before we even get there," Sean said. He was carrying a backpack of clothes. Several of the werewolves were, for when the battle was over and they were left standing naked in human form.

"I just want to get there." Kiernan bounced on his toes as though getting ready for a race.

Sean put a hand on his shoulder. "If you're the first one there, they're going to mow you down. You still need to stay with the group, no matter how bad you want to get to her. You're no good to her dead."

Kiernan made a frustrated sound. "Then the rest of these bastards better hurry up."

"Hey! We've got some bitches here, too." One young female werewolf grinned at them. She was standing with Alpha Edward's numbers, which, even with their Canadian friends, still constituted more than a third of the force.

"Apologies, ma'am," Sean said, tipping an imaginary hat.

Kiernan growled and began pacing again.

Finally, Alec had everyone gathered and ready to go. They took off at what would be considered an easy jog for werewolves, though quite fast to normal humans. Once they were out of sight of the hikers and tourists, they picked up speed.

Kiernan raced at the front of the pack, flanked by Sean and Alec. He wasn't necessarily the fastest werewolf of any of the packs, but he was definitely the most determined.

"Save some for the battle, yeah?" Sean told him.

"I'll have plenty left for the battle," Kiernan said.

Alec gave him a swat on the back. "That's the Kiernan I know!"

Kiernan just grunted and kept running.

CARLY

A loud voice startled Carly right out of sleep. She didn't even remember falling asleep but had been trying to stay awake for more than a day, waiting for Kiernan to come. Now she went to the window, pressing her ear against it.

"They're coming!" was the rallying cry. "They're dressed as marathoners, but it's them! Seven minutes out!"

Carly was annoyed on the pack's behalf that their disguise hadn't worked. They hadn't even arrived yet and the Hunters already knew who they were. Carly wondered how, but it was not the biggest concern on her mind. What concerned her the most was the seven nail-biting minutes it was going to take for them to get here.

There was activity in the barnyard as people finalized their positions, then nothing but quiet. Guns were trained on the long gravel driveway. White fences made it unlikely the werewolves would choose a different path.

Carly held her breath, going to the far side of her window and peeking as far as she could see down the driveway, her cheek pressed against the cool glass.

Seven minutes passed. Then eight. No one moved, no shots were fired, and Carly saw nothing.

Then, there was a commotion at the back of the farm. Carly could hear shouting and shooting, but her window did not allow her to see out the back of the house where the woods abutted the property. Just as she was turning her head towards her door, willing herself, just this once, to have x-ray vision, there was a commotion at the front.

The werewolves had not come over the driveway. Shifting into wolf form, sometimes in midair, they leapt over the white fences as though they weren't there at all. They dodged this way and that to avoid bullets and arrows hurtling at them. Carly tried to see if she recognized Kiernan's wolf, her heart nearly beating out of her chest.

Several wolves fell before they even reached the people firing at them, but once they broke through, it was carnage. Men were ripped apart by strong jaws, wolves were slashed open by silver knives. Shooting continued, and many more wolves went down.

Then Carly saw him, her beautiful sandy-haired wolf. Her hand flew over her mouth as a Hunter jumped on his back, striking downwards with a machete. Kiernan shook him off, however, and the Hunter went flying into a post. The Hunter didn't get back up.

Carly beat on the window with her fists. "Here! Kiernan, I'm up here!"

Kiernan glanced up, and his roar shook the farm down to the bedrock beneath it. Hunters and wolves alike stopped a moment to stare at him.

The interlude lasted only seconds, however. Brutal battle overtook every part of the farm. What Carly couldn't see, she could hear. Hunters and wolves mangled each other between Kiernan and the farmhouse, but Carly could see Kiernan making slow progress just the same.

"God, please let Kiernan be okay," Carly whispered as he muddled his way through the melee.

3 4

BREAKING IN, BREAKING OUT

Kiernan

Kiernan had one goal, and that was to get to Carly. Alec didn't even try to stop him, giving orders to the rest of the wolves, but leaving Kiernan to his own devices. There wasn't much ordering to do anyway—it was kill or be killed in the chaos around them now.

It took a few minutes, but Kiernan finally noticed Sean had joined him at his side and was helping to tear through the crowd on his behalf. Kiernan gave him a brief, wolfy grin before focusing his attention back on his mate.

MATE.

Mate.

Mate.

MATE.

Mate.

His wolf, at the fore, would not stop the chant in his head, but that was alright. They were aligned in a common goal.

Around him, wolves and Hunters were fighting and falling. When a Hunter popped into his path, either Kiernan or Sean tore through them like paper. This close to the battle, guns had become mostly useless, but there were those who kept firing just the same.

They'd almost made it to the front porch when Sean yelped in pain. Kiernan swung his head to the side, only to see a man he recognized on Sean's back, his knife buried deep into Sean's shoulder.

Matthew.

Kiernan snarled at him and bit his leg, just enough to make Matthew cry out and release the knife. Though it was dangerous, Kiernan shifted back into human form, ripping the knife out of Sean's shoulder and facing Matthew.

"Did you come looking for me, Matt?" Kiernan asked.

"No," Matthew said. "But I'm glad I found you just the same." He produced another knife from his boot and circled Kiernan. "You're going to regret what you did to my sister."

"Even if you kill me, I'll never regret it." Kiernan dodged a swipe from Matthew with superhuman speed.

When Matthew lashed out again, Kiernan did the same, dodging rather than fighting back.

"Come on, fight me!" Matthew shouted, stabbing several times at nothing but air.

"No. You're my mate's brother. There's no way I'm killing you." Kiernan got behind Matthew and, before Matthew could spin around, Kiernan flipped the knife over in his hand and clocked Matthew hard on the back of the head.

Matthew went down like a sack of potatoes, unconscious.

Then Kiernan turned to Sean.

'I'm fine,' Sean said over the mindlink, licking his wound in wolf form. 'Let's go get Carly.'

Kiernan patted Sean on the flank and shifted back into a wolf.

Together, they padded onto the porch.

CARLY

Tears rolled down Carly's cheeks seeing Matthew fight Kiernan, thinking one or the other would die. As they circled each other, and Kiernan feinted right and left, it seemed Matthew was the likely option. But then Kiernan had knocked him out, and Carly could see, even from her window, that Matthew was still breathing.

Carly lost sight of Kiernan and whom she assumed was either Alec or Sean when they stepped onto the porch. The window didn't allow her to see that far.

She did note the sound of a shotgun being cocked downstairs, however.

"Kiernan!" she yelled, banging her fists on the window. She wasn't sure if he could hear her.

Carly ran to her door and tried to get it open, pushing and pulling at it. She banged her shoulder into it once, twice, three times, but to no avail. Still, Carly couldn't let herself give up, and she slammed herself into the door again.

There was a metallic thud as something hit the floor. Carly looked under the door and saw the skeleton key lying there, just beyond the reach of her thin fingers. She tried reaching further, scraping the back of her hand, but to no avail. With a cry of frustration, Carly sat back, trying to figure out what to do.

She needed something that would fit under the door that she could use to hook it. Inspiration dawned suddenly and Carly ran to her closet, tossing one of her best dresses off a plastic hanger. She only wished she had wire ones. She hoped this would work.

Lying on her stomach, Carly worked the hanger under the door. She slid the hook of it behind the key and began dragging it forward. The hanger just wouldn't catch, however, and Carly sat back in frustration. Damn modern fashion technology anyhow.

Carly went back to her closet, looking for something, anything, that might work. If she'd known they'd left the key in the door, she would have ripped a page out of one of her larger books and done the paper trick —sliding the paper under the door to catch the key when she knocked it out. But she hadn't known, and it was too late now.

Finally, at the very back of her closet, Carly found a coat hanging on an ancient, pink silk-padded wire hanger. She grabbed it and began to try to undo the padded silk covering—it would never fit under the door with the thick covering on.

Precious minutes ticked by as Carly ripped at the cotton and fabric. She broke several fingernails, but she didn't care. Every second, Carly expected to hear the sound of a shotgun blast. She wondered why she hadn't heard it already.

Carly picked the rest of the cotton off. She looked at the twisted wire by the hook and realized she was going to need pliers. She didn't have pliers. Matthew had even taken her scissors.

There was nothing for it but to try without undoing the hanger. Carly slid back down by the bottom of the door and pushed the hanger underneath, trying to catch the key. She angled the hook at the handle, hoping to hook a hole in the decorative design of the key. It was slow going, the angle of the hook to the rest of the hanger making it extremely difficult.

Carly was just about to give up and try looking for something else in her room, when she heard it. The windows rattled. The light fixtures shook.

A shotgun blast broke the house's silence.

3 5

WEREWOLF DOWN

Kiernan

Sean and Kiernan carefully crept around the wraparound porch, sniffing the air and the ground. There was no motion in the windows, and the air was so polluted with wolfsbane it was impossible to smell anything else.

'I get the feeling we're about to be fucked,' Sean said over the mindlink.

Kiernan nodded. He was getting that feeling as well.

Carly pounding on the window above them, just barely audible even with wolf hearing over the din of battle, only added to their suspicions.

As the two wolves paced back and forth, though, nothing happened.

'They're waiting for us to make our move,' Sean observed.

'Let's not disappoint them,' Kiernan replied. He growled, and launched himself right at the front door, splintering it off its hinges.

That was when it happened. A shot went off, and a silver buckshot filled the air.

It would have hit Kiernan square in the face and chest, but Sean knocked him aside in a flying leap as Kiernan was hurling himself through the door. Buckshot riddled Sean's side and he went down with a loud thump.

Kiernan roared, standing protectively over his friend.

Henry prepared to unload the second barrel, but then a third wolf leapt over Kiernan's head and knocked the man flat on the ground. It tore out the Hunter's throat.

'Go!' Alec said, looking at Kiernan as he spat Henry's blood.

Kiernan whined and looked at Sean, rolling him with his paw.

Sean groaned.

'I've got this, go!' Alec repeated, nudging Kiernan off Sean.

Kiernan padded through the living room, coughing at the scent of wolfsbane in the air. Candles and incense were lit everywhere, answering the question of where it was coming from.

"Hey there, wolf. You planning on blowing the house down?" a Hunter asked, appearing suddenly with a Glock in his hand.

Kiernan growled, baring his teeth at the newcomer. He could see through the hall to the kitchen that there were more of them. With Alec protecting the front door, Kiernan had little hope of help and knew he'd need to retreat for the time being, but he didn't want to. His mate was up the stairs behind this asshole. He was so close.

MATE!!!

The Hunter fired, and Kiernan dodged to the side, this time his shoulder only getting grazed. He was going to have to write a letter of apology to his left shoulder when this was all over.

"Come on, werewolf. Just sit still and prepare to meet your maker," the Hunter said, taking aim again.

Like hell. Kiernan dove at the Hunter, who got off another shot, this time hitting Kiernan in the foreleg. Kiernan grunted, but it was too late for the Hunter. Kiernan quickly clawed him to death.

The other Hunters had guns and knives out as well and began converging on him. Kiernan's only saving grace was the hall, which forced them to narrow their assault to a single file line.

One at a time, Kiernan figured he could do. He faced down his attackers, his hackles raised, his lips and claws dripping the blood of his enemies.

There was no going back now.

***

CARLY

The shots fired below gave Carly hope. Mainly that, if they were still shooting, there were still werewolves in the house, and it was possible, just possible, that Kiernan was still alive.

With that in mind, Carly redoubled her efforts on getting the key. She pulled the hanger back under the door and bent the hook ever so slightly, so that it could still fit under the door, but would have an easier time grabbing a hole in the handle of the key.

She slid the hanger back towards the key. It still wasn't catching, and Carly let out an exasperated cry. She brought the hanger back to her, bent the hook as far as it would go while still fitting under the door, and tried again.

Carly had just gotten the hook to graze into one of the holes, pulling it towards her by increments, when a boot came down hard on the hanger and key.

"Oh Carly," Jamison said. "I'd be proud, except that you're working for the wrong side." He yanked the hanger out of her hands and the key off the floor.

"You sonofabitch!" Carly shouted, banging her fists on the floor.

"That's no way to talk to your father, young lady." Jamison leaned down and looked under the door, locking green eyes with green.

"Go to hell!" Carly hoped her father could see her flipping him off, but she doubted it.

Still, Jamison clearly got the sentiment. "Your brother thinks you can be rehabilitated, but I don't think so. When this is over, I'm going to kill you myself."

"When this is over, you're gonna be dead," Carly promised. She hoped it was the truth.

"Hmm. We'll see," Jamison said. He stood up and his boots moved away down the hall.

Carly sat back on her knees and put her face in her hands. How was she supposed to help Kiernan now?

She looked back at her window, the only other exit. Carly went over and examined the latch, which had been welded shut. She put a shoulder to her dresser and, with effort, moved it aside. Then she dragged one end of her bed under the window.

Wearing only slippers, Carly laid on her back and started kicking the window with her heels. She hoped the slippers would be enough to protect her feet, but if they weren't, she would deal with the conse-quences later.

Fighting and gunfire continued downstairs, but Carly tuned it out, concentrating on breaking the glass. Finally, the first pane cracked, then shattered.

Carly kicked out the largest shards of glass so as not to cut herself as she moved her feet in, then started kicking the second and final pane.

Soon, that shattered as well.

Carly allowed herself a little fist pump of victory before covering her hands with her comforter and picking and punching the last of the big shards of glass away. Then she folded her comforter in half and placed it over the jagged bottom of the window.

"Here goes nothing," she murmured and crawled out onto the roof.

3 6

DEATH DEFYING

Kiernan

Kiernan mauled the first few Hunters, but then they got smart, retreating behind the safety of the kitchen walls and turning down the hall to fire at him, not letting him get close. Kiernan found himself backing up to avoid gunfire, frustration invading every cell of his body as he watched the staircase get further and further away.

Then, over the gunfire, he heard shattering overhead.

'Fuck,' Alec said in his mind, confirming his worst suspicions. 'You'd better get out here, Kiernan. Your mate is pulling a Spider-Man.'

Kiernan didn't know whether to be proud, angry, or terrified. Carly had just put herself in harm's way with the battle raging below her. He turned and loped out of the house, skidding to a stop in the farmyard.

Carly was kicking off her slippers and moving barefoot across the gently angled rooftop, her feet gaining purchase on the shingles.

'Fuck.' Kiernan looked around and found a trellis leading up the side of the house. He let out a loud whine, catching Carly's attention, then trotted over to the trellis and bumped his head against it.

Carly saw, and began moving in that direction.

Kiernan watched her anxiously, Alec watching his back. Sean had been dragged to the side of the porch, still breathing and out of harm's way. The tide was turning, with the werewolves coming out on top.

A few of the kitchen attackers made it to the front door. Kiernan turned his attention to them, ready to pounce, but fur and fangs dragged them back into the house. Soon there was nothing but Hunter screams.

'We're winning,' Kiernan observed to Alec.

'Yeah, but the losses are tremendous,' his Alpha replied sadly.

Indeed, the farmyard was littered with bodies, werewolf, and Hunter. Kiernan had hardly noticed before, he'd been so focused on Carly. His stomach turned as he recognized Liam, back in human form in death. Kiernan had just ridden over two hours in Sean's SUV with him. He rather liked the guy.

With his attention turned from Carly, however, Kiernan failed to see Jamison Waite's booted foot coming out of Carly's window.

'What the holy fuck?!' Alec's voice made Kiernan look at him. Alec jerked his head upwards, and Kiernan looked up.

As Jamison Waite came into view, and it could be no one else, given how much the older man resembled Matthew, Kiernan growled, low and loud.

Carly looked down at him, then at the motion of Kiernan's head, she looked behind her. She gave an alarmed squeak and started moving faster towards the trellis.

Kiernan didn't think this was a good idea, and whined at his mate.

As he feared, Carly's foot slipped. She began tumbling down the roof.

CARLY

The shingles were nearly burning hot under the sunlight, but Carly didn't care. All that mattered was getting down the trellis and to Kiernan.

She was picking her way carefully along when Kiernan alerted her to her father's presence. Carly looked behind her and panicked. She tried moving faster, hoping to outrun her father. But the elder Waite was wearing boots, which protected his feet from the hot shingles.

Carly slipped then. With a scream, she grabbed at the shingles.

A hand gripped her arm, dragging her back up. "You are such a pain in the ass," Jamison said.

"Dad?" Carly was confused.

"I can't let you fall, now can I? You're still going to be useful to me." Then Jamison dragged her back towards the window.

Kiernan growled and jumped at the roof, but could only catch the edge, no matter how he scrabbled with his claws.

"Dad, just let me go," Carly said, looking out over the field and seeing Hunters now dropping like flies. "It's over."

"It's not." Jamison hauled Carly back into her bedroom and plonked her down on the floor.

Carly gestured at the window. "Dad, look. The Hunters are either dead, dying, or surrendering. It's over. You've got to let me go."

"Never," Jamison hissed. He grabbed Carly by the hair then. Carly squealed.

Jamison marched his daughter out her now-open bedroom door and down the stairs, holding a gun to her head. The wolves at the bottom of the stairs growled, but backed off.

"Are you really going to shoot me, Dad?" Carly asked.

"Yes," Jamison said. "If I don't get what I want."

"What do you want?" Carly felt she knew the answer and her heart filled with dread.

Jamison didn't answer right away. Instead, he paraded Carly out onto the porch.

Kiernan and the wolf who'd entered the house after him rounded on Carly and her father. Both growled, but did not move.

Carly looked to the side and saw the other wolf bleeding, but breathing. She wondered if it was Alec or Sean. She assumed whichever it wasn't was now standing with Kiernan.

"I want the asshole who bit my daughter," Jamison said, holding Carly in front of him like a shield.

With the battle winding down, Alec shifted back into human form. "Surrender or be killed, Jamison Waite."

"Alpha Alec." Jamison's smile was chilling. "So good of you to join us. I have no intention of surrendering."

"You must have some intention of dying, then," Alec rumbled.

Jamison laughed. "Maybe. Maybe not. If I go, she's going with me. Unless her 'mate' answers my challenge."

Kiernan shifted then, standing in front of Jamison naked but fierce. "I'm Carly's mate."

"Good," Jamison said. "I thought so. You're going to die for what you did to my daughter."

"We'll see. What do you want from me?" Kiernan asked.

Jamison pointed his gun at Kiernan. "I want you to die."

DEAL MAKING

Kiernan

"Are you going to shoot me, Mr. Waite?" Kiernan asked, staring down Jamison and his gun.

"I was rather hoping we could settle this like men, actually." Jamison looked past Kiernan's shoulder. "Wake him up."

Kiernan turned around and saw Matthew lying on the ground just where he'd left him. "That might not be easy."

"Try," Jamison said.

Alec walked over and grabbed Matthew by his hair. He slapped Matthew's cheeks. "Wakey, wakey. Daddy wants you."

Matthew groaned and blinked his eyes open.

"Matt, I need you to come over here and take care of your sister. See that she doesn't interfere. She's becoming prone to rebellion." Jamison frowned at Carly.

"What's going on?" Matthew asked. He looked Alec up and down as the Alpha dropped him back on the ground.

"You lost, but your dad's still trying to hold onto his little kingdom. That's what's going on," Alec informed him.

Matthew looked around. "Shit."

"Matt, get up here now!" Jamison's tone was like a whip crack.

Matthew got up, got his legs under him, then walked onto the porch. "Dad, what are you planning to do?"

"If she moves, or they move, shoot her," Jamison said, handing Matthew the gun. Then Jamison strode down the three steps to the farmyard.

"You know you're no match for me, right?" Kiernan sighed, looking at Jamison. The man must have been in his fifties.

Jamison pulled out a silver Bowie knife. "That's what your father said to mine."

Kiernan growled. "Let's do this, then."

"Winner walks out of here with Carly," Jamison said.

That gave Kiernan pause. "I figured Carly would walk out of here with whomever she chooses."

"That doesn't sound particularly fair to my side, now does it?" Jamison raised an eyebrow at Kiernan.

"So, let me get this straight. The stakes are, I walk out of here with Carly, you walk out of here with Carly, or Carly gets shot?" Kiernan asked.

"Now you're getting it," Jamison said.

Kiernan ground his teeth. "Gee, since you've left me so many choices..."

"I thought you'd see things my way." Jamison began to circle Kieran.

'I'll kill the brother if he kills Carly,' Alec said. 'Whether you live or die.'

'Thanks.' Dying was not an option today. If he died, Kiernan knew there was no guarantee Alec would go after Carly again, no matter how much he might want to. The death toll of this foray had been high. Alec had to make those kinds of difficult command decisions, and the smart choice would be to protect the pack.

That meant Kiernan had one shot at getting Carly to safety. He wasn't about to blow it.

Jamison took a stab at Kiernan, but Kiernan jumped back. The older man was faster than he looked.

Kiernan knew he'd have to get close enough to Jamison to do

damage, but he wasn't going to underestimate Jamison's expertise with the knife. Not now that he'd seen Jamison move.

Jamison slashed at Kiernan again. "You just going to fiddle around, boy, or are you going to do something?"

As Jamison said, Kiernan had to do something, or they'd be circling each other like this forever. With a hiss, he dove at Jamison.

CARLY

Carly gasped as Kiernan launched himself at her father. He got a slice down his back for his trouble. "Matt, this is madness," Carly said, looking at her brother.

"This is war." Matthew's hand did not waver.

"You don't think you're really going to shoot me, do you?" Carly asked.

Matthew blew out a long breath. "I don't think I'll have to. Either way, you're going home with somebody."

Carly hoped it would be Kiernan. She honestly didn't know what would happen if her father won. He'd probably shoot her as he promised. Still, it was difficult not to be torn. Jamison was her father. Kiernan was her mate. She'd rather neither of them died. "Can't you stop this, Matt?"

"I really don't think so," Matthew said.

Jamison and Kiernan grappled with each other, Kiernan's fingers elongated and clawed, both of them drawing blood.

"Oh God," Carly groaned, her hands going to her cheeks. She would have covered her eyes, but she was too worried she'd miss one of them dying.

"Are you hoping he kills Dad?" Matthew asked, sounding bitter.

"I'm hoping nobody else dies today," Carly said.

Jamison kicked Kiernan down onto the dirt, pressing a silver-heeled boot to the naked man's shoulder. There was an awful hiss.

"Stop!" Carly pleaded. She started forward, but Matt's firm grip on her shoulder stopped her.

"Listen to your 'mate,' begging for your life." Jamison sneered down at Kiernan. "You weak, pathetic thing. Even your father put up more of a fight."

Kiernan growled and twisted Jamison's ankle with an awful crack. Jamison cried out and tumbled to the ground. Kiernan pinned Jamison, his knee on Jamison's knife hand, his hands around her father's throat.

"Oh God, Kiernan, please don't kill him!" Carly said.

Kiernan stared down hatefully at Jamison for a long time. "You're lucky your daughter loves you, even if you don't love her. Yield!" Kiernan ordered.

"Fuck you," Jamison spat.

Kiernan punched him. "Yield!"

"Dad, just... live to fight another day, okay?" Matthew said.

"Please," Carly added.

Jamison was quiet a moment. Then he let go of his knife. "Fine. Since Matt seems so adamant about keeping me alive, I'll yield."

Kiernan nodded. "Good." Kiernan stood and kicked the knife away.

Jamison sat up and rolled his shoulders. Then Kiernan hauled Jamison up by the arm and began duck marching him over to Alec.

Matthew removed the gun from Carly's temple with a shaky breath.

Just as they were about to reach Alec, Jamison turned suddenly, a knife slipping out of his sleeve. "I'm not in the business of leaving werewolves alive," he snapped as he plunged the knife into Kiernan's chest.

3 8

DEAL BREAKING

Carly

"Dad!" Matthew shouted, holding out a hand to stop him, even though he was far too many yards away.

"Oh my God!" Carly ran down the steps. "Oh my God!"

Alec grabbed Jamison and snapped his neck. He dropped their father's lifeless body to the ground.

"Kiernan! Kiernan!" Carly skidded to her knees in the scrubby grass and dirt.

Alec dropped down next to her. "Teams, report!" he yelled to the other wolves.

Everyone was shifting back now. "Area is secure, Alpha Alec," one of the werewolves reported.

Alec's eyes went unfocused. Then he looked at Carly. "I've called in the healers."

Carly put shaking hands on Kiernan. Her fingers found his neck, and she felt a pulse. She put a hand in front of his nose and mouth, and felt his breath. Carly sagged. "He's alive."

"Good." Alec also looked relieved. "As long as he's alive, there are still things the healers can do."

Carly glanced at where the knife was protruding from her mate's chest. "His wound isn't really bleeding. Is that a good thing or a bad thing?"

"I'm not sure," Alec confessed. "We'll have to wait for the healers. Sean's wounded, too."

"Oh no." Carly felt a tear roll down her cheek.

"Don't cry yet. We're still not sure if either of them can be saved," Alec said gruffly.

Carly swept a hand around her. "Look at all this. Oh my God."

Alec looked around and nodded. "Yes, you're right. There is all this. I'm not looking forward to all the families I'm going to have to tell have lost a loved one. Though Alpha Edward's going to have the biggest job."

"I didn't think this was just your pack," Carly said.

"It's not. We're four combined packs here." Alec took Kiernan's hand while Carly stroked Kiernan's forehead.

"Four packs?" Carly asked.

"Two from Canada, one from Minnesota, and us," Alec confirmed.

"Canada?!" Carly couldn't imagine how he'd gotten them all here.

"What can I say? Your mate is very persuasive when he's pissed off." Alec gave a stressed-out half-smile.

Carly gave a small laugh. "I've noticed. Seriously, how did you get them all here?"

"Alpha Edward did. I called him. He called Canada. He's not a big fan of Hunters."

Kiernan's breaths began to stutter, and Carly reached for his other free hand , gripping it between both of hers. "Kiernan, please. Just hang on. Healers are coming."

"If you die on me, you big dumb dog, I'm going to have Carly mate with Sean," Alec threatened.

A low, feeble growl was Kiernan's response to that statement.

"That's right. Ah, here's Doc. Hey, Doc, how's it going?" Alec asked.

Doc snorted. "A whole field of dead and you're asking me how it's going."

"That good, huh? Look, I'd rather Kiernan not die today. Is there any way we can make that happen?" Alec's voice was casual, but his eyes were troubled.

Doc examined Kiernan quickly, holding his ear against Kiernan's chest, then nodded. "It sounds like they missed the vital organs."

"Good. Say, would you mind stitching Kiernan up here? I need to go check on Sean," Alec said.

"I'm waiting for the day when I'm not sewing this man up," Doc grumbled. "Stitch girl, sit back a bit. This might get a little gory."

Carly sat back as, very carefully, Doc pulled the knife out of Kiernan's chest.

Kiernan

The burning was unbearable. Kiernan had never been in so much pain. The only reason he held onto consciousness was because he could hear Carly. He thought she was talking to Alec, but his wolf was only focused on the fact that his mate was there and sounded alright.

Mate.

His wolf was weakened, but still had enough strength left in him to keep Kiernan's heart beating and breath going. They needed to be there for their mate. They needed to make sure she was safe.

There was a terrible, slow tug at his chest, and then the burning stopped. Another voice was there with Carly. As his senses started to return, Kiernan realized it was Doc.

"... just there. There we go, excellent work," Doc was saying.

"Stitch here as well?" Carly asked.

"Yes. Good instincts," Doc replied.

Kiernan blinked his eyes open. "Carly?"

"Kiernan!" Carly plastered herself over his chest, still holding the needle and thread in one hand.

"Could we please finish stitching him up first?" Doc grumped.

"Right. Yes, sorry." Carly sat up and looked down at his chest with an expression of deep concentration.

"That last section there, and he'll be done," Doc said. "Now, if you'll excuse me, I need to tend to other patients."

Carly stopped Doc with a hand on his arm. "Thank you."

Doc smiled at her. "You're welcome." Then he walked away.

"At least you didn't kiss him," Kiernan wheezed.

"You're still being ridiculous about that? Because I have news for you. If Sean pulls through, he's getting one heck of a smacker," Carly said.

Kiernan grunted. "I think I could live with that. He did save my life."

"There's hope for you yet." Carly finished up in a few silent minutes, then bandaged him up and laid herself over Kiernan, careful of his chest wound.

"Doc must be getting tired of stitching me up," Kiernan coughed.

Carly laughed. "He said as much."

"Well, hopefully this time's the last time," Kiernan said.

Carly sighed. She cupped his face and kissed him. "Don't make promises you can't keep."

Kiernan couldn't argue with the truth, so he just grunted. He tried to sit up.

"Just where do you think you're going?!" Carly asked, shoving him back down by the shoulders.

"Sean. Gotta see if he made it." Kiernan tried getting up again, groaning at the pain.

"Look, I just stitched you up. You shouldn't be getting up already," Carly said, trying to encourage him back onto the ground, but this time Kiernan didn't let her.

"I need to see if Sean is okay."

"You mean me?" Sean asked, standing over them. Like just about every other werewolf there, he was naked.

Kiernan laid back down. "Thought you were a goner."

"What can I say?" Sean said. "Wolf pelt is thicker than most buckshot. They just had to pull the shrapnel out and then I was good to shift. That burning was absolutely no fun, though. Can't imagine what it's like to have a knife through your chest."

"Don't. Don't imagine it." Kiernan shuddered. "You don't want to know."

Then there was another shadow over him, a clothed one this time. Kiernan growled when he realized it was Matthew.

"Matt!" Carly blocked Matthew's path to Kiernan and so did Sean.

"You got a death wish, Hunter?" Sean snarled.

"I... I can't believe he stabbed you." Matthew was staring down at Kiernan in disbelief. "He yielded. That should have been the end of it. There's no... honor... in what Dad did. I don't... I don't get it."

"Welcome to reality, Hunter," Sean said.

Carly grabbed Sean's arm and started marching him away. "You have to get out of here," Kiernan heard her saying. "They're not going to have any mercy on you if they catch you—"

"Carly, don't be shy." Alec came striding through the bodies, his tone tight with anger. "Introduce me to your brother."

"Shit," Kiernan groaned.

3 9

DONE

CARLY

Carly swallowed. "Ale-Alpha Alec, this is my brother, Matthew Jamison Waite. We call him Matt."

"Jamison. Figures." Alec walked around Matthew, looking him over. "They sure do make you Waites deceptively skinny."

"I'll be sure to take it up with God when I get there," Matthew said.

Alec smirked. "You do that. So, what should we do with you...?" His eyes flicked to the combine.

Carly followed his gaze and her eyes went wide. "Ale-Alpha Alec, no! Please just let him go."

"So he can go round up his other Hunter buddies?" Alec snorted. "Yeah, right."

"Do you really eat Doritos?" Matthew asked.

This startled Alec. "What?"

"Carly says werewolves eat Doritos. I figured if I'm going to die, I might as well get a real answer," Matthew said.

Alec stared at Matthew a moment. "Sure, Matt, I eat Doritos. I like to dip them in the fresh blood of newborn human babies."

"That's not a straight answer," Matthew objected.

"I didn't say I was going to kill you," Alec said. "Guess that makes us even."

"What are you going to do with him?" Carly asked.

Alec shrugged. "We had been planning to take your father alive and put him in the basement for the rest of his natural life. We were hoping he could lead us to other groups of Hunters. I don't see why Matt here can't take his place."

"The basement? For the rest of his life?" Carly felt panic building in her chest. "My baby brother?"

"You'd rather we kill him?" Alec replied.

"I'd rather you kill me," Matthew said.

Alec gestured to the combine. "You want to hop on in or do you want me to knock you out first?"

"Alec!!!" Carly protested.

"Your sister doesn't seem to like the idea," Alec said.

Matthew shrugged. He took off his leather jacket and handed it to Alec. "Shame for that to get eaten up in the combine. Maybe you can find a wolfy ten-year-old who can fit it."

"You two are unbelievable! This is a joke. Tell me this is a joke!" Carly looked from one to the other, horrified.

Then Alec cracked a smile. "I like you. Too bad I do have to keep you in our basement. Nice jacket, though."

"Would still rather die," Matthew said. He pulled a gun out of the holster at his side.

Alec pushed Carly behind him. "What do you think you're—"

Matthew put the gun to his temple.

"No!" Carly screamed.

Kiernan

Carly's scream got Kiernan on his feet as nothing else could. He took in the full situation, then gave Matthew a placating look. "Matt, just put the gun down. Alec didn't really mean he was going to put you in the basement."

"Yes he did." Matthew's finger curled around the trigger.

"He doesn't mean it anymore. I mean, don't you have women and children who need you to show up and tell them what happened?" Kiernan asked.

"I'm not telling you where the safe house is." Matthew looked over at Carly. "Close your eyes," he said kindly to his sister.

"No, Matt! No!" Carly cried. Tears were streaming down her cheeks.

If there was anything in this world Kiernan hated more than anything, it was seeing his mate cry. "Matt. Put the gun down. Let's talk about this."

"Fine, talk. But I'm not putting the gun down," Matthew said.

"Okay. Okay, then you hold the gun, but take your finger off the trigger, okay? We don't want there to be any accidents." Kiernan held out his hands. "We're all friends here, right?"

Matthew took his finger off the trigger, but still gave a bitter laugh. "Friends? Are you shitting me? Didn't I shoot you once?"

"Friends forgive things like that," Kiernan said.

"Alright, friend. You planning on defying your Alpha and getting me out of here?" Matthew asked sarcastically.

"He better not be," Alec rumbled.

Kiernan decided playing referee between Matthew and Alec was just about the worst job he'd ever had. "I was thinking maybe we could all go our separate ways and call it a day."

"What?!" Alec said. "No. No way. Alpha Edward will never agree to that."

"He's my mate's brother. I already pled for his life. I figured letting him go free at the end was part of the deal," Kiernan argued.

Alec crossed his arms. "That was before Jamison Waite decided he was going to be more trouble than he was worth."

"As I recall, you're the one who killed him," Kiernan said.

"As I recall, he'd just about killed you, after surrendering. I wasn't about to let him get another shot." Alec was grumbling now.

A crowd of those who were still upright began gathering around them. There was growling and snarling from the ones who were still in wolf form, and shouting and jeers from those who were human.

Matthew's finger moved back to the trigger.

"Hey, let's have none of that now! We're not done talking," Kiernan said.

"Let him kill himself. Who cares? He's a Hunter," someone in the crowd yelled.

Another spat at the ground near Matthew. "Coward."

Kiernan turned to Alec. "Alec, please. Just let the kid go, before this gets any worse."

Alec was about to answer, then his eyes went unfocused. A slow grin spread across his face. It was not a nice grin. "We've found two safe houses."

Matthew and Carly both made a similar noise of distress.

"Where?" Carly asked.

"How?" Matthew whispered.

"You people reek of wolfsbane. You think it's that hard to find in a town as small as Vermillion?" Alec chuckled.

"I wasn't aware we were looking for the safe houses," Kiernan said.

Alec made a vague gesture. "Alpha Edward thought it would be best to be prepared. Isn't that what you've always said? Be prepared?"

"Be prepared to what, stoop to their level? Slaughter women and children?" Kiernan growled.

Alec blinked. "Shit, Kiernan, of course not! We were going to use them as leverage for a hostage trade if we needed to. Where's your mind at?"

Kiernan shook his head. "Sorry, sorry."

"You should be sorry." Alec looked at Matthew again and sighed. "I suppose if we have them, we don't really need him. Run along, Hunter."

Loud protests roared through the crowd, but Alec silenced them with a snarl. "I'm Alpha in command here, and I say he goes. Don't you dare touch him, either."

"If you keep me, will you let them go?" Matthew asked.

Alec stared at Matthew. "That's surprisingly chivalrous of you. No, there's no need to keep you. We've got four Hunter guards from the safe houses, that should be enough. Besides, I did sort of promise we'd leave you alone."

"Go find Mom and Dawn," Carly chimed in. "They need someone to look after them now."

Matthew looked at their father's body on the ground, then back up at Carly. "It's over. I'm calling it. It's done."

"Good," Carly said. "Now you can—"

Matthew shook his head. "We're done, too."

4 0

GUILT

CARLY

Carly felt as though part of her soul was being ripped away. "What?"

Matthew didn't answer. He simply walked away.

The crowd parted for him, albeit reluctantly. At the far end of the field, Carly could see women and children gathered between about twelve werewolves. Matthew spotted them as well and headed that way.

Carly looked from her brother's retreating back to her father lying dead on the ground and felt her world shifting for the second time in a week. She felt as though the Earth had lost gravity, a sick, faint, floaty feeling coursing through her.

Kiernan caught her to his side before she actually fainted, which Carly appreciated. She didn't want to do that before the crowd of werewolves. There were a lot of things she wanted to do right now that she didn't want witnesses to.

"Take her out of here," Alec said before anyone even asked him.

Someone in the crowd passed Kiernan and Sean a set of clothes, which they quickly pulled on. With a nod from Kiernan, Sean scooped Carly up, carrying her beside Kiernan as they made their way... somewhere. Away from the farm, at least. Carly wasn't sure quite where they were going, and she didn't much care. She just knew they walked for a long time. Neither of the men talked to her, which was also fine. Carly didn't feel like talking.

When they reached it, Carly recognized Schaar's Bluff. She remembered her family and friends of her family had gone picnicking there when she was younger, under one of the covered shelters. Barbecuing weenies.

That's when the floodgates opened. Carly burst into terrible, wracking sobs.

Sean quickly got Carly into the back of his Jeep, setting her in Kiernan's lap. He then closed the door and stood outside it, guarding Carly and Kiernan's alone time.

"Carly..." Kiernan whispered, hugging her to him. "I'm so sorry. I'm so sorry, Babe."

"I can't breathe," Carly gasped. "Oh God, how do I ever breathe again?"

"Shhh." Kiernan held Carly to him and rocked her.

Carly gripped Kiernan's shirt, a My Little Pony number he'd clearly not picked out himself. She sobbed into the white and pink fabric, getting a little glitter on her cheeks.

"We're going to figure this out, okay? You and me, we're a team," Kiernan said.

"What is there to figure out? My father's dead. My family hates me. I think my best friend is about to disown me. I'm being cut out of my whole life!" Carly wailed. She wondered if this was how a weed felt when it was mercilessly torn from the ground.

Kiernan forced Carly to look at him. "Listen to me. You've got me. And you've got Jenny. And you've got Sean. And you've even got Alec. You're not alone in the world. I promise. I promise you. I will always be there for you, and if you're ever lost, I will always come for you. You're my mate, and I love you."

Carly's tears of loss flowed over his fingers, but she nodded. "I love you, too."

Kiernan kissed her, then tried thumbing some of the glitter off her face, but it just made it worse, as he'd somehow also gotten some flecks on his hands. "When we get home, we'll take a nice hot shower, curl up on the sofa, and watch some Hallmark romance movies with bad plots. How does that sound?"

"What if Jenny wants to watch her Lifetime movies?" Carly sniffled.

"Jenny's had plenty of time to watch Lifetime movies. Between that and ESPN, we never get to use our own TV anyway. It's our turn," Kiernan said firmly.

"What if I just want to go to bed?" Carly asked.

Kiernan shrugged. "Then we'll just go to bed. Sean and Jenny can fight over the remote and we can get the first good night's sleep either of us have had in days." Kiernan gave her a slow smile. "Unless you meant something else."

Carly let out a wet laugh. "Your chest was slashed open. I think that's off the table for a while, Mister."

"I don't remember Doc specifically saying anything..." Kiernan said.

"He was too busy going to see to the other injured." Carly's face fell again. "Oh my God, so many people died."

"Yes," Kiernan conceded. "Many people did die."

"Just to get me back," Carly whispered. "Oh my God, I got all those people killed!"

Kiernan

Kiernan saw where she was going with this and shook his head vehemently. "No. No, Babe, this is not your fault. This was coming one way or another. You were just a convenient excuse. Alpha Edward wanted a war. Your father wanted a war. So there was a war. You had absolutely nothing to do with it."

"I feel like Helen of Troy," Carly said miserably.

"Well, you are beautiful and special enough to launch a thousand ships, but I don't remember her having much to do with the war except being taken. That's you. You were just taken away, and that got all the packs thinking of all the times we've had Hunters take people from us. And all the packs were tired of it. That's all." Kiernan kissed her temple and rocked her some more.

"If you say so," Carly murmured, still looking glum.

Kiernan expected she would be that way for some time, but he also knew he'd be able to be there for her through the grieving process, and that gave him comfort. He nuzzled her hair, breathing in her scent. His wolf curled up inside, content.

Near sundown, werewolves in all kinds of mismatching clothes came loping back to the parking lot. Kiernan noted Carly had fallen asleep, so used the mindlink to communicate with Sean. 'What's going on?'

'They're taking some of the cars into Vermillion to pick up the dead,' Sean replied.

Kiernan looked around as black SUVs began pulling away. 'And the Hunters?'

'Alpha Edward said the combine, but Alec managed to convince him to let the women and children bury their own dead,' Sean said.

'Good. That's good.' Kiernan stroked Carly's hair. 'I suppose Matt took Jamison to be buried.'

'They left him.' Sean's mental tone of thought did not denote he cared in the slightest.

'What?' Kiernan asked.

'Matt took his mom and Dawn and they left,' Sean explained.

Kiernan turned his head to make eye contact with Sean. 'He's just sitting out there and rotting?'

Sean's eyes slid to Carly and back to Kiernan's. 'I think they're thinking the combine.'

4 1

BACK HOME

Kiernan

Kiernan waited patiently for Alec to return. Since Carly was asleep, Sean had slid into the driver's seat and was running the air conditioning. Luckily, the engine igniting hadn't woken Carly up.

Alec showed up wearing a Care Bears shirt, and not looking particularly happy about it. Kiernan began to wonder who had been in charge of getting replacement clothes.

'Is it over?' Kiernan asked Alec via mindlink as Alec got into the passenger seat.

Alec looked back, saw Carly was asleep, and closed his door as quietly as possible. 'It's over.'

Kiernan glanced at Carly, then back at Alec. 'Jamison Waite?'

'Fertilizer,' Alec replied.

Kiernan winced. 'I really didn't want to have to tell Carly that.'

'Then don't,' Alec said.

There was a mental sigh as Kiernan tried to formulate his next thought into something polite, but the disgusted emotion got away from him before he could make a complete sentence.

'What?' Alec asked peevishly.

'I think you need to understand that this is part of the reason

213

Jenny's mad at you, thinking you can keep things like this from her,' Kiernan said.

Alec's mood turned darker than it had been after the battle. 'It's not wrong to want to protect your mate from bad things.'

'It's infantilizing and if I were her, I'd throttle you.' Kiernan's words were stern. 'You know what infantilize means, right?'

"Drive," Alec snapped to Sean, who threw the Jeep into gear. 'You think I'm treating Jenny like a child,' he said to Kiernan via the mindlink.

'Yes, I do,' Kiernan said.

Alec growled. 'I'm getting really tired of how you keep jumping into our relationship, Kiernan.'

'She's my sister. Her family helped raise me. What do you expect me to do when she's upset?' Kiernan asked.

Alec stared out the windshield for a long time. Kiernan could feel over the mindlink that he was seething, but he didn't seem ready to talk, so Kiernan didn't push it.

'Could you try seeing things from my perspective for once?' Alec finally said angrily.

'I could if you shared your perspective,' Kiernan replied. Carly snuggled more into his shoulder and Kiernan smiled fondly. Still, she didn't wake, which he considered a good thing. She needed the rest.

'There's a lot of shit that goes down that Jenny doesn't need to know about or be a part of,' Alec explained. 'She doesn't need to be concerned about things like war and uneasy alliances and Hunters encroaching on our territory and vacationing near the resort. She doesn't need to worry about the fact that all the building going up around us is reducing our forest land. She just needs to worry about the welfare of the pack. That's her job.'

Now Kiernan wanted to throttle him. 'And you don't think any of those things have to do with the welfare of the pack?'

'Not if I can help it. Now I've got you, so we've got two people on these problems,' Alec said. 'So there's even less reason for her to be involved. It's my job to protect her.'

Kiernan pinched the bridge of his nose. 'Alec. It's your job to include her. She's your mate, your right hand.'

Alec became sullen and closed the mindlink. "I guess we'll have to agree to disagree."

"What are we disagreeing about?" Carly mumbled, waking with a yawn. She rubbed her eyes in a very cute way that had Kiernan kissing her eyelids when she was done. He also glared daggers at Alec for waking her up.

"Nothing you need to worry about," Alec said, his arms folded as he stubbornly stared out at the road.

"Oh yeah, that's going to stop her from asking questions," Sean snorted.

Alec glared at him. "Did I ask you?"

"Nope," Sean said, unapologetic.

"It's okay. I'll just ask Kiernan later." Carly looked around them. "Where are we?"

Sean read a sign as they passed it and he had to slow down for a town. "Clayton. Unincorporated."

"Well, as long as they have a gas station, a bar, and a church, they usually still call it a town," Kiernan chuckled. "Let's check."

Carly was distracted by the game, much to Kiernan's relief. As they had to slow down for small unincorporated town after small unincorporated town, she and Kiernan began ticking off whether or not they saw a gas station, a church, and a bar.

But when they hit another long stretch of highway, Carly grew quiet again.

Kiernan bumped his forehead to hers. "We'll be home soon."

A tear rolled down Carly's cheek, and she nodded. "Good."

***

CARLY

They played the gas station, church, and bar game again once they ran into more small towns, but Carly's heart wasn't really in it this time. The events of the last week flooded over her, overwhelming her. It was all she could do not to cry in front of Alec.

When they got to Crescent Moon Path Resort, Carly scrambled out of Kiernan's lap and headed off towards their cabin.

Kiernan was not far behind, and then he was striding beside her. Sean took up the rear. Carly wondered if Sean was going to continue to stay with them, then remembered Jenny was there. She figured as long as Jenny needed protecting, Sean would be there.

"Carly!" Jenny ran up and hugged her as soon as Carly burst through the door. "Thank goodness! How are you? Are you okay?"

Carly sniffled. "I'm really not."

Kiernan nodded at Jenny, then took Carly by the arm. "We'll be in the bedroom if you need us."

"Of course," Jenny said. "I'm just so glad to have you back, Carly."

"Thanks." Carly went with Kiernan to their bedroom, vaguely hearing Sean telling Jenny about how the battle had gone. Jenny asked Sean if Alec was alright. Carly was a little pleased about that, given the way Alec had saved Kiernan's life.

Kiernan pulled Carly down onto the edge of the bed and embraced her. "Okay now. Nobody here but us."

Carly dissolved into wrenching sobs.

4 2

LIFE AND DEATH

Kiernan

Kiernan's heart broke for his mate. He stroked her hair and the nape of her neck, holding her against his wounded chest. It hurt a bit, but he didn't care.

"Did they—did they put any bodies through the combine?" Carly asked after a while.

Ah. The dreaded question. "Just one," Kiernan said. "The rest were taken away by family members."

"Who went through the combine?" Carly asked the question, but Kiernan could tell from her tone she already suspected the answer.

"Your father. Matthew left with your mother and Dawn. They didn't take the body. I'm sorry." Kiernan hugged Carly more tightly.

Carly curled closer to Kiernan. "I kind of figured."

"I'm sorry, I didn't think to ask you before they did it. I—"

Carly put her fingers over Kiernan's lips. "Don't worry about it. I wouldn't have... wanted him around here anyway. I wouldn't have known what to do. I mean, he was my father, but he also told me he was going to shoot me, so..."

"He said that?" Kiernan growled.

"He's not winning a father-of-the-year award," Carly sighed.

"No, I think not." Kiernan kissed Carly's temple. "How are you feeling? Are you hungry? Tired? Need some more time to cry? I'm a great shoulder to cry on."

Carly gave a tearful laugh. "You do know you're basically covered in glitter, right? It keeps rubbing off your shirt."

Kiernan grinned. "I guess we're going to be a bit sparkly, then."

"Like little disco balls," Carly agreed. She stroked Kiernan's cheek. "I love you, you know that, right?"

"Of course. I don't think grieving your father or mourning the loss of your family makes you love me less. You can be upset and angry over what's happened, even so far as meeting me, but that doesn't mean I think you don't love me," Kiernan said.

"Good. I'm glad we met, but I'm also sad over what it's meant for other parts of my life. I wish... I wish everyone had just been more understanding." Carly tucked her head under Kiernan's chin.

Kiernan nodded. "I get that."

"Do you think I'll ever see Matt again? Or Dawn? Or my mom?" Carly asked softly.

"Yes." Because Kiernan was going to make it happen if it killed him.

———

KIERNAN LEFT CARLY sleeping and went out, going to help others unload bodies from the SUVs. The Superior and Canada groups had all taken theirs home, but the Crescent Moon Pack had three fallen, and they needed to be honored.

"Carly?" Alec asked when Kiernan approached.

"I don't think she's up to this. I don't think she will be for a long time." Kiernan helped Alec put Liam's body down on a tarp.

"His parents are coming to the cremation. They've asked for it to be private." Alec looked up as three hearses approached. "I'm just glad the funeral home doesn't ask questions."

"We pay them enough not to ask questions," Kiernan pointed out.

Alec nodded. "True. We'll have a ceremony in a couple of days. I think everyone will understand if you can't make it."

"I have to take care of Carly. If she's doing okay, I'll come. If not, I'll be sure to follow up with the families myself," Kiernan said.

"Good," Alec agreed. "I think the families will really appreciate that."

"I owe it to them." Kiernan looked back towards his cabin. "I think I should get back to Carly."

Alec clapped him on the shoulder. "Good luck, brother."

<hr>

Carly

Carly didn't emerge from their room for several days. Kiernan brought her meals and made sure she showered and brushed her teeth. She was so deep in grief that she sometimes forgot.

In the meantime, Kiernan healed. Carly saw, with relief, that his wound closed up, the stitches dissolved, and all that was left was a whitening three-inch scar.

"That's truly remarkable, you know," she said, stroking his chest one night as he lay naked next to her. They hadn't had sex since she'd been rescued, but Carly didn't mind him going back to his preferred way of sleeping. She herself had taken over the My Little Pony shirt for the evening and a pair of shorts.

Kiernan captured her hand and kissed it. "Werewolf healing. Gotta love it."

Carly kissed the scar on his chest. Her hand idly played at his abs.

"Carly?" Kiernan stroked her hair. "Do you... want something, babe?"

Carly's hand stilled. She propped herself up on her elbows and stared down at her mate. He'd been there for her through the worst of her grief, patiently waiting for her to feel well enough for him, she knew. Carly also knew if she needed more time, he'd wait even longer.

Even though the pain of loss still throbbed in her heart, though, it had always been lessened by her love of this man. Carly realized she didn't need any more time. She leaned down and kissed Kiernan fiercely. "Make love to me, Kiernan."

Kiernan groaned and rolled her underneath him. "Are you sure?" he asked, caressing her cheeks. "We don't have to. There's no time limit or anything. I mean, we have the whole rest of our lives—"

Carly silenced him with another kiss. "I want to. Please be inside me, Kiernan."

Kiernan nuzzled her neck and reached into the bedside dresser, pulling out a condom. "Okay, babe. Whatever you say." He kneeled up and stripped off her shirt and shorts leaving her naked beneath him.

When he came back over her, he licked her mark in one long, slow lap.

Carly shivered and ran her palms over his nipples.

Kiernan growled and nipped her mark, then let his hands wander to her breasts, squeezing them and rolling her nipples between his thumbs and forefingers.

Carly kissed him and her hands descended to his ass, pulling him closer to her. She could hardly believe how much she yearned for him, how much she'd missed this. "Kiernan," she begged. "Kiernan, now. It's been so long..."

With a groan, Kiernan handed Carly the condom packet. "Do you want to do the honors?"

"Yes." Carly tore open the packet and carefully rolled the condom onto Kiernan's cock. She gave his shaft a little stroke before pulling her hand back, just for good measure.

"Minx." Kiernan kissed Carly as she widened her legs for him and inched his way inside her.

It was maddening and Carly writhed beneath him. "Kiernan..."

"Shh, we'll get there. There's no rush," Kiernan murmured, holding her hips still as he continued to push slowly inside.

"Speak for yourself!" Carly moaned. She tried bucking her hips, but it was no use, his hold on her was too tight.

Kiernan's chuckle rumbled through her as he leaned down and gave her a kiss that promised everything she wanted.

Then he was fully inside her, his hips fused to hers. "Kiernan..." Carly sighed.

"Yeah, babe. I know. It feels amazing," Kiernan said, pausing there, buried deep inside her without moving.

Carly whimpered, rubbing her hips against his, enjoying the delicious friction. "Please, Kiernan. Please."

Kiernan groaned and seized her lips in a searing kiss as he started to thrust, hard and deep. His hands found her breasts once more and started playing with them as gently as he was thrusting powerfully inside her.

Carly wrapped her legs around his waist and moved with him. She clung to his shoulders, squeezing the back of his neck where his mark was.

Kiernan shivered and thrust harder and faster. Their breath mingled as they kissed each other desperately, reaching for their pleasure and finding it together.

As Carly trembled in the last throes of her orgasm, Kiernan stroked her and made a path of little nibbles up the side of her neck. He rolled on his back so she was sprawled across him, tickling his fingers up and down her spine.

"Better?" Kiernan asked, kissing her hair.

Carly smoothed a hand over his chest, then grinned impishly at him. "I don't know. We might have to try again."

4 3

A MAN WALKED INTO A BAR

Kiernan

They spent several hours satisfying each other. Of course, in that amount of time, a particularly murderous Lifetime movie blared louder and louder, but Kiernan and Carly just laughed about it. Poor Sean might never get to watch ESPN again.

Carly was now sleeping on Kiernan's chest, while Kiernan thought over the last two weeks and the whirlwind it had created of both their lives. He was glad he had Carly as his port in the storm. She was his mate.

Mate, his wolf agreed happily. It was as though his wolf were curled next to a glowing, warm fire. At least, that's the best way Kiernan could describe it. He had no doubt in his mind what, or rather who, the fire was.

Something felt incomplete, though. Kiernan frowned as he thought it over, rubbing Carly's back. Then it hit him. While Carly was his for all to see in his world, they might as well just be dating in hers. No special formal ceremony had taken place according to normal human standards.

Kiernan didn't like that. He wanted Carly to be his in every world. "I think we should get married," he murmured into the darkness.

223

Carly stiffened. Kiernan hadn't even been aware she was awake, he'd been so deep in thought. "You what?"

Kiernan looked down at his mate and smiled. "I think we should get married," he said with more strength.

"Do werewolves... do that?" Carly asked.

Kiernan popped a kiss on her nose. "No, not usually. But we do. I want you to belong to me before your God and Fate and everyone."

Carly inclined her head, her forehead scrunching up as she thought about it. "As long as you belong to me, too."

"Always," Kiernan said. "I will always belong to you."

<hr>

KIERNAN SAT at Tony's Riverside in Spooner, a sports bar with wooden tables, wood paneling, a pool table, and a friendly atmosphere. The padded metal chair beneath him creaked as he turned and looked at the door again, his hand around a cooling Alaskan Amber.

Just as Kiernan was starting to think he wouldn't show, Matthew walked through the door. He uncomfortably shrugged in the same leather jacket Alec had admired, rolling his shoulders as he went to sit across the table from Kiernan.

"I wasn't sure you'd actually show up." Kiernan nodded to the waitress, who came over.

"Budweiser, please." The waitress nodded and headed back to the bar. Matthew leaned back in his chair, his arms folded. "I wasn't expecting your call. I suppose that'll teach me to change my number. How did you get my number? Carly give it to you?"

"In a roundabout way, I guess," Kiernan replied. "Jenny, a mutual friend, is planning our wedding. Carly gave your number to her. I think she'd like you to come."

Matthew snorted. "Werewolves don't have weddings."

"Not usually," Kiernan admitted. "But Carly comes from your world, and normal humans do have weddings. I want to respect that. I'd also appreciate it if you came."

"You didn't bring Carly with you. Afraid I'll upset her when I say no?" Matthew asked.

"Are you going to say no?" Kiernan responded.

Matthew regarded Kiernan for a long time—so long that the waitress came and went by the time he spoke. "I haven't quite figured it all out for myself yet. I don't know if showing up as a Hunter in a church full of werewolves is such a good idea."

"You don't smell as much like Hunter anymore," Kiernan observed.

"Mom stopped burning the candles and incense once Dad was gone. Combine?" Matthew asked.

Kiernan fidgeted with his bottle. "Yes."

Matthew nodded. "Poetic." He took a long swig from his Bud.

"My sources tell me you haven't been back to the farm," Kiernan said.

"Mom doesn't want to. And frankly, neither do I," Matthew replied. "We're looking for a real estate agent right now. Know any good ones?"

"Not in the Twin Cities metro area, but I can ask around." Kiernan leaned forward. "Why did you come today?"

Matthew sighed and raked a hand over his hair. "I don't know. Curiosity, I guess? I don't know if I'm in a make love, not war place yet, but I'm certainly done with war."

"No more hunting?" Kiernan asked.

"Maybe the odd pheasant, but no. No more hunting. I'm sick of the whole thing. It's all bullshit." Matthew took another swig of his drink. He rolled the bottle back and forth between his hands, smearing a path of condensation on the table. "How is Carly?"

"Sad," Kiernan said. "But getting better."

Matthew nodded. "Same here."

"I think you both might be a lot less sad if you reconnected," Kiernan added.

"Thanks, Dr. Phil." Matthew laughed bitterly.

Kiernan shrugged. "Your loss. Anyway—" Kiernan set a pretty white, embossed envelope on the table. "This is for you."

Matthew looked at it as though it might bite him. Then he picked it up and tucked it into his jacket pocket. "Thanks."

"Think about coming, okay?" Kiernan stood and put a twenty on the table. "This is on me."

Matthew saluted him with his bottle. "I'll think about it."

***

CARLY

"You're still planning on hitting the road?" Carly asked as Jenny played with the hem of Carly's dress.

She took a pin out of her mouth and marked a fold she'd made in the white satin. Carly was standing on the coffee table in front of the TV in her silver heels while Jenny fitted her.

"Yes. Right after the wedding. Alec and I need some space, and he's not giving it to me here. Plus, I want to make sure that the Superior Pack guy is doing a good job selling Kiernan's furniture. Besides, my ears are going to start bleeding if we turn the TV up any higher." Jenny grinned up at Carly.

Carly blushed. "Yeah, sorry about that. I guess we've been a bit... enthusiastic... lately."

"I would be. You just got out of a terrible ordeal, and... well, I don't want to make you cry again before your wedding. Have to save up those tears for when he says 'I do.'" Jenny pinned another spot.

"Incoming," Sean said from where he was sitting in front of them, watching ESPN on mute with subtitles.

"Augh! I told him to mindlink me when he was coming home!" Jenny helped Carly step down from the coffee table. "Go in my bedroom, quick! I'll head him off."

Carly started moving in a rustle of skirts. She smiled as she heard Jenny scold Kiernan on the other side of the door. Carly undid the side zip of her dress and carefully stepped out of it, laying it on Jenny's bed. She pulled on her tank top and shorts and stepped back out, closing the door behind her.

"I wasn't trying to see the bride, I swear!" Kiernan said, holding his hands up in surrender.

Jenny poked him in the chest. "Yeah, right! I told you to mindlink me, and you didn't."

"I forgot." Kiernan beamed when he laid eyes on Carly.

Carly knew she was wearing the same besotted expression.

"You two are just too cute," Jenny said.

Kiernan walked over to Carly and wrapped his arms around her. "Gotta say, heels and jean shorts are becoming my new favorite look."

Carly looked down and laughed, realizing she'd changed clothes but not shoes. "It's your fault, coming in unannounced."

"Babe, you're living with a bunch of werewolves. There's no such thing as unannounced." Kiernan trailed his fingers up over the bare skin at the top of her back.

Carly's pulse quickened. "You do that on purpose."

"Every time," Kiernan agreed.

4 4

MELTING MOMENTS

Carly was just preparing to head out the door when Kiernan was called away on urgent pack business. That meant she still couldn't go to the store in Hayward to pick up the yarn that was on hold for Kiernan's sweater. Then again, she hadn't wanted to go there with Kiernan anyway. It would ruin the surprise.

But Kiernan was determined that she not ever leave the pack grounds alone after the incident with the Hunters. Sure they'd all been killed or were rotting in a dungeon with the Superior Pack to garner more information from them, but Kiernan had wanted to be extra careful.

Sean was out seeing a movie with Jenny, the same rules applying to her, so there was little for Carly to do but flop on the sofa and play with her phone. She was shocked when it started to ring—and even more shocked when she saw who it was.

"Matt?!" Carly stuttered into the phone.

"Hi." Matthew's voice was measured, as though not sure what to expect from her.

"I'm so glad you called! How are you doing? How's Mom? Is Dawn with you?" Carly asked.

There was a short silence, then a chuckle. "I'm fine. Mom is doing pretty well, considering. Dawn is with us."

"Where are you living these days? Or can't you tell me?" Carly asked. "Are you back on the farm?

"No. Mom's not ready, and frankly, neither am I." Matthew sighed on the other end of the line. "We're in Eagan. Temporary apartment."

Carly chewed her lip. "Is it nice? Bad?"

"Eh, it's okay," Matthew said.

"Okay," Carly remembered having a million questions she wanted to ask him, but couldn't think of one now.

"I met with your... mate." Matthew had trouble saying the last word.

"Oh?" Carly was surprised. "What did you meet about?"

"I hear you're getting officially married, even though that's not a werewolf thing." Matthew's voice held a lot of complicated emotions.

"Yeah. It was even Kiernan's idea. I'm pretty excited." Carly toyed with a fraying thread on the sofa. "You know you're invited, right?"

"I know," Matthew said.

Carly sat up, anxious about her next question. "Are you... coming?"

Matthew sighed. "I don't know yet."

Kiernan

Kiernan left the meeting with Alec feeling ever so slightly over-whelmed. It was just a week until the wedding, and since Jenny had not changed her mind, Alec had been inundating Kiernan with all the duties the Alpha of the pack had. At least the dumb bastard intended to go after her. The downside to this was that Kiernan would be left doing the work of the Alpha, and the Gamma, as Sean was leaving with Jenny.

Not that Sean had much on his plate. Alec had taken the lion's share of the work. His explanation had been he'd been waiting for Kiernan to return and become his Beta. But Kiernan suspected Alec might be a compulsive workaholic—or may have been using work to avoid problems at home.

Speaking of home, Kiernan smelled something delicious as he walked towards the cabin. This was both a good and bad thing. Good because, from the smell of it, there were going to be many, many chocolate chip cookies to eat over the next week. Bad because Kiernan had learned that Carly was a bit of a stress baker. She blamed not having her yarn. No one had been able to bring themselves to go back to the farm to get it yet.

"Babe?" Kiernan asked as he walked in the door.

"Oh, hi." Carly was wearing a flour-powdered apron.

Kiernan walked into the kitchen and hugged her, letting his clothes get all full of flour. "How are you doing? Are you okay?"

"Yeah." Carly sounded glum.

"You don't sound okay," Kieran said.

"Matt called." Carly leaned her head against him as though absorbing his strength.

Kiernan was happy to give it to her. "I take it that wasn't a good thing? Is he still angry?"

"I don't know. He didn't yell at me, but he also didn't know if he was coming to the wedding or not." Carly shook her head sadly. "I really wish he would."

"I think he's still getting his head around a lot of stuff. Don't count him out yet," Kiernan said, kissing the top of her head.

"Okay." Carly looked despondently at her cookies.

Kiernan stole one off the drying rack and popped it in his mouth. "Mmm, good."

Carly laughed and shook a finger at him. "How do you know those are for you, mister?"

"I bit it. I claimed it. It's mine ." Kiernan's voice rumbled as he said it. Then he took one of the cookies and popped it in Carly's mouth.

Carly munched thoughtfully. "Maybe I should bite you back."

"That would certainly start a new tradition," Kiernan chuckled. He kissed the chocolate off her lips. "But I'd let you bite me anytime you wanted."

"You say that now, but you freaked out the one time I even gave you a hickey," Carly reminded him.

Kiernan felt his cheeks get hot. "That was different. I had a council meeting an hour later."

"Ahuh." Carly booped him on the nose. "I think you just might be a big baby."

"Are you questioning my manliness, woman?" Kiernan asked with a grin.

"I might be. What are you gonna do about it?" Carly teased.

Kiernan set the third cookie he'd been grabbing back down and scooped Carly off the floor.

"Hey! I was going to put the next batch in the oven!" Carly protested, but laughed while she did so.

"They'll still be there when we get back." Kiernan began carrying her towards the bedroom.

"I'm all full of flour! The sheets!" Carly said.

Kiernan shrugged. "Guess they're gonna get some white dust on them."

Carly wriggled in his arms. "What about the chocolate and the cookie dough? I'm all sticky!"

"Then I guess I'm going to be sticky, too, in a minute." Kiernan dropped Carly on the bed and gave her a kiss.

Carly groaned and gave in. "You're doing the laundry."

"We're taking a shower," Kiernan countered.

"But what about the cookies?!"

Kiernan silenced her with a kiss.

4 5

GETTING READY

Jenny bent over Carly's dress, straightening the train as they stood before the mirror in the makeshift bride's dressing room in the lodge. As werewolves didn't tend to have weddings, and the resort was mostly frequented by werewolves, there wasn't exactly a formal dressing room for the bride. But they'd made do with a first-floor suite.

"Does Sean have the Jeep all stocked up? Kiernan said the RV's ready and waiting in Minnesota," Carly said, smoothing her hands over the eyelet bodice of her dress.

"Yep. Sean even has the directions already. We're leaving first thing in the morning." Jenny finished arranging Carly's train. Then she cocked her head and sniffed the air. She smiled. "We have visitors."

"Visitors? Seriously, Kiernan is NOT supposed to see me before the wedding. When will he get that through his head?!" Carly started bustling towards the bedroom, but Jenny stopped her.

"No, not Kiernan." Jenny went to the door and opened it.

Matthew was standing there with his fist raised to knock. "Er... hi."

Two female heads poked around him. "Oh Carolyne, you look lovely," Carly's mother said while Dawn clapped her hands.

Carly had to hold herself up on the desk. "You came!"

"Sure did." Matthew walked in but Jenny put a hand on his chest before he got to Carly.

"Later, we haven't taken the pictures yet and you're going to wrinkle her," Jenny said sternly.

Matthew and Carly both laughed. "We wouldn't want that."

"How about the way the French do it?" Dawn asked. She walked over to Carly and took her hands, then gave her an air kiss on each cheek.

"That works." Matthew did the same, as well as her mother, though Rose Waite did not let go of her daughter's hands.

"I'm just so happy for you, Carolyne," Rose said, tears brimming in her eyes.

"You're not angry?" Carly asked.

"A little surprised, perhaps, but no. Not angry at all. There's this lovely young lady from the Superior Pack that has been helping us get the farm on the market." Rose began fussing Carly's sleeves.

"You're selling the farm." Carly couldn't say she was surprised they were selling the farm. She was surprised Alpha Edward had allowed one of his pack to help a Hunter family. Carly suspected Alec and Kiernan had something to do with it.

Rose shuddered. "I never want to go back there. Matthew has been kind enough to gather the things we want and need, but everything else can burn for all I care."

Carly's heart went out to her mother. "I'm sorry things were so awful for you, Mom."

"Oh," Rose said, getting a bit flustered, "it wasn't that bad. I had you kids."

Carly smiled sadly. Then she noticed that her mother and Dawn were both wearing wine-colored dresses , and Matthew was wearing a suit that would match Alec's and Sean's in gray. "How... what?"

"Jenny figured you should have your two best girlfriends there. And Kiernan said if Matt comes, he wants him to stand up with him, so we did some last-minute shopping with Jenny's Internet search savvy," Dawn said. "Nice colors for an October wedding, by the way."

"Thanks." Carly felt her own eyes welling up.

"Not the mascara! Not the mascara!" Jenny yelped, and then she and Dawn were both fanning Carly's face with wedding programs.

"You'd better run along and see where the groom is hiding," Rose told Matthew.

"Right." Matthew headed for the door. "See you in there, sis. Oh, we figured you'd want Mom to walk you down the aisle?"

Carly sniffled and nodded. "Yes, that's what I was hoping for. I never expected I'd get it."

"See? We should all believe in wedding miracles," Dawn said .

Kiernan

"If you don't stand still, we're never going to get it on straight," Alec grumbled, trying to straighten Kiernan's red rose boutonniere.

"I am standing still. You just have no coordination." Kiernan tapped his foot. "At this rate, we're going to be an hour late."

"I'd try, but I'm all thumbs," Sean said from where he was lounging on a sofa.

The door opened, drawing the attention of all three werewolves.

Matthew took one look at the situation and waved Alec off. "Stand aside. Trust me, I've been in five weddings. There's a trick to these things."

Sean blinked at Matthew. "Didn't you stab me once?"

"Yeah... about that..." Matthew winced.

"We're calling it a bad life choice." Kiernan stood still as Matthew fixed his boutonniere.

"I hope you're not planning on making any more bad life choices today," Sean growled.

Matthew shook his head. "Nope. All done with bad life choices for this decade." He patted Kiernan's lapels as he finished. "There you go."

Kiernan looked in the mirror. "Good work. Now you can fix the other two's."

"What's wrong with mine?" Sean asked while Alec stepped up to have his boutonniere adjusted.

"It's basically sideways," Matthew said, glancing over.

Sean looked down. "Oh. I guess it is."

Matthew finished Alec, then went over to Sean. "Sorry about the shoulder."

"It's fine now. Just a couple days I couldn't practice my back swing," Sean grinned as Matthew worked.

When Matthew was done, Kieran came over and gave him a strong hug, pounding him on the back. "Thanks for coming."

"I can't go missing my sister's big day, now can I? Thanks for including me in the wedding party," Matthew said.

"We're about to be brothers. Seemed appropriate." Kiernan released Matthew and took one last look in the mirror. "We good to go, gentlemen?"

The three men assembled behind Kiernan.

"Let's do this," Alec said.

4 6

SHE SAID YES

Kiernan

Kiernan stood on the hall's raised platform, by the podium, behind which a werewolf Justice of the Peace was standing. Alec, then Sean, then Matthew were all standing to his left, hands clasped respectfully in front of them.

The werewolves were in their best finery again, only this time no one was going to be bitten. Kiernan wondered with good humor whether or not that would disappoint them.

"What's so funny?" Alec whispered.

"Nothing." Kiernan straightened, as did the other three, when the music started.

Jenny came walking down the aisle first, followed by Dawn, both carrying bouquets of white roses. Alec smiled at Jenny and she gave him a tentative smile back before going to stand at the other side of the podium.

Then the music changed, and every eye turned to the door.

Carly walked gracefully towards Kiernan, arm-in-arm with who Kiernan assumed was her mother. She was resplendent in white with little pearl seed beads sewn here and there. Her long black hair was half pulled back, with some of it trailing over her shoulder.

Kiernan saw the toes of her silver heels poke out from under the dress with a few of the steps she took. Those would be fun to remove later. For now, he was full to bursting with pride, happiness, and love. His mate was the most beautiful, wonderful creature in the world, and he was a very, very lucky man.

He held out his hand when Carly got close enough, and Carly put her hand in his. Rose put her hands over both of theirs and leaned up to kiss Kiernan on the cheek.

"You be good to my little girl," Rose said, patting his wrist.

"I promise," Kiernan replied.

Rose seemed happy with that and went to join the other two women on the bride's side.

Kiernan turned with Carly to face the Justice of the Peace. He ran his thumb over the back of Carly's hand and felt her pulse pick up. Kiernan smiled to himself, wondering if he was going to earn himself a swift kick in the shin later. It would be worth it.

The Justice of the Peace smiled at them. "Welcome everyone and thank you for being with us today as we celebrate the union of Kiernan James Peters and Carolyne Noelle Waite..."

⁂

CARLY

Carly wasn't sure whether she wanted to kill Kiernan for getting her flushed before they'd even said their vows, or thank him for distracting her from her nervousness. Either way, his thumb rubbing circles on the back of her hand was both comforting and maddening at the same time.

"...bride and groom have written their own vows," the Justice of the Peace said.

Kiernan turned to Carly and took her other hand as well. "Caroline Noelle Waite. I love you more than the moon. You were the piece of my soul I didn't even know I was missing. We've been together for the hard times. I'm looking forward to being there for all the good

238

times as well. Nothing will ever break us apart or diminish my love for you. I am so happy and grateful that Fate brought us together."

Tears rolled down Carly's cheeks. She heard Jenny softly bemoan behind her, "Mascara."

Carly squeezed Kiernan's hands. "Kiernan James Peters. You are the light of my life. We've had bad times, and good times, and come through the other side better people and stronger in our relationship. I love you. I want more than anything to spend the rest of my life with you."

Kiernan released one of Carly's hands to wipe at his eyes.

"Who has the rings?" the Justice of the Peace asked.

Alec reached into his jacket and pulled out two simple platinum rings. He handed them to the Justice of the Peace.

The Justice of the Peace handed a ring to Kiernan. "Repeat after me. With this ring, I thee wed."

"With this ring, I thee wed," Kiernan said. He slipped the ring on Carly's finger. He kissed the ring once it was on her finger, and Carly thought her heart might burst.

Then the Justice of the Peace handed the other ring to Carly. "Repeat after me. With this ring, I thee wed."

The ring was cool in Carly's hand. She knew Kiernan would warm it right up, just as he'd done with her heart. "With this ring, I thee wed," Carly whispered, sliding the ring onto Kiernan's finger.

"I love you," Kiernan murmured.

"I love you," Carly replied.

The Justice of the Peace smiled. "I now pronounce you husband and wife. You may kiss the bride."

Kiernan pulled Carly in for a searing kiss.

Carly kissed him back, tears still rolling down her cheeks.

The kiss was longer and more passionate than was strictly decent, but Carly didn't care. Laughter broke out through the hall, and Carly still didn't care.

When their lips finally parted, Kiernan kept his arms wrapped around Carly.

"Ladies and gentlemen, I present to you Mr. and Mrs. Peters," the Justice of the Peace said.

Loud clapping and whoops of congratulations filled the hall.

Carly blushed and Kiernan finally released her, but took her hand in a gentle but firm grip. They both smiled as they faced the pack.

Rose was sobbing. Doc came forward and handed her a handkerchief .

Jenny dabbed her eyes while Dawn cried openly.

Kiernan leaned in and whispered in Carly's ear. "What do you say? Are you ready to be Mrs. Peters for the rest of your life?"

Carly leaned up on her toes and kissed him again, which instigated laughter and more whooping. "Yes."

KISS KISS KISS!

Kiernan

The wedding party went outside for pictures, taking many down by the lake. Then Jenny carefully removed Carly's train. "I'll just pop this into the house."

"Thanks, Jenny," Carly said.

They returned to the hall. Tables were brought in after a DJ came in and set up his equipment. Each table had a crystal vase centerpiece with red roses.

Kiernan pulled out a chair for Carly once their table was set up. His beautiful bride sat down, and despite Jenny's fears, her mascara hadn't run. Carly was radiant and smiling, and Kiernan felt like the luckiest sonofabitch who ever lived.

A side table went up and a large tiered white cake set upon it. It had real roses interspersed on the tiers.

Alec and Sean had slipped out and returned shortly thereafter with a large something covered in red cloth. Sean winked at Kiernan, who grinned.

"What's that?" Carly asked, watching Alec and Sean set the something next to the cake.

Kiernan was about to answer when Matthew began clinking his champagne flute with his knife.

The werewolves present stared at the head table in confusion.

"Kiss, kiss, kiss!" Dawn added helpfully.

Carly pulled Kiernan's face to her for a long kiss.

The werewolves laughed, and got the gist of this convention. Kiernan and Carly had barely come up for air when werewolves began clinking their glasses as well.

"Do we ever get to breathe?" Kiernan chuckled and kissed Carly again.

"Probably during our first dance, but we'll see." A lovely, rosy color had suffused Carly's cheeks, and Kiernan rubbed his thumbs over them.

"You're sexy when you blush," he said.

"You're the sexy one." Carly dissolved into giggles when the clinking started again.

"I could just eat you up." Kiernan went in for another kiss.

Carly grinned at him when they were finished. "Are you my Big Bad Wolf?"

"You know it," Kiernan said.

Matthew came over then and helped Kiernan shrug out of his jacket. He draped it on the back of Kiernan's chair. "Congratulations." Matthew kissed Carly on the cheek and clapped Kiernan on the shoulder.

"Thanks, Matt." Carly turned and hugged him.

"Yes, thank you, Matt." Kiernan gave him a wide smile.

Kiernan clasped hands with Carly under the table, resting their joined hands on her thigh. He'd never been so happy and content in all his life.

"So, what's under the red cloth?" Carly asked again.

Kiernan kissed her temple, then treated her to a mischievous smirk. "It's a surprise."

"Should I start guessing?" Carly's green eyes sparkled as she looked up at him.

There was more clinking and Kiernan chuckled. "Are you going to have time?"

Carly laughed softly and looped her arms around Kiernan's neck. "Probably not."

CARLY

The clinking didn't let up, even during dinner, but Carly didn't mind. It just meant she got to kiss her husband and mate more in front of God and everyone.

Kiernan's kisses did get more passionate as the night wore on, and Carly felt hot under her dress. They got up and cut the cake, and everyone laughed as they smushed small pieces into each other's mouths, getting frosting all over their faces.

"We really need to start incorporating some of this into our mating ceremonies," Alec said as the DJ called Kiernan and Carly up for their first dance.

"Oh!" Carly looked at Alec in surprise. "I didn't know you had mating ceremonies."

"We do, but it's more like a less formal reception," Alec replied. "Everyone still dresses up, and there's dinner and dancing, but I like this glass-tapping kiss thing and the cake exchange. It's fun."

"It is fun," Kiernan agreed. Then he swept Carly onto the dance floor.

The DJ cued Chantal Kreviazuk's "Feels Like Home."

Carly hummed along, pressing her cheek to Kiernan's chest as they swayed to the music.

'Something in your eyes makes me wanna lose myself, makes me wanna lose myself, in your arms...'

Kiernan stroked Carly's back and the nape of her neck, playing with little pieces of her hair. "I like this song."

"It's my favorite." Carly snuggled into him, basking in his love and warmth.

'Feels like home to me. Feels like home to me. Feels like I'm all the way back where I belong.'

Kiernan kissed Carly. "You're my home, too."

Carly could have melted right there. Tears sprang to her eyes. "I wonder how many times I'm going to cry today."

"As many times as you want, babe." Kiernan held her impossibly closer.

The song stopped and people clapped. Carly and Kiernan kissed again.

"Ready for your surprise?" Kiernan asked.

Carly nodded eagerly, just dying to know what it was.

Kiernan signaled the DJ.

"And now, the groom has a very special gift for the bride!" the DJ said over the loudspeaker.

Alec and Sean brought the covered something over to Carly and Kiernan.

Carly ran her hand over the soft, red fabric covering it. "May I?"

"I'd be deeply disappointed if you didn't," Kiernan said.

Carly pulled the covering away, then gasped, her hands flying over her mouth.

Sitting in the middle of the dance floor was an oak spinning wheel.

"Oh my God, Kiernan!" Carly hugged him, then went over to examine the intricate spinning wheel. She was completely over-whelmed. Carly didn't know what to say. "Did you... did you make this yourself?!"

"Sure did." Kiernan beamed with pride.

Carly touched the different parts and spindles, then ran back to Kiernan and gave him a kiss. "This is so incredible! I can't believe you did this." She choked back more tears, and kissed him again. "It's so beautiful I... thank you, Kiernan."

"I'd do anything for you, babe," Kiernan said.

4 8

WHAT IF?

Kiernan

Kiernan made the rounds with Carly, thanking people for coming, accepting congratulations, and chatting briefly here and there. Rose was having a conversation with Doc. She laughed often. Kiernan and Carly decided not to disturb her .

"Mom seems to have made a new friend," Carly smiled as she chatted with Matthew and Dawn.

Matthew looked over at their mother and grinned. "Mom sure deserves one. Maybe werewolves are catching."

Dawn swatted him. "I sure hope not. Otherwise, how does a girl stand a chance?"

Carly's mouth formed a big "O" of shock. "You're dating?!"

Matthew rubbed the back of his neck. "Yeah. That's the big headline of the day."

Carly squealed and Kiernan had to cover his ears. So did the closest werewolves. "I can't believe it! That's wonderful news!"

"I thought you'd been planning to get a cat." Kiernan grinned at Dawn, and she blushed.

"Yeah, well, I have two. Figured I might try something more high maintenance just one more time," Dawn said.

Matthew gave her a soft kiss on the lips. "There's only gonna be the one more time."

Kiernan excused himself while Carly gushed, going over to where Alec was sitting alone. Not far off, Jenny and Sean were discussing their upcoming trip. Alec was sulking.

"So, did you buy an RV for yourself?" Kiernan asked, sitting down next to Alec.

"Yeah," Alec said. "I'm picking it up tomorrow. Gonna tow the Range Rover behind it."

Kiernan nodded. "Short honeymoon for me, then."

Alec winced. "Sorry about that. I can't let her get away, though."

"I hope you're not still worried about Sean." Kiernan followed Alec's gaze as the other man glowered.

"No. Just..." Alec opened the mindlink. 'Jealous.'

Kiernan sighed. 'You could have that, you know. If you get your shit together.'

'I've got my shit together,' Alec protested.

Kiernan shook his head. 'Brother, you don't. But I think some time away from pack duties will give you time to get some perspective.' He squeezed Alec's shoulder. 'In the meantime, why don't you ask your wife to dance?'

'What if she says no?' Alec asked.

'Only one way to find out.' Kiernan gave Alec a nudge, and Alec stood.

Kiernan watched as Alec walked over to Jenny and Sean. He held his breath as Alec held out his hand.

Jenny paused only briefly, then put her hand in Alec's.

Kiernan exhaled and sagged in his chair with relief.

Carly sat down next to him in a rustle of skirts. "That's nice to see," she said as Alec pulled Jenny out onto the dance floor.

"I think they might make it. How are you holding up?" Kiernan asked, taking Carly's hand and kissing it.

"Let's just say I'm going to be really happy when you take my heels off." Carly winced as she toed off a shoe and rolled the ball of her foot against the wood floor.

"Why, wait?" Kiernan scooped her legs into his lap. He pushed her skirts up a little and took off her other shoe, then began massaging her feet.

Carly moaned, and the sound went straight to his groin. "If I could bottle you, I'd make a fortune."

"'Fraid not, Babe. You're the only one who gets to have me," Kiernan rumbled.

Carly smiled. "I like that, too. Actually, I like that more."

"Getting all possessive on me?" Kiernan asked. He tickled the sole of her foot.

Carly writhed and giggled. "Hey, werewolves aren't the only ones who can be possessive of their mates."

"Good," Kiernan said. He leaned in and kissed her.

———

CARLY

That last kiss did her in. "You know," she murmured in his ear, "the bride and groom usually leave first."

Kiernan raised his eyebrows. His face broke into a lustful grin that made her hot all over. "I think that's my favorite part of this tradition."

Before she could do more than squeak, Kiernan had Carly up over his shoulder in a fireman's carry. "Hey! This is NOT the way you carry your new bride!"

Kiernan bent and picked up her shoes. "It is now." He gave her a playful swat on the bottom.

Wolf whistles and whoops filled the space, and people clapped as Kiernan headed for the door.

"I am so getting you back for this," Carly promised, feeling herself blush down to her toes.

"Oh, I hope so," Kiernan said.

He walked out of the lodge and down the path with Carly still slung over his shoulder. Carly stopped protesting by the first dim light on the path and decided to just enjoy the ride.

The crisp October air was cool on her skin, and she could smell the turning leaves. They rustled as a light breeze blew through them.

Kiernan kicked open the door to their cabin, dropped Carly's shoes on the floor, then closed the door behind them. "I believe you said something about carrying you over the threshold?"

"You're supposed to do it with me in your arms." Carly squealed then and Kiernan bounced her down off his shoulders and into his waiting arms.

"Let's try it again, then," he said. Kiernan stepped out the door and carried Carly back inside.

Carly's pulse pounded a mile a minute. Kiernan was staring unabashedly as her chest heaved up and down.

"Eyes on the goodies already?" Carly teased.

"You're lucky I ever take my eyes off the goodies," Kiernan muttered. He carried her to the bedroom and set her on the floor. Kiernan looked the dress over in frustration. "Where's the zipper on this thing?"

Carly laughed and raised her arm. "Side zip."

"Oh good. I was about to rip it right off you." Kiernan slowly pulled the zipper down, brushing his knuckles against her skin as his eyes met hers.

Carly swallowed. "Jenny would have killed you."

"Mmm. Worth it." Kiernan opened the dress and let it fall away. He openly ogled her lacy white bra and panties.

"Jenny picked them out." Carly turned in a slow circle, letting him get a real eyeful. "You like?"

"I should buy Jenny a nicer RV." Kiernan shed his clothes. His black silk boxers were tented at the front.

Carly ran her palm over the front of his boxers. "Your RV is already really nice. I know I liked it."

Kiernan growled and picked Carly up, then laid her on the bed. He took off his boxers, then made short work of her panties and bra, kissing and sucking his favorite assets.

As he was fumbling in the bedside drawer for a condom, Carly came to a decision over what she'd been thinking about the last several weeks.

Kiernan pulled out a condom, but just as he was going to rip the packet, Carly put a hand over his. "What if we don't use a condom this time?" she whispered.

UP TO FATE

Kiernan

Kiernan froze and stared at Carly, her soft hand over his. "Are you... serious?"

"I've never been more serious." Carly's steady gaze told him she was ready.

But was he? "That's a big decision, babe."

"I know." Carly's gaze didn't waver.

Kiernan had to laugh, though it came out sounding nervous. "You've been thinking about it without me?"

"I didn't decide until just now," Carly said. She sat up and put her arms around him, leaning her cheek against his shoulder.

"Just now? Where was I?" Kiernan asked, still laughing.

"See? This is why I said I was going to be jealous of your mindlink thing." Carly snuggled him, but didn't try anything else, waiting for Kiernan to make his decision. Kiernan appreciated that.

Kiernan turned the condom over in his hands, thinking. He knew he wanted to have pups with Carly someday. Kiernan imagined Carly big as a house, swollen with his pup. He liked the image.

He also liked the idea of running around with a little tyke, rolling around on the floor while he or she played with his fur. Probably getting it all sticky. When they were older, he could take the whole family fishing on the lake. Carly would like that.

Kiernan grinned and decided to leave it up to Fate. He put the condom back in the drawer. "Let's see what happens, then," he whispered to Carly, rolling her underneath him.

Carly wrapped her arms around the back of Kiernan's neck and kissed him. She played gently with his hair and the mark on the back of his neck.

Kiernan hiked one of her legs over his hip and stroked the bottom of her thigh. His cock was poised at her entrance. "I love you, Carly."

"I love you, too," Carly said.

A tear slid down Carly's cheek as Kiernan entered her. He groaned and got harder at the warm, wet feel of her. "Carly..." he whispered.

Carly kissed him and Kiernan felt it like an electric force. Something about the potential of creating life with his beautiful, strong mate made Kiernan wild with desire. He started thrusting hard, devouring her with his lips. He couldn't get enough.

When Carly came with a shout, Kiernan spilled his seed in her, but didn't stop. The biological imperative was just too strong. He thrust sharply into her, fiddling her clit between his fingers.

Carly clung to him and sobbed when she came a second time. Kiernan groaned and released in her, burying himself deep.

"I love you." Kiernan kissed Carly's tears and stroked her tenderly. "I love you. I love you."

"I love you, too," Carly sniffled.

Kiernan didn't even realize he'd been crying until Carly began kissing his tears as well.

CARLY

Carly laid beneath Kiernan, silently sending a petition to the Almighty to give them a child. Or pup, as the werewolves called them.

Kiernan rolled them so they were on their sides, but didn't pull out. Carly was happy about that. She felt she needed the closeness.

He kissed her neck and the mark on her shoulder, and Carly combed her fingers through his hair. "Kiernan?" Carly asked.

"Mmm... yeah, babe?" Kiernan gave her nipple a long, slow lick.

Carly shivered. "Do you think we did it?"

"Twice, as I recall," Kiernan chuckled against the swell of her breast.

Carly whacked him on the back. "I mean do you think I'm going to get pregnant?"

"I'm sure you're going to get pregnant. Because we're going to keep trying until you are." Kiernan smiled at her.

"Work, work, work," Carly teased. "It'll be a wonder if you can still run things at the lodge."

"I'm good at multitasking." Kiernan tangled his fingers in her hair and kissed her. "I do know where my top priorities lie, however."

"'Top priorities,' plural?" Carly asked.

Kiernan's laugh made her tingle all over. "Let's see here. Being with you. Eating with you. Sleeping with you. Making love with you... it's a long list."

"Good to know I made the list." Carly nuzzled Kiernan's cheek.

"Babe, you are the list." Kiernan cuddled her closer and then sighed. "I can't believe that asshole is making me work tomorrow. I can't imagine ever leaving this bed."

"I'm just glad he's going after Jenny. I find that very... hopeful," Carly said.

"I suppose it is." Kiernan stroked his fingers up and down Carly's back, making her writhe against him.

"That tickles!"

"Does it?" Kiernan asked innocently.

Carly laughed and swatted him again. "You know it does, you sex beast."

"I think you mean sex-y beast," Kiernan said.

"No, I said it exactly the way I meant it. I know you want to go again. I can feel you, you know."

Kiernan swiveled his hips in the most delicious way, and Carly moaned. "Can you feel me?" he murmured in her ear.

"Ahuh." Carly was already starting to lose upper brain function when Kiernan rolled onto his back so she was straddling him.

Carly braced herself on his chest.

"Want to take me for a spin?" Kiernan purred, massaging her hips.

"This is why I'm never going to visit you at the office." Carly bit her lip and started to ride him. He was so deep, and it felt so good.

"You say that now, but I'll bet I can convince you to have lunch with me. A long lunch." Kiernan's hands moved to her ass, and he encouraged her along.

Carly panted. "You just... want... to... christen... your desk." She started moving on him faster.

"See? You can read my mind." Kiernan began bucking his hips upwards, groaning with need.

Carly came then, falling forward and trembling against his chest.

Kiernan came as well with a shout and Carly felt the warm rush inside her.

"We are not christening the desk," Carly gasped sternly.

"I think we are," Kiernan said.

"You'll never convince me." Carly was sure she could hold onto her resolve.

"Pretty sure I will." Kiernan sounded equally certain.

* * *

THEY CHRISTENED the desk the next day.

50

KNOWING

Carly

Hayward was cold in November, but luckily it hadn't yet snowed. Carly walked beside Matthew to the quilt shop where, as far as she knew, the proprietress was still holding on to the yarn Jenny had bought for her.

"You bought it back in August, and you think it's still here? What makes you think she didn't sell it to someone else? You should have picked it up sooner," Matthew said.

Carly gave him a peevish glare. "I was a little busy. I'd have picked it up the same day, but someone decided I needed to spend some quality time in Vermillion."

"Dunno who that asshat could be," Matthew replied with a slight grin.

"Of course not." Carly stepped into the shop. Matthew walked in behind her, hands shoved in his jeans pockets. It was approaching the single digits that day, but he still refused to give up his leather jacket for something warmer.

"There you are!" the store owner said, leaning over her counter to look at them. "I thought you'd never come back!" She dug underneath the desk and produced two bags of burgundy yarn.

"Sorry. It's been a crazy few months." Carly started to take the yarn, but Matthew took it instead, carrying it at his sides.

The store owner chuckled. "You always come in with the most handsome men, I have to say."

"You should see my husband," Carly smiled.

"Oh, really? Then I can't wait," the store owner said.

"I hope we'll be back soon. He's been so busy with work." Carly put a twenty on the desk. "This is for holding the yarn and for letting me take that tourist map. I know they're not free."

"You don't need to worry about that, dear." The store owner pushed the twenty back at Carly. "I was happy to help."

Reluctantly, Carly put the twenty back in her wallet. "Thank you."

"You're more than welcome. Stop by and see an old lady now and again. I don't usually get as much excitement as when you're around," the shop owner grinned.

"It's a promise," Carly said. She and Matt then ventured back out into the cold.

Matthew kept his hands balled around the handles of the bags, clearly freezing his thumbs off. "You making something for Kiernan?"

"You still wearing that jacket because Dawn thinks it looks cool?" Carly retorted.

Matthew laughed, his breath clouding the air. "So I guess we can stop asking the obvious questions."

"How are you guys settling in? Is Mom liking the new house? I feel like I never get to see her anymore," Carly said.

"Dawn keeps decorating. Mom couldn't care less. I'm surprised you don't see her—she's always at the resort. Pretty sure she's just decided to shack up with Doc." Matthew gave a soft chuckle. "Good for her."

"Maybe I don't see her because she's shacked up with Doc." Carly bumped shoulders playfully with her brother.

"Probably." Matthew escorted Carly all the way back to Kiernan's SUV.

Carly took the bags from Matthew and popped them in the back, then turned back to him. "You want a ride home?"

"It's three blocks away. I can make it," Matthew said manfully .

"You sure?" Carly asked.

Matthew opened the driver's side door and shooed her in. "Don't worry so much. You'll have enough to worry about nine months from now."

"Shh!" Carly put a hand over his mouth. "I haven't told Kiernan yet!"

"He's not going to slither up out of the storm drain," Matthew laughed.

"You don't know that." Carly's eyes darted around. When she finally satisfied herself that Kiernan wasn't there, she relaxed back into her seat. "You take care. Get Dawn something nice for your two-month dating anniversary."

"You're not going to try to knit all that yarn into something by your one-month wedding anniversary, are you?" Matthew asked.

Carly shook her head. "No. Christmas."

"Good. I don't think the stress would be good for the B-A-B-Y." Matthew winked.

Carly rolled her eyes. "He can spell, you know."

"I'll remember that at Thanksgiving." Matthew kissed Carly on the cheek. "Okay, off with you. I have to figure out if the two-month dating anniversary is the paperclip or three-ring-binder anniversary."

"For God's sake, get the woman some roses," Carly said.

"Just kidding. I definitely will." Matthew closed Carly's door, then waved goodbye as she pulled away from the curb.

Carly smiled to herself all the way back to the Crescent Moon Path Resort. She was telling Kiernan tonight.

Kiernan

"Yes, Alpha Edward bought another twelve acres of property on the other side of the road, provided anyone from the Superior Pack gets to stay here for free until we pay off the debt," Kiernan said into the phone. "He was happy to do it. Well, yes, I guess that does mean if and when he goes to war, we lend a hand. But after his help with Carly, it wasn't like we weren't doing that anyway. It was a good idea, Alec. Give Sean some credit." Kiernan paced his living room. It was technically after work hours, but when the Alpha called, you answered.

Carly came skipping back into the cabin. She caught sight of Kiernan and quickly hid something crinkly behind her back.

Kiernan grinned and held up a finger. Then he turned his back so she could get away with whatever she was trying to get away with. "You really should have made Sean your Beta, Alec. He's a good man with good ideas. Now, Gamma isn't Beta, is it?" Kiernan winced at Alec's loud, expletive-laden response. "Alright, fine. I won't bring it up again."

Carly disappeared into Kiernan's old bedroom, or as she liked to call it, the craft room . Kiernan smiled fondly and sniffed the air. He wondered when she was going to tell him. "Yes, I'm listening. As far as I know, there's just the one family of Hunters on the lake right now. Unfortunately, I think they're buying the place they're renting. No, you don't need to come home. I've sent pictures to Alpha Edward's real estate agent. I think he might buy it out from under them, but for himself. It's a nice place."

After a few minutes, Carly reappeared and began shuffling around the kitchen. Kiernan was soon smelling pot roast just starting to cook, and his mouth watered. "Yes, I agree we're getting far too many tourists around here but, you know, wolves aren't the only creatures getting their habitat encroached on these days. I think we're just going to have to live with it. Not even the Superior Pack can buy up the whole lake."

Kiernan could hear Carly tossing a salad, and wanted to get in there to help her. Or at least set the table. "Listen, Alec, I've got to go. And stop talking about coming home. I'm not letting you come home until you come home WITH Jenny."

Even Carly could have heard Alec's sigh on the other end. "Good luck, Brother," Kiernan said, and ended the call. He walked into the kitchen and wrapped his arms around Carly from behind. He rubbed his nose up the side of her neck. "Something smells delicious."

Carly turned in the circle of his arms and kissed him. "I've got something to tell you." She bit her lip, but still couldn't quite hold back her smile as she placed one of his hands on her belly.

Kiernan grinned, a very proud papa indeed. "I know," he whispered in her ear.

5 1

THE GIFT

Kiernan

Kiernan carefully cut a curve in the wood, following the line he'd drawn. It was March, and temperatures were rising, but he still wore the red sweater Carly had knitted him for Christmas under his smock. It reminded him of the time they'd met at the Dream Weaver booth at the Minnesota Renaissance Festival. Sure, the sweater came a little bit later than expected, but it touched him that she still remembered, too. If he had a choice in the matter, he wouldn't wear anything else.

Jenny appeared just as he finished cutting the curve in the cedar. "Hi," she said.

"Hi," Kiernan replied, turning off the saw and pushing up his goggles. "Good to see you back."

"I've been back for a week," Jenny laughed.

"Still good to see you." Kiernan wiped sawdust off his hands and smock and went over and gave her a hug.

Jenny hugged him back, then looked at the cedar lying on the workbench. "Whatcha makin'?"

"A present for Carly. Well, a present for Carly and Squish," Kiernan said.

"I still love that you call him or her that. Still no interest in finding out the sex? It makes gift buying a little easier for the rest of us," Jenny wheedled.

Kiernan shook his head. "You can beg all you want, but we're waiting until Squish is born."

"But I could do such a fabulous gender reveal party!" Jenny tugged Kiernan's arm like a child asking for a cookie.

"I know. But we've decided. Maybe next time." Kiernan pulled his arm out of Jenny's grasp.

Jenny sighed and walked over to the workbench. She fluttered through the pages of Kiernan's design until she found the completed schematic. "Kiernan, wow! She's going to love it!"

"That's the idea," Kiernan said. "So, you and Alec haven't killed each other yet, I see. I'm taking that as a good sign."

"What can I say? He grows on you after a while. Like fungus." Jenny giggled at her own joke and Kiernan couldn't help but join in. "Besides, he did chase me all over the country. I figure that's something."

"Jenny, he would have chased you all over the world." Kiernan took a protractor and began roughing out another piece of the present.

"I know. We're going to make it work. I think he really thought I might elope with Sean," Jenny said.

Kiernan snorted. "Like you'd ever do that to Alec. Or Sean. Speaking of which, where's he at now?"

"He's still in Arizona. Their festival isn't over until the beginning of April." Jenny smiled wistfully. "It was so nice and warm there."

"I used to go to Oklahoma this time of year. I like how he's jumping around different venues. Sorry to hear he hasn't found his mate yet." Kiernan finished drawing another curve on the wood.

"Not for lack of trying on his part," Jenny agreed.

Kiernan set the protractor aside. "I'm really glad Alec isn't being an asshole about the Gamma being gone."

Jenny shook her head ruefully. "I think Alec is trying to stay in my good graces. That, and I don't know that he's ready to deal with Sean yet after all that time we spent together. He's a jealous wolf, my man is."

"We all know that. Luckily he's a jealous man who knows how to run a pack. He prepped me before he left and I still couldn't believe the amount of work he has to deal with. I'm just glad he's back so we can split it," Kiernan said.

Jenny patted him on the shoulder. "Thanks for making that time for him and me. I really appreciate it, more than you know, Kiernan."

Kiernan smiled. "What are brothers for?"

Carly

Carly laid back in bed, sweat still beaded on her brow as she watched Kiernan holding their daughter, Rosie. He rocked Rosie and made little babbling baby talk at her, and it made Carly's heart ache with happiness.

"And then Daddy's going to take you fishing," Kiernan was explaining to their daughter. "Yes, he is. Yes, he is. You're going to catch one whopper of a Northern. Yes, you are. Okay, maybe not in this lake—d-stupid tourists—but Daddy's going to take you up to Alpha Trevor's territory someday and THEN you'll catch a whopper of a Northern."

"I hope you're not planning on going without me," Carly said, pretending to be miffed.

Kiernan chuckled. "Mommy wants to go fishing, too. Should we all go together? I think we should. Yes. We'll go camping in a tent, and have tasty fish fries. Daddy makes the best fish fries, yes he does."

The tiny bright pink little girl in Kiernan's arms just made small snuffles and grunts. Her tiny mouth formed a huge yawn.

"I think it's time we use the present." Carly gestured to the side of the bed.

Kiernan sulked. "But I don't wanna let her go."

"She'll still be there after a little nap. Then we have to try to get her to latch on again." Carly grimaced at the idea. It was harder than it looked.

"We'll get there." Kiernan reluctantly laid Rosie in the cedar cradle he'd made her. He rocked it gently with his toe. Then he leaned over the bed and gave Carly a kiss. "I love you, Mommy."

Carly kissed him back. "I love you, too, Daddy."